Praise for Geo[rgia Beers]

The Do-O[ver]

"You can count on Beers to give you a [...] and every time."—*The Romantic Reader Blog*

"*The Do-Over* is a shining example of the brilliance of Georgia Beers as a contemporary romance author."—*Rainbow Reflections*

"[T]he two leads are genuine and likable, their chemistry is palpable... The romance builds up slowly and naturally, and the angst level is just right. The supporting characters are equally well developed. Don't miss this one!"—*Melina Bickard, Librarian, Waterloo Library (UK)*

Calendar Girl

"*Calendar Girl* is a perfect masterclass on how to write a breathtakingly beautiful romance novel...Georgia Beers had me captivated from the start with this story. Two skilfully crafted characters, an enthralling plot and the best kissing scene ever!"—*Kitty Kat's Book Review Blog*

"*Calendar Girl* by Georgia Beers is a well-written sweet workplace romance. It has all the elements of a good contemporary romance... It even has an ice queen for a major character."—*Rainbow Reflections*

"A sweet, sweet romcom of a story...*Calendar Girl* is a nice read, which you may find yourself returning to when you want a hot-chocolate-and-warm-comfort-hug in your life."—*Best Lesbian Erotica*

The Shape of You

"I know I always say this about Georgia Beers's books, but there is no one that writes first kisses like her. They are hot, steamy and all too much!"—*Les Rêveur*

The Shape of You "catches you right in the feels and does not let go. It is a must for every person out there who has struggled with self-esteem, questioned their judgment, and settled for a less than perfect but safe lover. If you've ever been convinced you have to trade passion for emotional safety, this book is for you."—*Writing While Distracted*

Blend

"Georgia Beers hits all the right notes with this romance set in a wine bar…A low-angst read, it still delivers a story rich in heart-rending moments before the characters get their happy ever after. A well-crafted novel, *Blend* is a marvelous way to spend an evening curled up with a large glass of your favorite vintage."—*Writing While Distracted*

"You know a book is good, first, when you don't want to put it down. Second, you know it's damn good when you're reading it and thinking, I'm totally going to read this one again. Great read and absolutely a 5-star romance."—*The Romantic Reader Blog*

"This is a lovely romantic story with relatable characters that have depth and chemistry. A charming easy story that kept me reading until the end. Very enjoyable."—*Kat Adams, Bookseller, QBD (Australia)*

"*Blend* has that classic Georgia Beers feel to it, while giving us another unique setting to enjoy. The pacing is excellent and the chemistry between Piper and Lindsay is palpable."—*The Lesbian Review*

Right Here, Right Now

"The angst was written well, but not overpoweringly so, just enough for you to have the heart-sinking moment of 'will they make it,' and then you realize they have to because they are made for each other." —*Les Reveur*

Right Here, Right Now "is full of humor (yep, I laughed out loud), romance, and kick-ass characters!"—*Illustrious Illusions*

"[A] successful and entertaining queer romance novel. The main characters are appealing, and the situations they deal with are realistic and well-managed. I would recommend this book to anyone who enjoys a good queer romance novel, and particularly one grounded in real world situations."—*Books at the End of the Alphabet*

"[A]n engaging odd-couple romance. Beers creates a romance of gentle humor that allows no-nonsense Lacey to relax and easygoing Alicia to find a trusting heart."—*RT Book Reviews*

By the Author

Visit us at www.boldstrokesbooks.com

FEAR OF FALLING

by
Georgia Beers

2019

FEAR OF FALLING

ISBN 13: 978-1-63555-443-4

This Trade Paperback Original Is Published By
Bold Strokes Books, Inc.
P.O. Box 249
Valley Falls, NY 12185

First Edition: June 2019

CREDITS
EDITORS: LYNDA SANDOVAL AND STACIA SEAMAN
PRODUCTION DESIGN: STACIA SEAMAN
COVER DESIGN BY ANN MCMAN

Acknowledgments

As always, thank you to Bold Strokes Books and everybody there for continuing to make the publishing process smooth and stress-free for me.

Thank you to my editors, Lynda Sandoval and Stacia Seaman, for catching my mistakes and teaching me along the way. You're never too old to improve on your craft, and they help me do that with every book I write.

Thank you to my author friends who get me, hold me accountable on word counts, help me with titles, talk me up when I need it or off the ledge when I need that. Writing is an inherently solitary career, but they make it feel less lonely and more like a group effort.

Finally, and always, I am forever grateful to my amazing readers whose emails and messages lift me up when I need it and keep me going when I feel stuck. Thank you never seems like enough, so I'll keep writing.

Chapter One

D id something crawl into her mouth and die?

That was only one of the many questions that ran through Sophie James's mind like the bulls stampeding through Pamplona. Some of the others: Why was the sunshine trying to slice through her eyelids? Who was running the jackhammer inside her skull? Could somebody please give her all the water on the planet, like, right now?

Sophie groaned and laid her arm gingerly across her eyes, wanting to get up and away from the bright and cheerful rays of sunlight that obviously hated her, but the rest of her body didn't seem to want to move; her legs felt like they were made of sandbags. It took her another five minutes to realize she was on her couch and not in her bed. When that happened, her eyes popped open and a few slivers of memory from the night before began to pierce through her brain.

There had been loud, thumping music.

There had been lots of dancing.

There had been *waaaay* too many shots.

Oh, God. The shots…

It's funny how, when vomiting is imminent, a body that previously wouldn't move suddenly does so at great speed. Sophie made it to the powder room toilet in the nick of time, and anything at all that had remained in her stomach as she slept evacuated her body in a hot, putrid rush.

She groaned in exhausted relief and sat back against the wall. The ceramic tile was cool under her bare legs and for a serious moment, she thought about just lying down and going back to sleep right there on the bathroom floor. She was sliding slowly down the wall to do just that when she heard her cell ringing from somewhere in the living room.

Another groan. Why was every part of her body so freaking heavy?

Standing was too hard. She crawled instead. Out of the bathroom, down the hardwood hallway, to the leather couch. Once there, she turned herself so she sat on the floor with her back against it, closed her eyes, and blew out a breath. Yeah, that was more than enough exertion for one day. She was pretty much done.

She saw the note when she reached for the phone.

Soph-a-licious—
Take the Advil. Drink the water. Call me.
—A

For the first time since opening her eyes, Sophie saw the water bottle on the coffee table, now sparkling in the sun, looking inviting. She grabbed it and twisted the top off, drank greedily as her phone beeped to remind her that she'd been too slow in answering and now she had a text.

No. Seventeen texts, she saw now as she downed the four orange tablets.

Seventeen.

That was a lot for somebody who rarely gave out her number.

She sucked down more water, as if hoping it would fortify her against the text onslaught she knew was right there in her hand, and she unlocked the screen.

Four from Andrew, all asking if she was alive. He'd show up at her door if she didn't respond, so she jotted off a quick text to let him know she did actually open her eyes that morning.

Feel like shit, but I'm breathing, so there's that, she sent.

Unsurprising, came Andrew's reply. *You and tequila made a beautiful couple last night.*

Just the mention of the alcohol made Sophie's stomach roil in protest, and she grimaced as she waited for it to pass. Andrew said he'd be over later.

Three texts were from Michaela, who had also been out with her and Andrew last night. Before sending her a note like she had to him, she quickly scrolled through the rest of them. Ten more, all from the same person: Vincent D'Angelo. Her agent.

WTF did you do, Sophie? was the first one. The rest were similar in tone. The last one, which had come in while she was crawling from the bathroom like a loser, said simply *Turn on Pop!*

The feeling that settled in the pit of her stomach as she read that one was different than the overdid-it-last-night-probably-gonna-puke feeling she'd had since she opened her eyes. No, this feeling was something else entirely. This feeling was dread.

With a hard swallow, Sophie grabbed the remote and turned on the TV, switched to the Pop Network. She didn't have to wait long. It was the top of the hour and Pop always did a quick recap of the top entertainment news of the day then. Brooke Kramer stood there in all her blond Hollywood mannequin glory, looked right at the camera, and said seriously, "Has Sophie James lost it completely over the death of her manager?"

It was like a gut punch. Sophie's entire body deflated, like it wanted to sink down into the floor and become one with the hardwood. There was grainy video of her, wearing the same royal blue dress she realized she still wore, being half dragged, half carried out of Glitter last night.

"Two months after the death of her longtime manager, Ray Cooper, singer Sophie James was seen last night at Glitter, a hot new Manhattan nightclub. Obviously over-served, Ms. James had to be escorted out by her companions. This is the third time since Cooper's death that Ms. James has been seen exiting a New York establishment in questionable condition—"

Sophie clicked the TV off with Brooke in mid-sentence. She couldn't listen to it anymore. In that moment, she didn't care that she'd been caught on camera doing her best impression of a rag doll. She didn't care that this was the third time, according to Brooke's Hollywood sources. Her brain would only focus on one piece of information. Just one from that entire story.

Ray was gone.

When her phone rang in her hand, instead of cursing the name on the screen, she felt a surge of relief. Anything that kept her from dissolving into a pathetic puddle of emotion these days was welcome. Even Vincent D'Angelo, who was about to lambast her, she was pretty sure.

"Hi, Vince," she said, surprised by the hoarseness of her own voice.

"What the fuck, Sophie?" Vince's voice was deep and smooth as silk, like warm melted chocolate. Like always. It was only because Sophie had known him for the past ten years that she knew how upset he really was with her. That and the F-bombs. "I mean, seriously. What the actual fuck?"

"I know. I'm sorry." It was all she could say. She had no excuses.

"You're making it easy for the media. You know that, right?"

Sophie inhaled quietly and repeated herself. "I know. I'm sorry." She hated how small her voice sounded, but she couldn't seem to put anything more into it. She let her head fall back against the couch and closed her eyes.

"Look." Vince's voice softened, veered toward the more fatherly tone he often used with her. Sophie sometimes wondered if he even realized it. "I know this has been hard. I know you miss Ray. We all do. But you have to stop this. Miracle is starting to freak out." He was referring to Sophie's record company. "Your audience doesn't handle public drunkenness or profanity-laden meltdowns well. You know this." When Sophie didn't answer, he added, his voice going softer yet, "They'll only cut you slack for so long. You know?"

"Yeah."

There was a beat of silence, a beat filled with so much for Sophie. But all she could do was sit, helpless against the tear that coursed slowly down one cheek. She swallowed audibly, then was pretty sure Vince heard it, as he cleared his throat and spoke again.

"So, listen, Miracle is assigning you a new manager and publicist. One person who'll handle both."

That made Sophie sit up. "What?" She swiped at the errant tear and furrowed her brow. "What do you mean?"

"Soph, you can't not have a manager. I know it's always been Ray, and I know you miss him. We all do. But you have to have a manager. And you need a publicist, especially now." It seemed like he actually tried to keep the sarcasm out of the last two words. He didn't quite succeed.

"Already?" This information got her blood moving. A new manager? For real?

"You're due to meet with the producers for the next album next week, Soph. You need somebody to start handling things, setting the schedule, get you appearances, do damage control."

"But…" Again with the small voice. "It's only been two months."

"I know." This time, "fatherly" was the only way to describe Vince's tone. "I know. And I want to give you more time, but…"

"Miracle needs me to do my job." Sophie's tone was resigned. She was the number one artist in the record company's Adult Contemporary category, and they wanted to keep her right there, cranking out the same old ballads, making them reliable piles of money.

"Yeah." Vince also sounded resigned, and for that, Sophie was thankful.

All right. Maybe getting back to work was the thing she needed. Maybe jumping back in with both feet would help her keep from drowning. She squinted at the metaphors that didn't quite match up. Damn hangover. She scanned the room, her eyes landing on a framed photo of her and Ray taken in Sydney a couple years ago, and she sighed. "When do I meet him?"

"Her," Vince said. "Can you be ready tomorrow?"

A small snort escaped her. "Do I have a choice?"

CHAPTER TWO

D ana Landon was not thrilled.
    It was true that she knew why she'd been assigned to this one. She understood it. She'd handled this kind of thing many times before and she was good at it. The higher-ups at Miracle trusted her implicitly to get things back on track. None of that was a surprise.

But Dana was tired.

Tired of divas. Tired of entitled young artists who wanted the world on a silver platter after they had one hit. Tired of the drama and the rumor mill and the paparazzi. Her curse was her ability to handle all of these things with organized authority and keep everybody happy in the process.

And now they wanted her to handle Sophie James.

Dana sat in her Manhattan office and gazed out the window at the sliver of gray sky she could see between other buildings. It was going to rain; she could feel it. It had been a lovely, crisp and sunny, fall weekend, folks out in Central Park, walking their dogs, jogging, soaking up what may very well have been the last nice day of the season. But it was Monday now, and, as if Mother Nature had decided to make sure people went to work, she took away the nice weather and reminded everybody it was fall, soon-to-be winter. Gray and gloomy and very, very Monday.

The ringing of her cell yanked her attention away from the weather.

"Sophie James, huh?" Anya Reeves asked without preamble or greeting.

"Wow. News travels fast." Dana chuckled, not really surprised. The grapevine in the entertainment management world was less a vine and more a lightning bolt.

"You see the coverage?"

Dana sighed. "I did." It was surprising, the footage of Sophie James, darling of the Adult Contemporary charts for more than a decade, slurring her swear words, half stumbling, and half being carried by her companions.

"What is that, the third time? Fourth?"

"Third."

Anya scoffed, then seemed to think slightly better of it. "I suppose I could cut her a little slack. Ray was a good guy and was with her... how long?"

Dana slowly shook her head, even though Anya couldn't see it. "I don't know, but Sophie was just a teenager. It's got to be like losing a father."

"Or something more..." Anya let the innuendo hang in the air.

"Ew, no." Dana paused, thought about it. "You think? He was way older. Like, what? Twenty-five years? Thirty?" She shook her head again. "Ew. No."

"I don't know," Anya said, drawing it out like she had information.

Dana didn't want to think about it. "Regardless. Losing him had to be hard on her. She's young."

"She's twenty-nine. Not that young."

"Still."

"How do you feel about taking her on?" Anya knew Dana well. They'd been friends for nearly ten years, started together at Starshine, the talent agency Anya now ran. "I know you wanted to scale back. Repping Sophie James is anything but that. Especially with her recent... escapades. She's looking like she could be a real handful."

Anya wasn't wrong. The Sophie James of last year had a pretty sterling—albeit kind of boring—reputation. Adult contemporary ballads, a few appearances here and there on the occasional late-night talk show, a slew of fans age forty and up. Huge celebrity in Europe. Her star had faded slightly, it was true. A twenty-nine-year-old singing prodigy isn't quite as enamoring as a sixteen-year-old one. Sure, she continued to sell, but her numbers weren't quite the same. Still, she made Miracle boatloads of money and Dana knew the business well. Sophie was one of the steady contributors who helped keep the lights on so Miracle could experiment with some new acts and Indie bands.

"I'm not loving this...acting out," Dana said truthfully.

"That's why Miracle is giving her to you. I'm sure. You get the problem children."

Again, Anya wasn't wrong. "I know," Dana groaned.

"I bet she's a diva."

"Oh, don't say that. I can't do another Sheba." Dana didn't like to think about the country singer she'd managed for a mere six months. She'd had to ask her bosses to replace her before she murdered Sheba. And cut her up into little tiny pieces. And fed her to wild animals. Or a wood chipper.

"What? You don't enjoy telling people your client needs a massage therapist at her beck and call, Texas barbecue flown in whenever she wants, only round ice in her drinks, and an endless supply of Gummi Bears, but just the weird yellowy-gold-colored ones?"

"Jesus, right?" Dana could laugh at it now, but God, then? No. She'd seen a lot in her career, met a lot of people who thought they were better than everybody else. But Sheba took the cake easily. She was rude to everybody, was never satisfied, and was just a generally angry person.

"That woman needs to get laid," Anya said.

"Still does, according to Barb," Dana said, referring to the manager who'd taken Dana's place.

Anya barked a laugh. "Maybe you'll get lucky and Sophie James will be nice and demure."

"Oh, yeah, I'm sure that's exactly the case. At least she's here in Manhattan."

"You can work from home for a change."

"I'll have to travel with her eventually, but yeah, I'm happy to not have to set up camp in Nashville again."

"It's the little things. Dinner this weekend?" Anya asked. "Duncan says he misses your face."

"I miss his, too. Yes. I'll bring wine and fill you in."

They hung up, promising to text dinner details as the week progressed. Right now, she had to get ready to meet Sophie James, who'd be there in half an hour. Dana was not a nervous person. She'd been doing this job for a long time and she was good at it, had several clients she handled at once, and well. She knew that. She was manager of some, publicist for others, but for Sophie, she was going to be both. Normally, that wasn't daunting to her at all. Dana was not easily intimidated. For some reason, though, she was uneasy about this one…

Shifting in her chair, Dana got her things together so she could go over, one more time, items she'd need to address with Sophie James.

God, why did she feel so unprepared for this?

❖

Sophie hadn't been to the Miracle Records headquarters in years. She couldn't remember how many. When her first album had gone platinum, they'd invited her to a party. A "meet and greet" they'd called it, but it was really a gathering where the higher-ups could meet her, shake her hand, stare at her. She remembered it well: she'd never felt undressed by so many eyes in her entire life. It was disconcerting and she'd held Ray's arm the whole time like it had been a life preserver.

She was seventeen then.

Today was different. Ray had always handled this stuff for her. She'd never had to worry, never had to be concerned that she didn't know what she was doing, who she was talking with, whether she sounded stupid or naive or…young. No, today, she was on her own. Meeting a new version of Ray. The thought made her grimace. She couldn't think about it that way. There was no other version of Ray. Ray was gone. This was going to be like starting over, and Sophie hated it.

Sophie had agonized over what to wear. She'd called Andrew, made him come over and go through her closet with her. "Not too glitzy. Casual, but not too casual," she'd told him. "Professional. I need to look like I have my shit together."

He hadn't questioned her. Just did his job as her stylist and pulled out dark designer jeans, modest heels, and a relaxed sweater in blue and white stripes. He'd draped a navy blue scarf loosely around her neck, and when she'd looked in the mirror, she felt confident. That's what Andrew did for her. Every time. The guy was a magician.

"You don't have to impress anyone," he'd reminded her. "They're already sold on you. Remember that. This is just a formality. You meeting the new manager. Just be you."

Sophie often wondered if other people in her line of work—singers, actors, whatever—had stylists that also doubled as life coaches. Because that's what she often felt Andrew was for her. More than once, she'd thought about asking him if he had to reassure his other clients the same way he did her. But what if he said yes? What if she wasn't special? What if they weren't really friends, she was just part of his job? She wasn't sure she could take that. Not today. Not now. Not with Ray gone. So she stayed quiet and wondered instead.

This was an introduction, a simple meeting of two people, so

Sophie had decided to go alone. She could've coaxed Andrew into accompanying her. Or even Michaela, her makeup artist. But she had heard inklings her entire career of how the record executives often looked at her: as a young, naive girl who'd been coddled by her manager for the past decade and a half and who rarely made her own decisions. About anything. And while she would be forever grateful to Ray, it wasn't a reputation she was proud of…though she'd never stood up for herself with him either.

With a sigh, she took the offered hand of the driver and allowed him to help her out of the car that was stopped in front of the Miracle Records Building, not far from Central Park. Realistically, she could've walked. Also realistic was the fact that she would most likely be recognized and her quick jaunt along the Manhattan sidewalks would take much longer than it should. Thus, she'd opted for a car service.

The doorman held the door for her and tipped his hat as if he'd stepped out of a movie from the fifties. Once on the elevator, and surprisingly alone inside, Sophie took off her oversized sunglasses and inhaled deeply.

"You got this," she whispered to herself, suddenly more nervous than she cared to admit. She never did things like this without Ray. The thought brought a fresh sheen of wetness to her eyes, and she shook her head roughly. "No. No, no, no. You will not cry in front of your record execs. Or your new manager." Suddenly, as if he were standing right next to her, Sophie heard Ray's voice. "*Stand up straight. Chin up. Head high. Make eye contact. Command attention. You own the room and everybody in it. Remember that.*" Words he said to her before every show, before every appearance, before every interview. She took another deep breath, sniffed, dabbed under her eyes with a finger to make sure her makeup wasn't smudging. By the time the elevator dinged her arrival on the fifty-seventh floor, Sophie James had pulled herself together.

"Miss James," the receptionist at the desk said coolly, when she saw Sophie. She was probably thirty, her dark hair swept back into a complicated updo that made her Bluetooth earpiece visible, and her clothes were just this side of edgy: black and modern with silver accents that gave her a tiny sliver of flash. Sophie figured she was paid to have no outward reaction to the well-known singers and musicians and various celebrities who passed by her desk, and she was good at it. Her smile was neutrally pleasant as she said, "I'll let them know you're here," then spoke quietly to some unseen person.

The waiting area was such a stereotype, Sophie allowed herself to smile over it. Gold, silver, and platinum records in frames lined the walls, boasting musical acts from well before Sophie was born up to last month. It was impressive, she had to admit, though she did note the abundance of new bands and new individuals. She strolled slowly along and stopped in front of Gemma Day's debut album from two years ago. It had gone platinum a couple times over and was still generating singles. Gemma Day was not much younger than Sophie, but she was hot and sexy and in demand, and Sophie felt a pang of jealousy she didn't expect roll through the pit of her stomach.

"Miss James?" The receptionist's voice startled Sophie back to the present. "Follow me, please."

Sophie was led down a long, carpeted hallway, those walls also covered with various framed albums in different shades of metal. At a doorway on the left, the receptionist stopped and held out an arm, gesturing Sophie inside.

With a nod of thanks, Sophie stepped into what turned out to be a conference room. Long table surrounded by many ergonomically correct chairs, and a bevy of food and drink laid out on the surface. Fresh fruit, baked goods, cheese and crackers. Along one wall was a sort of sidebar that boasted wine, beer, sparkling water, champagne, soda, and Sophie was willing to bet she could choose the most obscure beverage possible and it would show up in this room within a few minutes.

"Sophie! How are you holding up, babe? You doing okay? It's so good to see you." Davis Silverstein was all huge grins and boisterous greetings and familiarity, his arms outstretched like Sophie was his niece and it was his job to comfort her over Ray's death. Didn't matter that they'd only actually met maybe four times in all the years Sophie had been making money for Miracle. She allowed the hug, the too-damp kiss on her cheek, tried not to stiffen at his large, meaty hand on the small of her back as he turned her to face the other three people in the room. "Sophie James, I'd like you to meet Brooks and Kettle, two of our terrific producers."

Sophie knew the names, knew they served as both producers and songwriters, and they'd been with Miracle probably longer than she had. They were older, looked like middle-aged dads instead of what somebody might picture a record producer or songwriter to look like, and they regarded Sophie with a small hint of interest, as if she were a stray cat that they weren't sure what to do with. She dutifully shook their hands—Damon Brooks and Tim Kettle—and smiled.

"And this is Dana Landon, your new manager and publicist."

How Sophie had entered the room and not seen this woman was a mystery, because when her eyes landed on her, weird things happened to Sophie's body. Her heart rate picked up speed. There was an unfamiliar flutter in her stomach. Her mouth went instantly dry.

"Hi, Sophie." Dana Landon held out a hand, her blue eyes not cold, but cool, like she was assessing things before relaxing completely. She was blond, her hair hanging in soft waves just past her shoulders. She wore an expensive dress—Sophie could spot specific designers the way Michaela could identify brands of makeup—in a soft blue that made her eyes stand out. Dark lashes and eyebrows said maybe the blond was artificial, but Sophie didn't care. It was perfect. "I've heard so much about you. It's nice to finally meet you in person."

Sophie put her hand in Dana's and suddenly the only thing she could focus on was the softness of Dana's skin, the warmth of her touch. After a beat or two went by, Sophie realized she'd held on a bit too long, hadn't said anything, so she scrambled to do so. Clearing her throat, she managed, "It's nice to meet you as well." *A complete sentence. Thank fucking God.*

Dana's smile only faltered slightly, and Sophie figured she was probably used to self-absorbed musicians acting like idiots in her presence.

"Dana's one of the best in the business," Silverstein said, pulling Sophie's attention away from the slight embarrassment that had set in. He rattled off half a dozen names, all people Sophie knew, and spent the next five minutes singing the praises of her new manager and publicist. Dana sat quietly and Sophie wasn't sure why, but she got the distinct impression that Davis Silverstein annoyed her no end. But he was the boss, so she smiled politely and let him talk. Then he moved on to the two producers and gave them the same treatment. Sophie did her best to listen and nodded where she thought she was supposed to. "So, I'm going to leave you to it," he said finally, after what felt like a good half hour to Sophie but was probably only about ten minutes. "Help yourself to whatever you'd like to eat or drink. If there's something you don't see, Dana can buzz Raquel and she'll get it for you." Plastering another wet kiss on Sophie's cheek, Silverstein bid them adieu and was gone.

A moment of quiet passed before Dana, her eyes on the closed door, broke it with, "Thank God. That was painful."

Tim Kettle laughed. "I mean, I like you a lot, Dana, but that was a bit much, even for him. He so wants you to be his next conquest."

"He's wanted that for the past five years," Damon Brooks added.

Dana seemed to find the whole thing amusing. "I've got a built-in deterrent." Her voice was matter-of-fact, and she shrugged to punctuate her point.

"Please. You think the fact that you dig chicks is gonna keep him from trying?" Tim chuckled his apparent enjoyment of that.

Damon snorted. "That just makes you more of a challenge."

Sophie watched the entire exchange, fascinated. She'd learned so much already. That Davis Silverstein was a huge creeper. That Brooks and Kettle were a bit hipper than she'd originally thought. That her new manager and publicist preferred women.

That was interesting information and it caused a weird tingling in Sophie's body. *What's that about?*

"So," Dana said, and Sophie realized she was talking to her. "That was all terribly unprofessional and I apologize." Her concerned expression seemed genuine to Sophie.

"No big deal," Sophie said with a shrug. And it really wasn't. She didn't care who thought what about Davis Silverstein. She'd formed her own opinion. "I'm a big girl."

"Good," Dana said. "That comes in handy."

Sophie smiled at her. There was an instant comfort around Dana Landon and it confused Sophie. She'd come here expecting to hate her new manager simply because he or she wasn't Ray. Ready and fully prepared to hate her. But there was something about Dana…

"All right then." Dana woke up the tablet Sophie just noticed on the table in front of her and scrolled. "You're scheduled to start working on the new album in two weeks." She looked up from the screen, her blue eyes suddenly much softer than when Sophie had first walked into the room. "Are you up for that?" she asked, her voice quiet.

Sophie didn't have to think about her answer. She gave a curt nod. "Absolutely. I think getting back to work is a good thing."

"I agree." Dana seemed to study her screen for a moment, but when she asked her next question, Sophie realized she'd just been formulating how to say what she needed to say. "And…are you done with the…clubbing?"

It was a very diplomatic way to say "public drunkenness" or "acting out" or "embarrassing yourself," and Sophie appreciated the effort. She inhaled deeply, let it out slowly, and noticed Brooks and Kettle suddenly pretending to be engrossed in their laptops.

You own the room and everybody in it.

Ray's voice was clear as day. Sophie sat up a little straighter, a little taller, did her best to command attention. "I lost somebody very close to me and it's been...difficult. To say the least." She nibbled on the inside of her cheek as she thought about how legit terrified she was by the thought of carrying on with her career without Ray. But she was not about to give these people the satisfaction of seeing that weakness. "I cut loose. I think any regular person would do the same."

"But you're not any regular person." Dana kept her tone gentle, but there was a firmness to it that Sophie could feel more than she could hear. Not scolding, but not far from it.

"That is the happy and the sad truth of it, isn't it?"

Dana nodded, gave her a small smile.

"I can tell you with all honesty that I'm not planning on cutting loose again."

"But it could happen."

"But it could happen." It was as honest as Sophie could be.

"Understood." Something about Dana seemed to...shutter then. It was the only word Sophie could come up with. Like a sheer blind came down in front of her and obscured her just a bit. Took her slightly out of focus. Which was a shame because Dana Landon was fun to look at. That was a fact. "All right. I'm going to go through some emails here, some appearances people are asking about, and I'll get them all lined up for us to talk about. While I'm doing that, why don't you talk to the guys here about the upcoming album?"

Damon jumped right in and Sophie tried to tamp down the disappointment at having her attention pulled from the beautiful blond woman across from her—a disappointment she didn't quite understand. "Okay, we've got a couple of great ideas for the next album, sort of a theme."

"Desire and unrequited love," Tim chimed in, and it was amusing to watch the two men merge onto one page. "An entire album devoted to it. It tells a story, from beginning to end."

The idea was an interesting one, Sophie had to admit. She'd never done any kind of a theme around her albums. She'd jumped to a conclusion about these guys and she felt guilty about that now. At the same time, they went on about this ballad and that ballad and Sophie listened for a while before holding up a hand.

"What if we went...a little edgier?"

Both producers stopped what they were doing and stared at her. Really stared. Blinked. Looked at her as if a third eye had popped out on her forehead. As Sophie moved her gaze from one guy to the other, she suddenly realized that Dana Landon had also tuned in. Sophie could feel her eyes. Feel them. Which was *so weird.*

"Edgier?" Damon asked, his face genuinely surprised.

Sophie nodded.

"What does that mean?" Tim asked, looking just as bewildered. "You sing ballads. I mean, you sing them amazingly well, but...you sing ballads."

Sophie sighed quietly, could almost hear Ray agreeing with them. "Yeah." She felt the determination slowly leak out of her like she was a balloon with a pinhole.

"Miracle has...expectations," Dana offered quietly, somehow making Sophie feel like she completely understood what she'd been thinking.

She was right. Sophie knew that. She motioned for the guys to continue and they dove right back in as if they'd never been interrupted. Sophie did her best to listen and seem at least somewhat interested. It was harder than she expected, but she managed.

The guys had some recordings on their computer and they played a few for Sophie, gave her a chance to get a taste of what they were thinking.

"Can you email me a couple of those so I can listen again at home?" she asked.

Damon looked surprised, like the idea of her offering opinions was a foreign one, but nodded. "Sure." She rattled off her address and he hit Send. "Done."

"I'll take a day or two and get back to you with any questions or suggestions."

"Sounds great," Dana said, smoothly reentering the conversation. "I just emailed you a suggested schedule for the next two months. Take a look. Tell me what you think. If it's too much or too little or whatever. Let me know." Her eye contact was direct. Firm... *Can eye contact be firm?* Sophie's mind tried to carry her off to the Land of Words, a place she really enjoyed wandering around, but she yanked it back to the table.

Sophie nodded. "I'll take a look later today."

Dana smiled at her, a small smile that was pleasant enough but gave Sophie the impression that there was much more behind it than most were allowed to see. *Reserved.* That was the right word to describe Dana Landon. Sophie felt better having put her finger on it.

"My number, email, etcetera is all in the email," Dana went on, gathering her things, sliding what little paperwork she'd brought with her into a neat pile, her tablet on top. "Any time, day or night, you call me. We're a team now."

A surprising lump formed in Sophie's throat. Ray used to say that all the time. They were a team, the two of them. Having somebody new take his place was…strange, odd, and Sophie wasn't sure what to do with the jumble of feelings that suddenly crowded her head, her chest. With a curt nod, she cleared her throat and stood.

Dana came around the table, sidled up close, said quietly, "You okay?"

The guys were oblivious to any change in the mood of the room— or at least they pretended to be—and Sophie was grateful. She could feel the warmth of Dana's hand at the small of her back—such a shockingly different feeling than when Davis Silverstein had done the same thing—as she nodded. "Yeah. I am. It sometimes just…"

"Comes out of nowhere? Yeah, that happened to me after my best friend passed away."

"I'm sorry," Sophie said, startled by the revelation. "That's awful."

"Thank you. It was a long time ago, but I remember very clearly how the grief would just sneak up on me when I wasn't expecting it and whack me in the head with a board."

Sophie's chuckle was short. "It feels just like that sometimes."

"It'll get better." Dana grimaced with a cute expression of self-deprecation. "God, that's such a clichéd thing to say, isn't it?"

Sophie nodded good-naturedly.

"But it's true. Just hang in there. I'm here if you need to talk."

"Thanks. I appreciate that." *Never happen*, she thought. There was no way she was about to talk about the pain of losing her manager— and friend—to her new manager. That just seemed…almost incestuous. Or something equally unpalatable.

With a pasted-on smile—a look Sophie had perfected over the

past three weeks—she bid the three goodbye and was surprised to find the receptionist waiting for her just outside the door to show her out.

Back in the safety of the car, she let out a long, slow breath as her driver inched them into downtown Manhattan traffic.

She'd survived. She'd taken the first step of moving forward in her career without Ray and she'd survived. She was still breathing.

Thank fucking God.

Moving forward in her *life*, however, already felt like it was going to be a whole different story. But now she had work. Something to focus on. She forced her brain away from thoughts of Ray and toward the things Brooks and Kettle had suggested. A theme album. She could work with that, absolutely.

From her purse, she pulled out the little notebook she'd started carrying everywhere with her a year or two ago and flipped it open, smiled as she read her own handwriting. Yeah, she had more to contribute to this album than her producers expected.

It was time to spread her wings.

CHAPTER THREE

The Reeveses' brownstone was unobtrusive on the outside, blending in with the rest of the brownstones up and down their street in Soho. Inside, however, was a slightly different story.

Duncan Reeves was a Wall Street broker by day and a master of DIY projects by night. Dana had stayed with them for a week last year when she'd had her floors redone in her place in Chelsea and she'd never seen anybody change out of a suit and into jeans and a T-shirt so fast in her life. With his rugged, dark-haired good looks, his broad-shouldered build, and how perfect he looked with a hammer in his hand, Dana was still surprised by his choice of career. Even after years of knowing the man.

"Hello there, you gorgeous creature," he said, as he let her in the door.

She placed her hand against his cheek, his five o'clock shadow as thick as if he hadn't shaved at all that day. "Hi there, handsome."

Duncan took her coat and called over his shoulder, "Honey! She brought that wine you were hoping for."

"Excellent," came Anya's voice from deep inside the house. "You can let her in then."

Dana wiped a hand across her brow in mock-relief. "I was so worried."

"Rightfully so." Duncan grinned and stepped aside to let her pass.

"Oh, I love this color." Dana ran her hand along the hallway wall as she walked, her fingertips skimming the deep rust color. Not quite orange, but not brown. Somewhere in between.

"Yeah?"

"I do. Anya tried to describe it to me, but seeing it is…it's very warm and inviting."

Duncan grinned. "I'm glad to hear that. It was not an easy battle."

"Oh, I know all about it," Dana said, and bumped him with her shoulder as the hall opened into a modern gourmet kitchen.

Anya came out from behind the granite countertop, wiping her hands on her apron. She held out her arms for a hug, wrapped Dana in her warm embrace. "I'm so happy to see your face," she said softly in Dana's ear. Even though they talked regularly on the phone, their schedules didn't often allow for personal visits, so seeing one another face-to-face was kind of rare.

Dana squeezed, then let go and held her friend at arm's length, always struck for a moment by how such a big personality fit into such a small frame. Anya's sleek, dark hair was pulled back. "You look beautiful and I hate you a little bit."

"Goal achieved." Dana followed Anya into the kitchen where a bottle of something red was breathing on the counter, two crystal wine glasses next to it. "I've got a Sangiovese. All right with you?"

"Is it wine?" Dana asked, and Anya chuckled as she poured. "God, it smells good in here." She wasn't kidding, the aromas in the air of oregano and garlic filling her nose, causing her mouth to water.

"I made ravioli," Anya said, holding out her glass for Dana to touch hers to it.

"Correction," Duncan said. "She made ravioli from scratch. And sauce. And bread. *From scratch.*" His smile was proud, and he kissed the top of Anya's head as he passed her and got a beer from the fridge.

"Wait," Dana said, holding up a finger.

Before she could say more, Anya stopped her with a hand and nodded. "That's right. This Korean American chick made Italian from scratch."

"I'm so confused right now."

Anya laughed and went back to the stovetop.

"Wow. I'm getting spoiled." Dana loved dinner with Anya and Duncan. The warmth and the welcome feeling always reminded her of home, of her parents and her siblings, how dinner every weeknight at the table together was a requirement. They could invite any of their friends over that they wanted to, but any and all kids had to be sitting at the dining room table by six.

Anya stirred her sauce with a wooden spoon while Dana took a seat on one of the stools tucked under the breakfast bar and helped herself to some of the cheese and crackers from the tray on the counter. She followed it with a sip from her glass.

The wine was a burst of complex flavor in Dana's mouth. She let it coat her tongue, rolling it around a bit before swallowing. Deep, but not heavy. A hint of fruit, but not sweet. "My God, between the wonderful smell of almost-dinner and this wine? I may never leave." Dana grinned as Anya glanced over her shoulder.

"I'd be totally happy with you here all the time," she said fondly.

Duncan raised his hand, never looking up from the laptop he had opened on the table. "Same."

"Of course, once you started bringing chicks home, I'd have to draw a line," Anya teased.

"I'd have no lines to draw," Duncan countered. "At all. Bring home all the chicks you want to. The hotter, the better."

They went back and forth a couple of times about Dana's nonexistent harem of women being filtered into her room in the Reeves house, which also didn't exist, and Dana shook her head, chuckling with fondness.

"Speaking of hot chicks," Anya said, using a mesh spoon to scoop ravioli out of the boiling water. "How did things go with your new diva?"

"There's a new diva?" Duncan asked, his dark brows raising.

"Babe, I told you." Anya rolled her eyes. Sighed. "You never listen when I talk."

"I absolutely listen."

"Dana's managing Sophie James now."

"Seriously?" Duncan's brows went higher. "You didn't tell me that."

Anya turned to look at Dana, nodding vigorously as she mouthed, *Yes, I did.*

"Is she as hot in real life as she looks on TV?" Duncan asked.

Dana thought about it, thought back to the meeting. Sophie was dressed smartly. She looked elegant, but casual. Classy, but approachable. Her skin was flawless, olive in shade, very little makeup. Her hair... Dana recalled how shiny it was. Dark. Lustrous. Her dark eyes accented by even darker brows and lashes. Her lips shimmering with a hint of gloss. The way she folded her manicured hands on the table in front of her...

"Hello?" Anya snapped her fingers and jerked Dana back to the present, then gave a knowing grin. "Well, that says a lot."

"What does?" Dana asked, clearing her throat.

"That dreamy look on your face."

"That wasn't dreamy."

Anya shot a look to her husband, her expression questioning.

"Totally dreamy," Duncan said with a determined nod. "So, I'm gonna take that response as, 'Yes, Duncan, you sexy hunk of a man, Sophie James is, in fact, as hot in person as she seems on television.'"

Dana shook her head and felt herself blush a little bit. Doing her best to reroute the conversation, she said, "She was surprisingly... steady? Does that make sense?" At the blank looks from her friends, she tried to explain. "Like, I expected her to be a little more lost. Or at least uncertain. Ray Cooper did everything for her, for her entire career—or so I've been led to believe. I sort of expected her to need some hand-holding. She didn't seem to." And that was nice, if Dana was being honest. Sophie had been the ultimate professional.

"Was it just the two of you?" Anya asked as she dished food onto three plates.

"Us and Brooks and Kettle." With a glance at Duncan, she clarified, "Songwriter/producers."

"Ah."

Anya tipped her head from one side to the other. "They're not bad."

Dana recalled the conversation and furrowed her brow. "Sophie did say something about being more...did she say edgy? Something like that."

"She is pretty vanilla." Anya delivered two plates to the table, went back for the third. "Love songs. Ballads. Adult contemporary stuff."

"True." Dana got up with a chuckle and grabbed the wine bottle. She topped off her glass and Anya's. "The guys looked like she'd started speaking Pig Latin."

Anya and Duncan both laughed. "I bet," Anya said. "They're not exactly cutting-edge kind of guys."

Dana recalled telling Sophie that the company had expectations and how her face fell just a little bit, how her shoulders had dropped subtly. "Yeah." It had bothered Dana some, and that was unexpected, but she'd shaken it off, just like she did now. "I've set some stuff up for her," she said, carrying the glasses back to the table. "A couple appearances. And I have some ideas for venues. She starts recording in a little over a week."

"Think she'll be okay?"

"With what? Recording?" Dana cut a ravioli with her fork and

popped half into her mouth. All thought ceased as she closed her eyes
and savored the flavors of cheese and tomatoes and… "Oh, my God,"
she muttered, eyes wide, fingers in front of her lips. "Anya. This…I…
oh, my God."

"Right?" Duncan asked, shoveling a whole ravioli into his own
mouth.

"This is friggin' *delicious*," Dana said, scooping up more.

Anya grinned, looking from one to the other. "Thanks, guys. Not
bad for my first attempt, if I do say so myself."

Dana and Duncan could only nod and grunt their agreement as
they ate. Dana tried to slow down, but it was all so good. Before she
knew it, her plate was empty and she was sopping up the remaining
sauce with a warm, crusty piece of bread.

"You didn't answer me," Anya pointed out. Somehow, she still
had three ravioli left on her plate.

"About?"

Anya sighed. "I asked you if you think Sophie will be all right
recording on her own."

Dana furrowed her brow for a second or two before catching up.
"Oh! Because Ray's gone."

Anya's eyes widened for a beat. She gave her head a quick shake,
and her expression clearly said, "Duh," as she opened her hands, palms
up.

"I guess?" Dana said. "I hadn't really thought much about it. She
seems okay."

"D. It's been what? Two months since the guy died?"

"Yes?"

Anya shook her head again, but this time it seemed like she was
backing off. Or giving up. "All I'm saying is maybe keep an eye on her.
You know?"

It wasn't that the thought hadn't occurred to Dana; it had. But it
had been fleeting. Sophie James seemed solid. Steady. In control. Fine.
"She seemed fine."

"Do you need me to pull up Instagram and show you how fine she
was last week?" Anya arched one eyebrow as she took a bite of dinner.

Dana picked up her glass. "You make a valid point, my friend."

"She does that," Duncan chimed in.

"I do." Anya pointed her fork at each of them. "It would do you
both well to remember that."

Dana grinned and looked at Duncan, who had the same dopey smile on his face. "Yes, ma'am," she said, and shot a look to Duncan, who nodded vigorously.

Later on, the trio sat in the Reeves's living room, soft jazz on the stereo. Anya sat on the couch, curled up in the crook of her husband's arm. Dana was in the overstuffed chair to their right. Each of them had a snifter of warm brandy, courtesy of Duncan's latest hobby. Dana watched how he held his glass, nestled in the palm of his hand, gently swirling the dark amber liquid, and she did the same.

"What do you think?" he asked, his eyes sparkling with excitement in the soft lighting as Dana took a sip.

"It's really smooth," Dana said truthfully. "I know nothing about brandy, but this is nice." To Anya, she asked, "Do you get to do tastings every night?"

Anya gave a snort. "Hopefully, not for long." She glanced up at Duncan, whose smile grew wide.

Dana looked from one of them to the other. "What does that mean?" She pointed at them, waved her finger back and forth. "What's that look? What are those weird grins?"

"We're trying," Anya said, her smile wide, her entire being seeming to light up the room.

"What?" Dana's eyes went round, her eyebrows shot up. "Trying… to get pregnant? *Oh, my God, are you guys trying to get pregnant?*"

"We are trying to get pregnant," Anya confirmed with a laugh and was on her feet in obvious anticipation of the hug from Dana that came instantly and almost knocked her off her feet.

"Oh, my God, I'm so happy!"

She felt Anya laugh in her arms. "We're just trying. We're not pregnant yet."

"I don't care," Dana said quietly, surprised to feel herself suddenly overwhelmed by emotion. "I'm still so happy." She cleared her throat.

Anya grasped her shoulders and pushed herself back from Dana so she could see her face. "Are you crying, D?"

"No." Dana wiped the tear that was coursing down her cheek. "I don't cry."

"Liar."

They stood there for a moment, two best friends sharing a moment. Duncan stood behind his wife, his tender smile filled with love, and Dana reached up and stroked his cheek.

As if suddenly snapped into action, Dana gave her head a shake and blinked rapidly as she glanced at her watch. "Gah! It's late. Why am I still here?" To Duncan, she pointed and ordered, "Go. Take her upstairs and put a baby in her!"

Dana left her friends laughing, arms around each other, waving at her as she got into an Uber. She loved visiting them, even though it was sometimes a titch bittersweet for her. She adored Anya and Duncan, would never think anything bad about them. Ever. She would, however, be envious of them on occasion. Like now. Not because she wanted a baby. Despite the obnoxiously loud ticking of her biological clock, Dana hadn't made a decision on that yet. No, she was envious of the Reeveses because *they had each other*. Always. Unconditionally. It had been a long time since Dana'd had a partner, and if that relationship had been half as strong as Anya's and Duncan's, she'd still be in it.

No, she seemed to be better off by herself.

Yeah.

No reason to be sad about that. It's just fact.

Alone was better for her. Much better.

Wasn't it?

CHAPTER FOUR

Sophie never sat at the window, which was sad.
Her penthouse had an enormous window seat, the view from the twenty-fourth floor stunningly overlooking Central Park. She'd actually picked out this place for exactly that. She could still remember running across the hardwood and flopping herself down on the red velvet cushions that had been there during the scheduled visit with the Realtor.

"Look at this," she'd said to Ray, her voice filled with wonder and enthusiasm. "You can practically see the whole park!" A huge exaggeration, but to her easily impressed younger self, it had seemed like it. "I want to just sit here forever."

That desire lasted until the first time a photo of her had shown up in a tabloid, a shot of her in her panties and a tank top at night, naively backlit by her own floor lamp. That was the last time she'd sat there.

Until today.

It was daylight, and that definitely helped in the decision. No photos could be taken if the inside of the penthouse wasn't lit. She'd also had blinds installed that made it impossible to see inside, but they kept out too much of the light, so Sophie barely used them. She hadn't been fodder for the paparazzi in quite some time...until her drunken performances of late. Now she had to be vigilant again. Make sure she didn't parade around her place naked. Or pick her nose. Or shove a giant slice of chocolate cake in her face.

With a sigh, Sophie tilted her head back against the deep purple pillows she loved—the only thing in the room a decorator hadn't chosen for her—and basked in the warmth of the sun. This, she remembered. This was what she'd loved about this place.

Opening her eyes again, she focused on her laptop, readjusted her earphones, and clicked on one of the sound clips Damon Brooks had sent her. A song titled "Across the Room." It wasn't bad. His email had said to imagine it with an orchestra behind her, and while the idea of strings was appealing, Sophie heard more. Guitar. Keyboards. A beat. She stroked a fingertip over her eyebrow as she played it again. The mainline wasn't bad. It could be catchy with the right tweaks...

Sophie spent the next hour listening to the cuts the guys had sent, rewinding, zeroing in on certain riffs or bridges, jotting notes in her notebook, losing herself in the music.

She felt more than heard the presence of another person, and when she looked up, Andrew was setting his things down on her table. Sophie grinned, realizing that most people might freak to look up from their laptop and see another person suddenly standing in their apartment. But she never felt that with Andrew. He had a key. He didn't knock, just let himself in. Didn't matter what state of dress Sophie was in. Andrew was gay and her best friend, so if she happened to be in her underwear, which had occurred more than once, he'd comment on the color or style or both, and she'd roll her eyes at him.

"Hey," Sophie said, tugging her earphones out. She took in Andrew's perfectly styled sandy hair, his dark jeans, brown leather shoes, and white oxford. "How do you make such simple clothes look so great all the time?"

"Honey, you've asked me that a million times and the answer is always the same: It's a gift." As Sophie grinned, he put his hand on his hip and studied her. "How're you doing, kiddo?"

Sophie tipped her head to one side, then the other. "I'm hanging in there." It was the truth.

Andrew crossed the open concept penthouse apartment, his shoes echoing on the hardwood floor, to the refrigerator. He pulled out a bottle of water and held it up for her to see. She nodded. He usually flitted around whatever space he was in like a six-foot-tall bird, but today, he took his time. Sauntered. Sophie realized he'd come by simply to check on her, and her heart warmed in her chest.

At the window seat, he handed her a bottle, then lifted her legs and sat under them so they were draped across his lap. "Talk to me."

Lifting one shoulder in a half shrug, Sophie said, "Not much new to say."

"You sleeping?"

"Some."

Andrew narrowed his blue eyes at her.

"Okay, fine. Not a lot."

"And what about the prescription?"

Sophie grimaced. Her doctor had given her some pills after Ray's death to help her sleep, and she'd taken them for a couple of nights, then stopped. "They make my head feel fuzzy in the morning. I don't like the feeling that my ears are full of cotton."

Andrew's hand was warm as he set it on her yoga pants–clad knee. "I know, sweetheart, but you have to sleep."

"I dream about Ray." Sophie's voice was barely a whisper and she felt her eyes well up. "I mean, sometimes, that's okay, but…"

"Sometimes, it's too hard," Andrew finished for her. "I went through that when I lost my dad."

The tears rolled down her face as she cried silently. Andrew squeezed her leg gently and was quiet, let her have her emotions. That was the best part of their relationship right now and Sophie thought about it often. Andrew got it. He got it. He didn't try to hold her because they both knew if he did, she'd lose herself completely…and she worried that she'd never be able to get it back. He simply sat with her, was present, while she dealt with whatever she was feeling, then tucked it back into its box and put it on a high, high shelf.

Several moments went by, Andrew looking at his hand on her leg, Sophie watching New York City out her window, until she felt like she could speak without the annoying lump—which seemed to have somehow become a regular part of her throat now—interfering. She cleared it as Andrew reached for her earphones.

"What're you listening to?" He put one in his ear as Sophie popped in the second one.

"New music the guys at Miracle sent." She hit play on "Across the Room," watched Andrew's face as he listened. His head moved slightly to it, not exactly a bob. He had a surprisingly good ear for musical style and song potential, and Sophie had found over the past couple of years, not only did they have similar taste in artists, but Andrew could pick out subtle nuances that Sophie also zeroed in on. Maybe it was his age, only four years older than her, but Sophie could talk to Andrew about music in a way she never could with Ray. "What do you think?"

He inhaled slowly, squinted as he thought. "I like it. I love the lyrics, the idea of loving someone from afar. Everybody can relate to that." He seemed like he had more to say, but couldn't grasp the right words.

"What if it had more…edge?" Sophie asked.

He looked at her, squinted again, pursed his lips. "Edge."

Sophie nodded.

Andrew tapped a finger against his lips. "Play it again."

Sophie did and they both listened. Andrew pointed, eyes closed, and she played it again. They repeated this, five more times before Andrew opened his eyes and met her gaze.

"Edge," he said, and Sophie nodded. "I see it."

"Yeah?"

"Definitely. You could kick it up a bit, give it a bit of a punch, but not lose the overall effect."

"Exactly." Sophie pushed at his shoulder affectionately. "I *knew* you'd get it."

His nose slightly wrinkled, he asked, "Would they let you do that, oh Ballad Queen of Adult Contemporary?"

Sophie sighed as she clicked the laptop shut. "No idea. My new manager says my record company has 'expectations.'" She made air quotes around the last word.

"Oh, right. How'd that go, meeting him?"

"Her," Sophie corrected. "Dana is a her and it went fine." She thought back to the other day, to Dana Landon, her blond waves and sparkling blue eyes and calm demeanor. "She seems to know her stuff. She's emailed me some upcoming appearances she's booked so I can start plugging."

"That's great. You want to forward it to me so I can add them to my schedule?"

"Way ahead of you. Sent it just before you got here."

"Perfect." Andrew took a sip of his water, then scrolled on his phone. "Yup. Got it. When do you hit the studio?"

"Soon. They're sending me a few more cuts later today, and then we meet on Thursday to talk."

Andrew indicated the notebook next to her with his eyes. "You have ideas." It's wasn't a question.

"Yeah."

"You gonna present them to these guys?"

"I don't know."

"Sweetie." Andrew shifted his body slightly so he was facing her directly. "You've had that notebook—or *a* notebook—for as long as I've known you."

Sophie gave a slow nod and faced the window again. Andrew knew her well but didn't know the half of the notes she actually had.

Ideas, song titles, lyrics. In a cedar box under her bed. Locked. "I know…" She let the sentence dangle, not even sure which direction to take it. When she glanced back at Andrew, his expression could only be described as "knowing." It was like he could see right through her, into her, read her thoughts as if they were written out for him.

He reached for her hand. "Ray's gone, babe." He took a beat, seemed to let his words sink in, let Sophie absorb them. "Maybe it's time for you to spread your wings a bit. You know?"

Sophie looked at their linked hands, Andrew's so much bigger than hers, his nails manicured, his skin alarmingly soft, and tried to focus on his words. On all of them. The same words she'd used in her own head. But she couldn't. Her heart wouldn't let her. Her heart only heard two.

Ray's gone.

That was still all that mattered.

God, when will this end? she asked herself as a tear spilled over and she felt the familiar pain squeeze her chest. *When?*

CHAPTER FIVE

S ophie had such mixed emotions about this appearance. *Brooke Talk* was popular and the exposure would be good, Dana had told her. And normally, Sophie would have no issues at all making a talk show appearance to plug her upcoming work, especially a live afternoon show that was right here in New York so she didn't have to travel far from home.

But she was unusually nervous.

She stood in front of the full-length mirror in her room and assessed her look. Andrew had chosen well, as always. She wasn't singing for this appearance, just chatting with Brooke Kramer for an eight-minute interview, so they'd decided to go somewhat casual with her look. The flowy black pants and printed halter-style top made her look effortlessly elegant. The silver heels made her tall, which was a power thing Andrew had explained to her. Sophie was tall anyway at five nine. But add another two, three, or even four inches when the outfit called for it and people couldn't help but notice her. She commanded attention. Owned the room and everybody in it, as Ray would say. Andrew agreed.

Michaela was going to meet her at the *Brooke Talk* studios and do her hair and makeup, so Sophie gathered her things and texted the doorman downstairs for a car. She was just putting her phone into her purse when it rang. Hardly anybody called her, and her heart skipped when she saw the screen.

"Hi, Mom," she said, trying to sound laid back but knowing she sounded happy to hear from her. It had been a while and Sophie had left a couple of messages since Ray had passed away. Her mother had been out of the country, on a trip to Japan that Sophie had given her as a gift, and hadn't come back for Ray's funeral. Sophie had gone through it all on her own. Sure, Andrew was there. Michaela. Ray's friends. But all she'd wanted was her mother, standing next to her, being her strength, telling her it was going to be okay, that her world hadn't just crumbled to bits around her.

"Hi, sweetie," her mother said, and there was chatter in the background, as if she was at a party. Or a mall.

"How are you? It's been a while. How was Japan?" She listened as she left her penthouse and rode the elevator down to the lobby as her mother went on and on about the beauty and intricacies and people and food she experienced on her trip. Sophie could picture Debbie James, the woman who grew up with nothing, who had nothing even when Ray discovered Sophie singing in a Christmas concert in their small North Carolina town. The woman who raised Sophie alone—and wasn't always good at it. Her bottle-blond hair, though a much more expensive bottle from a high-end salon since Sophie became successful; her year-round tan, from the trips she continually "casually" mentioned to Sophie and Sophie sent her on; her penchant to overdress, go glitzier and more designer now than she'd ever been able to. But she was the only mother Sophie had, would ever have, and Sophie loved her.

The fall air hit Sophie like a gentle slap, the unexpected breeze cutting through her long jacket as if it was made of cheesecloth. Sophie shivered and nodded at the driver who held the car door open for her as she kept the phone to her ear and slid inside. When there was finally a break where her mother needed to take a breath or pass out from lack of oxygen, Sophie said, "I'm about to do my first talk show appearance since Ray passed away, Mom." The lump formed in her throat—she was almost used to that now—but she held the tears at bay. A good thing, as she didn't want Michaela scolding her for having bloodshot eyes.

"Yeah? That's great," Debbie said. "What show?"

"*Brooke Talk*."

"Oh, she's so pretty." Debbie's voice was dreamy.

"Yeah…" Pretty wasn't the word that came to mind for Sophie when thinking about Brooke Kramer. Driven? Indelicate? A little vicious? Definitely. Pretty? Meh.

"Listen, sweetie, I was thinking I'd like to redo the master bathroom. Put in a Jacuzzi for my old bones, you know?" She let loose a staccato giggle and Sophie knew where the conversation was going. "I'm not getting any younger, you know."

"You're only fifty-two, Mom." Sophie tried to stifle her sigh, knowing this was nothing but a typical Debbie James phone call. The usual. "How much do you need?" Her mother rattled off a figure so easily that it was clear she'd had it ready. "I'll call Bradley and have him put it in your account."

"You are the absolute best, you know that?" Debbie's voice held a giddy quality to it now, something Sophie loved to hear even if it wasn't for the reasons she'd like.

The car came to a stop and Sophie glanced out the window. "I'm at the studio, Mom. I have to go."

"Okay. Thank you, sweetie. Knock 'em dead in there."

"Will you watch?" Sophie hated the slightly whiny quality to her voice just then.

"Actually, I'm headed out in a minute, but I'll record it. Or I'm sure I can find it on YouTube later."

"Sure." And just like that, Sophie was ten, home alone while her mother stayed at the restaurant well beyond her shift so she could have a couple drinks with her friends.

"Don't forget to call Bradley," was Debbie's parting comment and then the call was over.

As Sophie headed into the building, she swallowed hard, chastised herself for feeling so let down every time she talked to her mother.

Not once had she asked how Sophie was doing since Ray's death.

❖

"Don't let her rattle you. Do not let her rattle you." Dana said it softly, under her breath, so the others in the green room wouldn't hear as she watched her client on the wall-mounted television shift uncomfortably under Brooke Kramer's questions.

"Yeah. She's rattled." Michaela Dodd stood next to Dana, arms folded, as she shook her head slowly back and forth. They'd just met— the new manager and the hair and makeup artist who'd been with Sophie for a decade—but Dana liked her instantly. She wasn't sure what it was, but there was something surefooted and genuine about Michaela. No-nonsense. Dana suspected she was kind and easygoing but took no shit.

"I've seen her interviews," Dana whispered, a bit confused. "She's a champ at this kind of thing."

"When she got here, she was a little bit...off," Michaela offered.

"She didn't want to talk about it. Plus, I mean, let's cut the girl some slack. Ray's barely been gone for three months."

Dana nodded, knowing Michaela was right. This business didn't often allow for a performer to be human. To grieve, to be sad, to have anger. Superhuman is how they were viewed more often than not. "Oh, shit," she muttered as Brooke Kramer went to video and they played the grainy film of Sophie being helped out of the club, drunk, stumbling, slurring, swearing.

On the screen in the greenroom, Sophie briefly closed her eyes, obviously resigned to having to deal with this situation she'd much rather have disappear.

"On the bright side, she looks fabulous," Dana said, bumping Michaela with a shoulder.

Michaela's chuckle was soft. "What can I say? I'm good at what I do. Plus, it's a pretty amazing canvas to work on, you know?"

She wasn't kidding. Dana had tried not to notice at first, to not pay attention to just how naturally beautiful Sophie James was. And because Sophie had been in the spotlight since she was a teenager, for some reason, Dana had assumed she'd still look like one. She hadn't been expecting the gorgeous woman who'd walked into the conference room at Miracle and stolen Dana's breath right out of her lungs, as if she'd simply reached in and grabbed it. Dana studied her now on the television screen. The dark, furrowed brows made it clear that she wasn't loving this interview. Her long, dark hair was pulled partially back, the rest falling in large corkscrew curls around her shoulders, down the front of her chest, brushing along the ends of the collarbones her halter left visible. Her brown eyes were large and very dark, the lashes and liner only serving to accent them more fully. Her skin was more olive than creamy, and Dana absently wondered how dark she'd tan in the summer, if her shoulders would freckle. Her lips, even though they were in a straight, unamused line at the moment, were full and Michaela had opted for a tinted gloss rather than a lipstick, giving Sophie a younger, more playful look to offset the sophistication of her outfit.

In short, the woman was stunning. There was no way around that, and Dana felt a little twinge in the pit of her stomach.

"I'm not proud of my behavior," Sophie was saying now, and Dana forced herself to pay attention. "And I don't have an excuse other than to say that losing Ray was like losing a parent. It's been devastating, and I'm handling it as best I can."

It was a perfect answer, taking blame and responsibility, but also reminding Brooke Kramer that Sophie was only human.

It seemed to work, as Brooke nodded and said, "Well, we appreciate you sharing your thoughts, Sophie, we wish you all the best, and we're really looking forward to the new album." Then she turned to the camera to tease the next guest and they cut to commercial as the audience broke into enthusiastic applause. Sophie smiled as she stood and shook Brooke's hand. Dana didn't know Sophie that well yet, but she was pretty sure that smile didn't reach her eyes.

Less than five minutes later, Sophie walked into the green room.

"Get me the hell out of here," she said quietly to Dana.

"Absolutely." Dana waited until they had bid Michaela goodbye and were in the limo, driving, before she said anything more. "You okay?"

Sophie had been sitting with her arms folded, gazing out the side window. "That bitch ambushed me."

Dana grimaced. It was true.

Sophie turned to her, eyes crackling just a bit, and Dana got the impression she was holding her temper. "I thought you told her that stuff was off-limits."

Tipping her head from one side to the other, Dana said, "I told her not to go too deeply into it." When Sophie opened her mouth to protest, Dana held up a hand. "I think it was good to address it head-on, Sophie. Now it's done. The elephant in the room has been dealt with. You know? That's better than pretending it didn't happen, even though everybody with a computer or a phone or a television knows it did."

Sophie's shoulders sagged slightly, as if the fight simply left her, and she turned back to the window without comment.

Dana took that as a win. "Hey, are you hungry? I'm starving. Want to get something to eat? We can talk about your upcoming schedule…" She sort of let the sentence dangle, hoping Sophie would bite. It was time for Dana to get to know her newest client a little better.

Sophie sighed, but didn't turn to face her. "Can we order in? I just want to go home." She waved a hand over her torso. "I need to get out of these clothes and into my sweats."

"Did you know there are now lists of tips for how to wear sweatpants?"

Sophie did face her then. "There are?" When Dana nodded, she asked, "Like what?"

Dana tapped a finger against her lips as she tried to recall the article she'd recently read. "Let's see. You can add a loose button-down top. You should stick to basic, neutral colors of sweats."

"So it's not obvious you're wearing sweats."

"Exactly. You can wear a jean jacket with them. You should buy the ones that are tighter at the ankle so they don't look quite as slobby."

"Huh. Who knew you were such a wealth of information?" Sophie's expression softened and an almost-smile appeared.

"Just you wait. I know way too many useless things, and I'm always happy to share them."

"I look forward to it."

The car pulled up in front of Sophie's building on the Upper East Side and the driver helped them both out. Dana tried her best not to glance up—she'd been in New York long enough to not be easily impressed by architecture any longer—but she failed. Sophie's building was gorgeous, all intricately detailed stone and glass, an eclectic mix of old and new, of traditional and modern. She pulled her focus back down so she could follow Sophie.

As the doorman opened the door for her, Sophie turned to Dana and said, "Come into my parlor, said the spider to the fly…" Then she winked and headed in.

Something fluttered low in Dana's abdomen and caused her breath to catch in her lungs. She cleared her throat, exhaled slowly, and headed inside.

CHAPTER SIX

The ride in the elevator was quiet, Sophie lost in her thoughts. *What am I doing?*

She didn't invite very many people into her apartment. It was her sanctuary, her space away from the chaos that her career could be at times. Andrew and Michaela were both allowed because after so many years of working together, she considered them friends—no, family. Ray had had his own key as well. But that was about it. Anybody else she needed to see or meet with, she went to them.

Her suggestion that she and Dana order food and eat here had come out all on its own, as if Sophie hadn't even had control of it. Like it was perfectly natural for her to invite somebody she barely knew— had only met a few weeks ago, in fact—into her home, into her personal space, into her life.

Sophie slipped her key into the lock and turned. She couldn't very well uninvite Dana now, could she? *Too late now. What's done is done.*

"Welcome to my humble abode," she said, and waved her arm in a flourish as she stepped aside so Dana could enter.

"Oh, Sophie," Dana breathed out as she slowly took in the open-concept loft penthouse apartment. Sophie followed her gaze as she looked toward the white walls, then the bleached oak hardwoods, the enormous gas fireplace, and the huge windows. "This is gorgeous." She took several slow steps forward, and it was obvious she was taking it all in.

Sophie felt a gentle wave of pride wash over her. "You like it?"

"I love it." Dana set her purse and bag down on a side table and her footsteps echoed on the floor as she crossed to the window seat. "I would live right here," she said, as she sat.

"That's my favorite spot." Sophie crossed to the fireplace and clicked it on to take the chill out of the room.

"I can see why." Dana was looking out the window now, and Sophie knew she was lost in the stunning view of the park and the city beyond.

"That seat is why I bought the place. I've only recently started sitting there again." Sophie shed her coat and hung it in the closet, then crossed the room to sit near Dana. "The whole loft was super modern when I first looked at it. All white walls and white floors and chrome and glass. I mean, don't get me wrong. It was beautiful. Just..." She searched for the word, felt Dana's blue eyes on her.

"Cold," Dana supplied.

"Yes." Sophie pointed at her. "It was cold. So, I've gradually tried to change things, warm it up a bit. I replaced the floors. I picked more comfortable furniture. I expanded the fireplace."

"The fireplace is perfect." Dana had shifted in her seat so she could see it. "I love that kind of warmth, especially in fall."

"Fall is my favorite," Sophie said, feeling a tad dreamy. She gazed out the window as dusk hit and lights twinkled on. She turned to look at Dana as she held up a finger. "Don't get me wrong, I do not love winter. If we could go from fall to spring, I'd be totally fine with that."

Dana laughed, a softly feminine sound, and Sophie realized that was the first time she'd heard it. "I love winter."

Sophie scoffed. "Weirdo."

They sat in companionable silence for several moments, and Sophie tried not to analyze how or why it felt so comfortable to be there with Dana, saying nothing. It just did. She sat next to Dana, close enough to smell her perfume—something citrusy and fresh—and felt no need at all to fill the quiet. It was the most relaxed she'd been since before Ray had died.

"Still hungry?" Dana asked after a few more minutes. Her voice was soft, as if she was afraid of disturbing the comfort.

"I am. You?"

"Starving. What do you feel like?"

Sophie pursed her lips as she thought. She knew what she wanted, felt herself salivate, but pretended to waver. "Am I allowed to have pizza?" she finally asked, her voice small.

Dana's light brow furrowed and she wrinkled her nose. "Why wouldn't you be allowed to have pizza?"

Sophie lifted one shoulder. "Ray always wanted me to watch what

I ate." She lowered the pitch of her voice as she did an impression of him. "Size twos don't eat pizza, Sophia."

Dana groaned and rolled her eyes. "Goddamn Hollywood and its impossible standards. Sophie, I don't care what size you are. Be a two. Be a four. Doesn't matter to me."

"Good, 'cause I'm a six."

Dana grinned. "I'm an eight. Eat some pizza, Six."

"Don't mind if I do, Eight."

Half an hour later, the doorman buzzed to let Sophie know her pizza from Vincenzo's had arrived and he was bringing it up. The second she opened the door, the aromas of garlic and tomato sauce and pepperoni wafted into the loft. Dana lifted her nose like a puppy catching a scent, and Sophie couldn't help but laugh.

"You are hungry, aren't you?"

"I believe the word I used was 'starving,' thank you very much." Dana headed into the kitchen. "Plates?" she called.

"Top cupboard to the right of the sink." Sophie set the pizza box down on the coffee table, which she then dragged closer to the window seat. "Napkins are near the fridge."

"Did you know that nearly three billion pizzas are sold every year in the U.S.? Three *billion*."

"Seriously? That's a lot of pizza."

Dana appeared with two plates in one hand and a stack of white paper napkins in the other. "God, that has to be what heaven smells like."

"Right?" Sophie glanced over her shoulder at the view. "I thought we could eat right here. Is that okay?"

"It's perfect." Dana smiled, and not for the first time, Sophie marveled at how much it changed her face. Everything softened. Not that Dana was hard; she wasn't. But she was serious and professional and when she smiled, all that firmness fell away so she just looked... really pretty. "How do you feel about wine?"

Dana's eyebrows went up. "I feel very warm and happy about wine."

"Do you have a preference?" Sophie crossed the room to the wine fridge that was tucked in a corner next to a small liquor cabinet, and she could tell by Dana's surprised face that she hadn't noticed either of them.

"I...hmm." Dana did that thing again where she tapped her finger against her lips.

Sophie grinned.

"While I like wine a lot, I'm not terribly educated beyond the basics. I love Zinfandel. And Pinot Noir…" She let the sentence dangle, as if she wasn't sure how Sophie would react.

"Okay, so you like red."

"I do. I like white, too, but I like red more."

"All right." Sophie reached into the wine fridge to the red rack and pulled out a bottle. "Since you like Zinfandel, we're gonna go with that. But this one's a bit lighter than most, so it should work well with the pizza." She opened a cabinet next to the fridge and pulled out two glasses and a corkscrew. When she looked up, Dana was watching her.

"Why?"

"Why what?"

"Why should this wine work well with the pizza?"

Sophie removed the foil wrapping and twisted the corkscrew in, talking as she did so. "Pizza is made up of two main things besides the crust. Tomatoes and cheese. Tomatoes are acidic and there's fat in the cheese. To contrast with the cheese, you need something fairly high in acidity, and it's the same with the tomatoes. You don't want something with a lot of tannins either because that plus the acid in the tomatoes can taste…kind of metallic. Zinfandels can be quite robust and heavy, but some are a bit lighter and juicy with fruit." She held up the bottle. "Like this one. Should complement the pizza nicely."

She poured the wine, always slightly mesmerized by the beauty of the color as it settled into the glass. At the window seat, she handed a glass to Dana, who was regarding her with what looked like impressed curiosity.

"How do you know so much about wine?" she asked, taking her glass from Sophie's hand.

Sophie swirled her wine gently, put her nose in it and inhaled. "Ray knew wine. He owned a restaurant before he started managing me full-time, and he was taking classes on food and wine pairings so he could advise his customers. He wanted to be a certified sommelier one day."

Dana swirled her wine the way Sophie had, then sniffed.

"What do you smell?" Sophie asked, as she took a seat next to her.

"Cherries."

Sophie nodded.

"A little…" Dana squinted, her blue eyes narrowing. Sophie

smiled as she watched as she sniffed again. "Pepper?" She looked to Sophie for approval.

"There are no right or wrong answers. Everybody smells different things." She sniffed again. "I definitely get the cherries, though. This one's pretty fruity. Ready?"

"Yes," Dana said, and the enthusiasm in her tone warmed Sophie from the inside.

"Cheers." They touched their glasses to each other's and sipped.

It was one of Sophie's very favorite Zinfandels, and she closed her eyes as she let it coat her tongue, let the flavors mingle in her mouth. When she opened her eyes and turned to Dana, she was looking at her, blue eyes intense. Then she blinked rapidly and pulled her gaze away.

"This is delicious," she said, and there was something in her tone Sophie couldn't identify.

"Glad you like it. Now, let's try it with the pizza."

I could look at this view forever.

The thought ran through Dana's mind for the thirty-seventh time that evening as she sat sideways on the large window seat, her gaze alternating between the stunning sights of Central Park and New York City at night. They'd both kicked off their shoes early on, and she was facing Sophie, who sat on the opposite side, also sideways, so their feet were together in the middle. The purple pillows were ridiculously soft and cushiony and Dana felt like she was perched on a cloud. Her belly was full of some of the best pizza she'd ever had—and this was New York, so that was saying something—and she was on her third glass of the delicious wine. Sophie had opened a second bottle fifteen minutes ago.

Dana sighed, much louder than she'd intended, then laughed when Sophie shot her a puzzled look. "Sorry. I'm just really, really comfortable right now. Thank you for this." She held up her glass. "And this, especially."

"You're very welcome. Thank you for staying. It's nice to have somebody to talk to, you know?"

Dana tilted her head and studied Sophie. Her dark hair still held the curl Michaela had given it hours ago. After the pizza had arrived, she'd gone into her room and come out fresh-faced and looking stupidly adorable in black sweats that were tight at the ankle and an off-the-shoulder gray sweatshirt with a logo so faded, Dana couldn't make out what it was. Now, she looked so casual and comfortable, and though they didn't know each other that well, Dana realized it was the first time she'd seen Sophie not looking the least bit stressed or on edge. It was a very nice change.

"Tell me more about you," she said, burrowing down into the pillows, wine in hand. Her phone buzzed on the coffee table, as it had done many times throughout the evening, and she ignored it, as she had done many times throughout the evening. Her Google alerts were going off, telling her one or more of her clients had been mentioned somewhere. Probably Sophie, as she'd just done an appearance. But Dana didn't care right now. No, right now, she just wanted to sit where she was, drink wine, and talk to Sophie. "I mean, I've done my research, but tell me what I can't read online."

Sophie held Dana's gaze for a moment and there was a definite… something to it that Dana'd had too much wine to try and figure out. Then she turned to the window, and Dana thought maybe she wasn't going to answer at all.

"I've only met my dad once that I remember." She said it matter-of-factly, as if she was telling Dana she had a bagel for breakfast.

"Wow. Really?"

Sophie nodded, took a sip of wine. "Yeah. I was ten. It had been just me and my mom my whole life and she didn't like to talk about him. He was a truck driver who came through town every so often because we were right off the highway." She looked up at Dana, a sparkle of a smile on her face. "God, that sounds like the plot of a bad Lifetime movie, doesn't it? *Truck Driver Hook-up.*"

"*Highway Love.*"

"*Rest Stop for Lovers.*"

"*Eighteen Wheels to My Heart.*"

"*Exit Ramp to Love.*"

They laughed harder with each title, until they could barely form coherent words. Sophie was beautiful when she laughed openly. Seriously beautiful, and Dana tried hard not to stare.

"So, yeah," Sophie continued after they'd caught their breath. "He said hey and that was about the extent of it."

"I'm sorry."

Sophie shrugged, drank. "What about you?" She poked Dana's

leg with her foot. "I'll be honest. I didn't Google you. Yet." Waggled eyebrows punctuated the mock-threat.

"Let's see. I was adopted."

"You were?"

Dana nodded. "My parents live upstate. They had two kids already, but despite an emergency hysterectomy that my mom had to go through, they wanted one more kid. Their two were older, so I think that helped them to like me rather than hate my guts and be jealous of me, you know? My brother Sean was twelve and my sister Bethany was fifteen when they brought me home."

"Are you close now?"

"Very. Bethany's pretty much my best friend, despite our age difference. She gets me. And Sean is very big brother protective."

"That must be awesome. I'm an only child, so I have no idea what it's like to have siblings." Sophie lifted the lid on the pizza box and pulled out a piece of crust she'd left in there earlier. "When did your parents tell you that you were adopted? Was it weird?"

"Well…" Dana chuckled, because if Sophie saw her family, she'd get it. "If they'd never told me, it wouldn't have been hard to figure out. They are all redheads with green eyes. All four of them. I mean, my dad's gone silver now and my mom's hair has lightened a lot, but I so did not blend in with them."

Sophie smiled. "What? You with your gorgeous blond hair and beautiful blue eyes and tanned skin didn't fit in? I find it hard to believe you've ever not fit in anywhere." As if realizing she'd said more than she meant to, she shoved the crust into her mouth.

"You're sweet."

"What about relationships? I heard the guys at Miracle say you preferred girls. True?"

Dana tried not to shift in her seat, but it wasn't easy, as an odd tingle settled low in her body at not only the question, but the intensity of Sophie's dark eyes as they focused on her. "True," she said, as Sophie sipped her wine. Dana followed suit.

"Got a wife? Girlfriend?"

"Not at the moment, no." The answer came right out. No hesitation at all, which gave Dana a tiny, internal freak-out because she didn't answer personal questions. Not right off the bat like that. Not even if she was on a date, so certainly not personal questions posed by people she barely knew.

What is it about this girl?

The question bounced around in Dana's head, no answer to be found, as Sophie asked, "An ex?"

Dana nodded, wondering if her head had a mind of its own. "Oh, yes. There's an ex."

Sophie's small laugh was musical, and Dana didn't know why she expected any different from a musical sensation like her. "*That* sounds like a story."

"Laura." Dana sighed. "Laura Clarkson." Her brain tossed her an image of the woman she'd been certain she was going to spend her life with. Laura Clarkson had been beautiful—still was, probably, just on a different coast—all chestnut hair and those green eyes. She could hold Dana in place just by looking at her. Had always been able to. "She lives in California now."

"How long were you together?"

"Six years."

"Long time," Sophie observed. And there was that intense eye contact again. "What happened? Can I ask?"

"Well, since you just did…" Dana shot a half-smile across the window seat so Sophie would know she was teasing, and Sophie grinned back. "Laura's the regional sales manager for a national hotel chain. When they moved their headquarters to San Diego, they offered her a promotion to move with them."

"And she didn't ask you to go?"

"Oh, no, she did. But…" Dana took a swallow of wine as she tried to focus on the facts and not the emotions of the situation, which, if she wasn't careful, could still sometimes clobber her. "I was doing really well with Miracle. I'd been with them for five years and they were giving me bigger, more successful clients." She waved her hand up and down, encompassing Sophie's form. "Case in point. And I loved my job. Leaving wasn't even an option, as far as I was concerned."

"And as far as Laura was concerned?"

With a scoff, Dana said, "Yeah, she saw things differently. I offered to do the long- distance thing for a while—"

"Never works," Sophie interrupted. "Trust me."

"You're probably right, but I didn't get a chance to find out because Laura decided she didn't even want to try that. Six years and she was just done. Out. She packed up her stuff and headed for San Diego with barely a goodbye."

"Wow, that's cold."

"It really was," Dana said softly. She allowed herself a moment of melancholy before literally giving her head a shake. "What about you?"

"What about me?"

"Relationships? I remember you dating that one boy band guy... Cliff?"

"Clive," Sophie said, with a roll of her eyes. "Yeah, Ray set that up. Thought it would be good publicity."

"Was it?"

Sophie's brows went up and she shrugged and shook her head. "I have no idea, but that guy was so enamored of his own hair...I just... wow. I still can't get over it."

Dana laughed. "He does have good hair."

"Not a lie."

"Nobody else, though?" Dana was curious. There must have been somebody. "I mean, look at you." She felt her cheeks blossom with heat, but hoped staying quiet wouldn't call attention to her words.

"It's hard. I travel a lot when I'm not in the studio, when I'm not doing appearances, when I'm not trying to work on new material." Sophie sipped the last of her wine and set the glass down on the coffee table. "I don't have a lot of time. And I have yet to find somebody who gets that. Or who, like you, is willing to give the long-distance thing a shot."

"I thought you said that never works."

"It doesn't, but what choice do I have?" Sophie grinned, but the grin was interrupted by a yawn.

Dana looked at her watch and did a double take. "Oh, my God, is it midnight? How did that happen?"

"Yikes," Sophie said, but made no attempt to move. "Time flies when you're having fun, isn't that what they say?"

Dana swung her legs off the window seat and sat on the edge. "It is what they say, yes." She turned to Sophie, and those deep, dark eyes were focused on her. *God, those eyes.* "I had a nice time tonight. Thanks for inviting me up."

"You can stay." Judging from the way her eyes widened, Sophie must've blurted the words before thinking about them. She cleared her throat. "I mean, I have a guest room."

Dana inhaled and exhaled quietly, gave herself a beat because staying here in her fairly inebriated state was most definitely not a good idea. "Thank you. I'll just take a cab home. Rain check?" *Rain check? Really?* She clenched her jaw.

"Sure. Okay."

Her things gathered, goodbyes said, Dana crossed to the door. When her hand was on the knob, she turned back to Sophie, who had walked her to the door and was close—very close. "Hey, Sophie?"

"Hmm?"

"You handled yourself pretty well on *Brooke Talk* today."

Even though it was slight, Sophie's expression lit up just a bit, and that was worth it to Dana. "You think?"

"I do."

Their gazes held for a beat before Sophie said quietly, "Thanks, Dana."

"Sure. Talk to you soon." With that, she pulled the door open and escaped into the hall and the elevator. Once safely inside with the doors shut, she fell back against the elevator wall and let out a long, slow breath.

She had so much wrapped around Sophie already. Feelings, emotions, attraction, caution.

"Jesus, Dana, pull yourself together. You're a professional."

The words hovered in the air of the car as it slid downward, and Dana had a hard time believing them.

"Shit."

CHAPTER SEVEN

The studio audience burst into applause, a thundering sound that seemed to shake the building. The young boy onstage, Charlie Preston, sported a smile so wide it was almost comical. He was obviously thrilled by the reception.

"Well," said Gerard Timmons, from the chair next to Sophie. "I will admit to that being impressive." The unspoken, "however," was apparent to every person in the room, and Sophie felt herself stiffen in anticipation of whatever he would say next. *Sing It!* was his show. He'd created it and he'd been a judge for the past seven seasons, and the American audience loved to hate him. He was brutal, much of the time way more brutal than he needed to be, and he'd sent dozens—probably more—of hopeful contestants off the stage in tears. "I think it was ambitious—maybe too much so—to attempt such a classic as 'Unchained Melody.' It's a tough one to put your own spin on, and while your pitch and process was acceptable, I found it a bit on the boring side."

Sophie watched as the joy on Charlie's face dimmed considerably. His shoulders drooped a titch, and he blinked rapidly.

Timmons was met with a tiny smattering of applause but an overwhelming chorus of boos from the audience. "What?" he asked, turning around to face his critics, as he always did when the crowd thought he was being too harsh. Which was almost always. "I've been doing this for years. You guys know that!" Timmons pleaded his case, his brown eyes wide with what most people knew was mock-indignation. "I know what I'm talking about."

Sophie had turned down many requests to do a guest appearance as a judge on *Sing It!* Mostly because she really didn't like Gerard Timmons or his approach. While she understood his drama was for ratings—as was everything in television—it rubbed her the wrong way. The people who came on the show were pouring out their hearts on national television, standing there and giving voice to the biggest dreams of their lives. While it was inevitable that they weren't all good, Sophie just couldn't see the purpose behind cutting somebody down onstage. Making them feel awful while millions of people watched. She didn't have the stomach for it.

"I'm going to have to disagree with Gerard," she said, her voice level. The audience quieted. "I think it was ambitious, yes, and also very brave to come here and perform 'Unchained Melody.' What are you, Charlie? Twelve?"

"Eleven, ma'am." Even from the distance her chair sat from where the boy stood, Sophie could see the color bloom on his cheeks. "Next month."

"Eleven," Sophie repeated. "Wow. I mean, I started kinda young..." The audience chuckled, as they all knew who Sophie was and how she'd started. "But you've got me beat with eleven. Wow." She glanced down at the scraps of paper she jotted on for each performance, and before she could say more, Brennan Stevens, the country singer sitting next to her spoke.

"I want you guys all to know," he said in his signature charming Southern twang, "that Miss James here has notes. Actual *notes*."

On the other side of Stevens was Tamara, the hottest hip-hop artist on the charts right now. "That girl's making us all look bad," she said and the audience laughed as she reached around Brennan Stevens and gave Sophie a playful poke. "I have no notes."

"Me, neither," said Brennan. "We're terrible."

"We're the worst."

The banter went on for another moment, Sophie grinning the whole time at the gentle ribbing that actually did make her look good, before they finally turned the floor back over to her. "Continue, my queen," Stevens said.

Sophie shook her head with a grin. Brennan Stevens was a charmer, that was for sure. It wasn't the first time they'd met and he'd always stayed just this side of flirting. Sophie liked him.

With a clear of her throat, she focused on Charlie, who had stood there patiently—and probably dying inside—as they all joked and teased. "I think you were incredible, Charlie. You need a bit of direction on your pitch, but you have so much heart and so much courage. I definitely vote for you to come back."

The audience went crazy. It sounded like the house was coming down. Charlie's young face exploded in joy. Huge smile, bouncing on his feet, a clap of his hands, and Sophie couldn't help but mirror his expression.

This.

This was the only reason she agreed to do these gigs.

That boy's expression was everything.

❖

"Why are you going?" Anya had asked on the phone that day. "You don't have to show up at all her stuff, you know. She's been doing this a long time."

"I know." Dana had tried to sound more casual than she felt, but she instantly worried she'd overplayed it. "I mean, I like the show. I figured why not watch from backstage instead of on TV?" She made a wincing face but kept it silent and waited for Anya to pounce.

Which she didn't.

That baffled Dana a little bit, but she took it as a win and changed the subject immediately.

Now, as she stood backstage in the wings of *Sing It!* and watched the monitors, she was super happy she'd chosen to come. The show was immensely popular, the epitome of over-the-top variety special, and it was live. Sophie had balked initially, and her reasons were valid. Dana didn't care much for Gerard Timmons either, nor did she enjoy the way he condescended to contestants. Sophie, on the other hand, was the picture of sophistication and class, and it was obvious to the audience—just as Dana had predicted it would be. She smiled now as she watched the boy's entire being light up as Sophie contradicted Gerard.

"She's so nice," said the woman next to her, quietly.

Dana turned to look at her, thought she looked vaguely familiar. "She really is," she replied, almost to herself, and had trouble remembering why such a thing came as unexpected. Dana stuck out her hand. "Dana Landon. Sophie James's manager."

"Oh," the woman said, her eyes going wide for a second as she put her hand in Dana's. "Jenny Brisco. I work here at *Sing It!* I like to watch from back here. Less chaotic."

"I bet." Jenny was tiny. Maybe five feet tall. Her blond hair was pulled into a ponytail, making her look about fifteen, which Dana was sure she wasn't. She also had a lovely, positive energy about her that Dana liked immediately. "And there goes Brennan Stevens." She rolled her eyes. "Honestly, I'm surprised it took him this long to start flirting with her."

Dana watched the monitor as the country singer leaned in close to Sophie, pretended to peek at her notes, then glanced up at her face and smiled.

"My God, how adorable is it that she actually took notes?" Jenny's grin was wide, her eyes sparkled. "She's so nice."

Dana felt a small wave of pride wash over her, which was silly, she knew, as she had nothing at all to do with what kind of person Sophie was. Or even how she handled herself on national television, given that she'd only been managing her for a short time. But watching her talk to the young contestant, watching as she looked him in the eye, made sure he got all her attention, watching the look of stunned wonder on his face…yeah. Pride was exactly what she felt.

The next three contestants got the same treatment from Sophie. She was kind, but honest. Encouraging, but also pointed out what needed to be worked on. Each contestant fell a little in love; it was obvious. So did the audience.

Unlike Gerard Timmons, who seemed to be a bit put off by her, Brennan Stevens was in awe of Sophie, if the goofy look on his face was any indication. He hung on every word she said, leaned close whenever he could, laughed at anything even remotely funny that came out of her mouth. Dana wrinkled her nose, then decided not to dwell on why she found herself looking away each time the camera broadcast a double shot of the two of them.

By the time they wrapped and Sophie wandered backstage to the green room, Dana felt inexplicably tense. She tried to shake it off as her eyes landed on Sophie's tall form, her big, dark eyes. Her cheeks were tinted pink, but not from makeup. They were naturally pink, like she'd been running.

Or blushing.

"Hey," she said with a smile as she reached Dana and put a hand on her arm. "What did you think?"

Dana forced her eyes away. "You were great."

"Yeah?"

Dana gave one nod, shouldered her bag.

Sophie lowered her voice to a whisper. "Gerard Timmons is such a dick."

"He is."

Sophie squinted at her. "You okay?"

"Yup." Dana could feel Sophie's eyes on her and knew she was being ridiculous, so she forced a smile. "You ready?"

"Please get me out of here before I have to deal with—Brennan. Hi." The appearance of the country singer interrupted Sophie's escape request.

"Hey there. I was hoping to catch you." Brennan Stevens was very good looking. Very. Dana couldn't deny that. His sandy hair was a bit long, which caused him to do a little toss of his head to get it out of his eyes. Something the girls seemed to love. He wore jeans and cowboy boots, of course, and his black T-shirt seemed to cling to every muscle and tendon in his body. He might as well have been shirtless, that's how much it left to the imagination.

"Brennan Stevens, meet Dana Landon, my manager."

Brennan held out a hand, shook Dana's a bit too firmly, his eye contact way too intense. Dana wondered if she was supposed to read something into that. She decided not to.

"So…" Brennan shifted his weight from one foot to the other and tossed a sideways glance at Dana.

She held up her hands. "No worries. I can take a hint." She stepped away, pretending she didn't see Sophie's slight expression of panic.

The green rooms of most shows were filled with tons of food and drink, from simple appetizers like fruit and pastries to more complicated fare, such as champagne and caviar. *Sing It!* fell in the middle. Some fruit. Bottled water. Sandwiches. A small choice of wine and beer. Dana rarely partook, if for no other reason than she was in green rooms far too often and if she grabbed something each time, she'd have to spend a lot more time on her treadmill. But this was different somehow…and she didn't want to think about it. Instead, she hummed a little tune to herself to keep from hearing any of the nearby conversation happening, as she snagged a bunch of deep purple grapes and began to pop them, one by one, into her mouth.

"'Frère Jacques,' huh?" Sophie asked, startling Dana as she suddenly appeared next to her. "Interesting choice of tune to hum."

"Did you know grapes are actually berries?" Dana asked. "And that there are more than eight thousand different kinds?"

Sophie blinked at her, then pulled a grape off the bunch Dana held. "I did not know that, no." She popped the grape into her mouth and held Dana's gaze.

Dana had trouble looking away. "Well. It's true."

"You are a wealth of information."

With a shrug, Dana ate the last grape and tossed the stem into the trash.

"Also, that was weird." Sophie grimaced as she grabbed her purse, which she'd left with Dana.

"What was?"

Sophie waved a hand in the direction of where she'd stood a few minutes ago. Brennan Stevens was gone and the green room was empty now except for the two of them. "That whole…thing." At Dana's furrowed brow, she went on. "He asked me out. Ray used to handle those things. And by 'handle,' I mean, never let them happen at all." She gave a small chuckle, but Dana could tell it was more sadness than humor.

"What did you say?" Dana asked as they headed out. She couldn't help it; the question slipped out before she'd even realized it.

"I said no, of course." Sophie's scoff said there was no other answer option.

"How come? He's cute. Talented. Popular."

Sophie kept walking, didn't look at her. "He's not my type."

"No? What is your type?"

Again with the wave to empty space, Sophie said simply, "Not that."

Not that. Dana filed that away. "Well, okay then."

Not that. Okay, but…what did that mean?

❖

It's hard to explain, 'cuz he's handsome and kind
People might think that I'm out of my mind
But something is holding me back

It was close to two a.m. and Sophie sat on the window seat, looking out over the city that never sleeps. She'd lived in New York for years and it still never ceased to amaze her how very accurate that description was. There was always hustle and bustle, no matter how early in the morning or how late at night. Somebody was always moving. It fascinated her.

She'd had to turn her phone off because it was buzzing nonstop with alerts that she'd been mentioned somewhere. Instagram, Tumblr, headlines on several news sites, all mentioning her appearance on *Sing It!* Reviews and comments were mostly positive, save for the trolls and complainers who'd found a comfy home online where they could cut people down and not have to look any of them in the face as they did. Ray would've been pleased.

She clicked the pen in her hand, then smiled as she heard his voice in her head. *For the love of God, Sophia, stop that.*

Pen and paper were her thing. She knew a lot of songwriters, a lot of writers in general, and she knew many preferred the feel of jotting down lyrics with a pen rather than on their phones or tablets or laptops. Not all, but many. She always had a notebook with her, no matter what. Ray never really understood it; it wasn't like she wrote her own songs. She couldn't play an instrument.

But words.

She loved words.

Any given situation or event or conversation could lodge words in her head that she felt an urge to get down on paper for some reason. It had always been that way. She'd asked Ray once about writing her own lyrics. He'd seemed cautiously positive, but then it never came up again, and Sophie wondered now if that had been intentional.

Sophie exhaled heavily and it left a round circle of fogged glass on the window. She reached out, drew a smiley face with her finger before the fog faded. She missed Ray, especially at times like these, when she was alone and couldn't sleep.

At the same time... Sophie glanced down at the notebook, at the lines she'd written. They'd been inspired by her earlier conversation with Brennan Stevens. A nice enough guy. Handsome. Polite. Obvious in his desires. He'd asked her to join him for a drink. Nonchalantly and with manners, which was refreshing. Everything about him was perfect; Sophie knew instinctively that he'd be a gentleman, and that the paparazzi would love them as a couple.

She hadn't even hesitated to say no.

The weird part was that she knew why—if not exactly why. But Dana had asked her and she hadn't just come out and said it.

Instead of analyzing that further, she returned her focus to the words on the paper in front of her. She had a meeting with Brooks and Kettle tomorrow, and she had some things she wanted to bounce off them. Ideas. Suggestions. Tweaks.

Lyrics.

Ray would never have gone for that.

You sing, Sophia. That's what you do. Leave the rest to the pros.

"I love you and I miss you, Ray," she whispered into the night. "But it's time for me to take control of my own career, you know?"

She tried to ignore how hesitant and uncertain she sounded.

Chapter Eight

Sophie liked the studio the guys had chosen. It wasn't new, and it wasn't new to Miracle Records, but it was new to her, tucked in a corner of Manhattan. There was a lot of room, and even though they weren't actually recording today, it gave her a good idea of what it would be like once they began. The place had a comfortable feel to it, a warmth. It was a big building with many other recording studios in it and she could hear snippets of a handful of different types of music as she walked through the halls. She felt immediately creative the second she walked in the door to their little piece of the whole, and that brought her some relief.

"Hey, Sophie," Tim Kettle said with a smile. His long, graying hair was loose today, his face clean shaven around the goatee, and his blue eyes shining. "You made it. Come on in."

Sophie followed him down a hall to a sort of sitting room, complete with two couches, an overstuffed chair and ottoman, and a small kitchenette tucked in a corner. Lots of studios were outfitted for long meetings, sometimes days long, and Sophie knew there was most likely lots of water and Gatorade in the small fridge, as well as beer and maybe some other alcohol. Along the small countertop was a tray of fresh fruit and a large clamshell package of sandwiches.

Damon Brooks stood as they walked in, his thick glasses reflecting the fluorescent overhead lighting, which he glanced up at with obvious annoyance.

"We'll use the lamp and turn those off," Tim assured him as if reading his mind.

"Good. Hi, Sophie. Good to see you again." He didn't shake her hand this time, but moved in close and hugged her before she realized what was happening. Not a creepy hug. Just the hug of a nice guy. She squeezed him back.

"Not a fan of the lights, huh?" she asked, pointing to the ceiling.

"Ugh. They mess with my eyes and they can trigger a migraine for me if I'm not careful."

"Ray used to get migraines," she told him. "They were awful. He had medication, but if he didn't take it soon enough and missed the window, he could be down the whole day."

"Oh, yeah, that window can be small. If you miss it…" Damon grimaced. "I've lost entire weekends to a bad one." Tim clicked on a table lamp in the corner and Damon switched off the overheads. "Ah, relief." He gestured to the coffee table where papers were spread out next to an open laptop and a small electronic keyboard. "Wanna sit? We can go over some things in greater detail."

Sophie chose a couch and plopped down. She liked all the papers scattered about, the jotted notes, the scribbles. "Old school, I see."

Damon grinned as he sat next to her and Tim took the other couch across the table. "Yeah, does it bug you? I'm a paper guy."

"Not at all. I like paper, too."

"Don't get me wrong. I love technology as much as the next guy, but there's something more…immediate? Not sure that's the right word, but…I just like the reliability of writing something down with a pen."

"I totally feel you," Sophie said with a grin, as she patted the messenger bag next to her. "I have notes, too."

"Yeah? Excellent. Let's see 'em."

They spent the next couple of hours going over individual songs, lyrics, and styles. Sophie had psyched herself up to present some of her own twists and suggestions, but when faced with the chance to do so, hesitated. It wasn't that the guys wouldn't have listened to her—she was fairly sure they would—but it was more about speaking her mind, using her voice for something other than singing. But Ray's words would echo through her head again. *You sing, Sophia. That's what you do. Leave the rest to the pros.* And her lips stayed firmly closed. She sighed internally at her own lack of courage.

"Okay, let's look at one more and we'll call it a day," Tim said, much later. "You look beat." His voice was kind and his eyes matched it as he looked at Sophie.

A chuckle escaped her as she took in her own frame, slumped down on the couch like a teenager, her Chuck Taylors propped on the coffee table, her ankles crossed. "I'm close to tapped out," she agreed. "But I can go over one more."

"It's 'Across the Room,'" Damon said. "We think this one should be the first single."

Sophie sat up, took her feet off the table. "Yes. I love this one and I have some ideas." *Oh, my God, where did that come from?* The thought screamed through her head, but she did her best to ignore it as she rifled through her notes, flipping pages in the small notebook. She pushed forward. "I think we've got some possibility here."

Tim nodded, seemingly open. "Hit us."

"Remember when we first met and I said something about being edgier?"

It was Damon's turn to nod. "Sure do. Dana shut that right down." Tim chuckled in agreement.

"I think 'Across the Room' is a good one to play with a bit."

The men exchanged a look.

"I know, I know. 'Miracle has expectations.'" Sophie made air quotes as she repeated Dana's words. "I'm not suggesting we completely change my entire style. I know Miracle wants the steady income my music provides. I'm a smart girl." She smiled at the guys so they wouldn't think she was angry with them. "But I'm also not a kid anymore, and I feel like there's plenty of room to try…something new."

Tim held his arms out. "All right. Tell us what you're thinking." He looked to Damon, who shrugged and agreed.

"Okay, so 'Across the Room' is the first cut. It's the beginning of the story, yes?" At their nods, she went on. "It's how we pull people in. Hook them."

More nodding, and this time, Tim sat forward, his interest obviously piqued.

"I don't play, but I've been doing this long enough to know how to alter the sound a bit. So, what if we do this?" She sang the first couple of lines to the song, but changed up the rhythm, gave it a beat, which she tapped on her thigh, altered some of the rhyme and added her own line of lyrics. When she finished, she looked from Damon to Tim and back. "What do you think?"

Tim shook his head slowly, brow raised. "It's catchy."

"Damn right it is," Damon agreed.

Tim pulled his keyboard closer and tapped out the melody for "Across the Room." He played the chorus, but then changed it slightly.

"What about this?" It was hipper, more modern than your average Sophie James ballad.

"Yes!" Sophie said, unable to keep the excitement from her voice. "Exactly that."

Damon was bopping his head to the song as Tim messed around, changing things up, trying different chords, adding Sophie's lyrics from last night. "That's good stuff," he told her. "I like it. It's got heart."

"Thank you," Sophie said. She felt lighter than she had in a while. Excited by the possibility of being more involved in her own music. "I've never learned to play, but I love words. I have tons of lyrics in notebooks all over my apartment."

"It's *really* catchy," Damon said as Tim continued to play. "I love it."

"Me, too," Tim agreed.

Sophie couldn't remember the last time she'd been this happy, and she suddenly found herself so grateful for the team of Brooks and Kettle. And she decided then and there she would never call them anything but Damon and Tim. She felt somehow safe with them and the weirdest part was that, even though she knew she'd just gone against everything Ray would've said, she also knew he was smiling down on her right now. With pride.

Her eyes misted over as she continued to grin and listen to Tim play, but she'd honestly never felt so comfortable in her own skin as she did in that very moment. She wanted to share the feeling so badly. With Ray. With Andrew.

With Dana.

❖

"Hey, it's Sophie. Are you busy?"

"Too busy for my biggest client? I've got my eye on a new coat I saw in the window of a store on Fifth Avenue. Of course I'm not too busy for you."

"You're hilarious."

"I try. What's up?"

"I need a favor. I need moral support because I'm about to do something I've never done before. Can you meet me? Please?"

"Absolutely. Tell me where."

That's how things had started. That's how Dana had ended up

in Ink Jet, a tattoo parlor in the East Village. She held Sophie's right hand—pretty sure she could feel the bones of her own hand slowly being crushed—while an enormous bald man with a Paul Bunyan beard and the biggest forearms she'd ever seen used his needle on Sophie's left wrist.

Sophie hissed in air and squeezed harder. "Shit," she whispered, a step up from the, "damn it," she uttered earlier. "Shit, shit, shit, shit."

Dana was reasonably sure the tattoo artist had no idea who Sophie was. His name was Blake—he couldn't look less like a Blake to Dana if he tried—he was young, and the heavy metal blasting from some unseen speaker told Dana that adult contemporary ballads were probably not his music of choice. But he was nice to her and seemed to be doing his best to cause her as little pain as possible.

"You doing okay?" Dana asked softly, her eyes on Sophie's face, which had completely drained of any and all color as soon as the needle had punctured her skin.

Sophie nodded, hissed again, and gritted, "Son of a bitch," through her teeth.

"Tell us the truth," Dana said to Blake as his tattoo gun buzzed along. "Is the inside of the wrist the most painful place to get a tattoo?" She felt Sophie's eyes narrow at her, and she bit down on her lip to keep from laughing, then winced as Sophie gave her hand an extra hard squeeze.

Blake tipped his bald, bearded head from one side to the other as he wiped a cloth over his work. "It's pretty close. The ankles are rough, too. The sides. It depends on the person, but the wrist doesn't have a lot of meat, you know? Just bones and skin."

Sophie hissed again. "Motherfucker," she muttered.

Dana burst out laughing. "You are quickly traveling up the profanity scale, my friend."

"Almost done," Blake promised. "You're doing great." His smile was sweet and it was Dana's turn to squint, but in his direction this time. No, he might not know he was tattooing one of the most successful female singers of all time, but he knew an attractive woman when he saw one.

Sophie looked extra cute today. Casual. Jeans. Bulky red sweater. Hair in a messy ponytail. Little to no makeup. Maybe another reason she went unrecognized.

"There." Blake gave Sophie's wrist one more wipe and then studied his handiwork. "What do you think?"

Sophie looked at her new ink, studied it. She held Dana's hand the whole time; letting it go didn't seem to cross her mind. Dana saw her swallow. Then she cleared her throat and said, very quietly, "It's perfect."

Dana shifted her position so she could see the final product. It was a very small yellow sun with a couple of subtle rays shining down from it. The whole thing couldn't have been bigger than an inch, and it was surprisingly tasteful. Dana had never been a fan of tattoos, but this one, she understood.

"For Ray?" she asked when Sophie finally looked up at her, her dark eyes wet.

Sophie simply nodded.

"It's beautiful," Dana told her, still holding her hand. She could let go now. *Should* let go now. Didn't want to let go now.

Apparently, neither did Sophie, as she got out of the chair and followed Blake to the counter, tugging Dana with her. They stood there, quietly holding hands, while they listened to Blake go over the instructions for caring for Sophie's tattoo, what to watch out for, how to preserve the color. When it came time to pay, Sophie finally let go of Dana's hand.

Dana was sad about that, felt suddenly cold, which freaked her out a bit, so she refused to analyze it at all.

Once everything was all taken care of, they headed out the door and Sophie said, "I'm not ready to go home yet. Want to grab a drink with me?"

"Sure." No hesitation on Dana's part at all, which was interesting on its own.

"Cool. I know a little wine bar nearby." Sophie stepped to the curb and waved down a taxi, then held the door open for Dana. Once they slid inside and Sophie gave the driver the address, she let out a long, slow breath.

"You okay?" Dana asked, pretty sure she wasn't. They sat close enough that their thighs touched, and Dana laid her hand on Sophie's. "Soph?"

Sophie looked down at her wrist, at the rays, and Dana saw a drop fall from Sophie's nose onto the skin of her wrist. When she looked up at Dana, her face was colored with such a mix of emotion, of pain and joy, of love and sadness. "I think he'd like it," Sophie said, so softly Dana almost didn't hear her.

"I bet he would."

"I miss him so much."

"I know." It was all Dana could think of to say before Sophie leaned against her, one gentle sob escaping her. Dana wrapped her up, held her while she quietly cried in Dana's arms. She hesitated for a second with her hand hovering in the air before allowing it to settle against Sophie's head, let her fingers burrow into the softness of Sophie's dark hair.

Dana simply held her.

It had been a long time since Dana had felt this needed, this able to comfort someone. It had been an even longer time since she'd *wanted* to.

CHAPTER NINE

It was probably a good thing that her phone rang, because Dana had spent the better part of the morning staring out the window of her office, unable to concentrate on anything she was supposed to. She spun her chair around to the desk and snatched up the handset.

"Dana Landon."

"Dana! Davis Silverstein here." Dana cringed as his big voice boomed through the telephone line like that of a cartoon character. "Just wanted to check in and say hi. See how things are going with the diva. How ridiculous is she?"

This form of conversation was not unusual in the business Dana worked in—celebrities were often overly demanding and expectant—but something about the fact that Silverstein was talking about Sophie made her clench her jaw a little bit, the muscles on the side of her face flexing as she did so. She wanted to leap to Sophie's defense.

"She's been terrific," she responded, and grimaced at the clipped tone of her voice. "She's not a diva at all, nor is she ridiculous. Did you see her on *Sing It!*?"

"I did," Silverstein said, with a hearty chuckle, apparently missing any and all irritation from Dana. "She was good. The audience loved her."

"They did. And you know how that goes."

"The audience has the money."

"Exactly."

"Things are going well with the album, then?"

Dana nodded, even though Silverstein couldn't see her. "I spoke to Brooks and Kettle earlier today. They seem really excited by the work so far."

Silverstein grunted and made some sort of sound that told Dana he was only half listening. "Well, good. Good. Keep it up. We can always count on Sophie James to keep her demographic happy."

They signed off, Dana punctuating her hanging up with a roll of her eyes. She couldn't help it; that was the reaction she always had when finishing up any conversation with Davis Silverstein. She could picture him now, the epitome of a Hollywood fat cat. Sitting at his oversized desk, asking his secretary to bring him a cup of coffee— probably calling her "sweetheart" or "honey." He was a big man, but a big, round man, with a donut of salt and pepper hair circling his head and a belly that made the buttons on his shirts work much harder than they were intended to. Like so many rich white males in the entertainment industry, he acted like he was entitled to better treatment than others while simultaneously treating others with a very slight, subtle condescension. Especially women. Things were definitely improving in the wake of the #MeToo movement, but Dana still saw plenty of sexism in her world every day.

With a sigh, she turned to her computer and tried to focus on the schedule she was working on for an up-and-coming actor she repped. He'd had a few sidekick roles in the past year and got himself noticed. Those led to him landing a leading role in a film to be released in a couple weeks, so he was making the talk show rounds Dana set up for him. He'd mentioned really wanting to get a guest spot on *Brooke Talk*, so Dana had made it happen. One of the main reasons she played nice with everybody in the industry—whether or not she could stand them—was so she never let a client down. Luckily, this guy had no recent questionable behavior that Brooke could blindside him with live like she had with Sophie, so Dana wasn't worried.

And now she was thinking about Sophie, and within about fifteen seconds, her mind had wandered off again. They hadn't stayed out long after the visit to the tattoo shop. They'd ordered drinks, and Sophie was recognized almost immediately. Considering how emotionally spent she was, she'd been surprisingly gracious to the two fans who asked for a selfie and her autograph. After that, a few more got the courage to approach, and Sophie obliged them all. Dana watched from her chair, feeling oddly proud of the way Sophie handled herself, but when she saw a flicker of tension cross Sophie's face, she'd stepped in, played the bad guy and requested that everybody else "give Ms. James some space and privacy." They'd exited the wine bar and the cab dropped Sophie home first, leaving Dana with time alone in the back seat to ponder the evening. Her agreeing to be Sophie's "moral support," even though they were work colleagues, not friends—right? Her holding Sophie's hand the whole time…and enjoying the feel of her warm, soft skin, enjoying being Sophie's lifeline during a stressful moment. And most of all, her comforting Sophie as she cried. Grieved over a man who was essentially a father to her. The weight of her in Dana's arms. The warmth of her body. The feel of her hands holding on to Dana…they were things Dana'd had trouble getting out of her head. Having a thing for her client was not smart. It was not cool. She needed to nip that in the bud. Like, now.

She smelled so good, though.

Sophie James smelled like…vanilla and nutmeg and warmth and…home and… *Oh, my God, what am I thinking?*

The ringing of the phone startled Dana so thoroughly, she jumped in her chair and let out a little yip, which made her glance around the office in embarrassment, as if somebody else was there and might have heard.

"Dana Landon," she barked.

"Wow," said an achingly familiar voice. "I know that tone. Somebody's in trouble. Can't be me. I just got here."

Dana sat there and blinked. Just blinked. What in the world?

"Dana?" Laura asked. "You there?"

"Yeah," Dana croaked, then cleared her throat. "Yes. Yes, I'm here."

"So, hi. Surprised?"

"That's one word to describe it." Dana's mind was racing, her thoughts a whirlwind. She hadn't spoken to Laura since the day she'd left for California. Not once. Not even in a text. Not even online. It had been instant radio silence, and that had been more Dana than it had Laura. Cutting off all contact at the time seemed to be the only way to hold on to her sanity. Now she wanted to ask why Laura was calling, but it seemed so rude she couldn't seem to blurt it out.

"You're probably wondering why I'm calling you," Laura said, as if reading Dana's thoughts, the way she always used to. "You're probably a little freaked right now, am I right?"

Dana nodded, then realized she needed to actually speak. "A little bit, yeah. To be honest."

"Well, I'm in town." For the first time since she'd picked up the phone, Dana detected the slightest hesitation in Laura's voice, and it dawned on her that much of Laura's cheer was forced. She was nervous. "Here. In New York. I'm back."

Dana felt her brows meet at the top of her nose. "You're back. What does that mean?"

"It means I left my job and have a new one. I'm running the Carrington. Downtown."

"The...wow. The Carrington?" Dana couldn't keep the disbelief out of her voice. The Carrington was beyond ritzy. Diplomats and world leaders and royalty stayed there. "Wow."

"I know, right?" Laura cleared her throat then—again with the nerves, Dana thought—and said, "I'd love a chance to tell you all about it. Maybe over dinner?" She was quiet a moment, and Dana heard her swallow. "There's so much I want to say to you, Dana. And I know you might not want to talk to me. You might tell me to go fuck myself and you'd have every right. But...I've missed you so much, and I'd really like to have dinner with you."

Dana Landon was not often at a loss. She was rarely speechless. She was a strong-minded, intelligent woman who had no issues handling herself in a crisis. But this? This had her stopped dead in her tracks. She felt like she was standing in the middle of a busy street, feet rooted to the pavement, cars hurtling toward her, and she had absolutely no idea which way to leap.

When you don't know what to do, I often find the best course of action is to do nothing for a little while.

It was her father's voice and she heard this piece of advice often, reverberating through her head when she felt uncertain. It had worked for her on several occasions in life, and she trusted her dad implicitly.

"Can I think about it?" she finally said.

"Absolutely." Laura's relief was obvious, and Dana wondered if she'd just expected a flat-out no. Which was tempting, she had to admit, but she couldn't seem to. Analyzing why was not something she was ready to delve into yet, either, so this was good. "I called your office because I wasn't sure if your cell number was the same."

"Why wouldn't it be?" Dana knew exactly why Laura had called the office: because if she'd called her cell, Dana might've seen her name come up and would have had time to think about not answering. Or maybe she'd come up as an Unknown Caller, another thing Dana wouldn't answer. Laura wasn't stupid.

"Well." Laura took an audible breath. "I'll text you so you have mine. I'll probably get a new one with a New York number soon, but for now, it's still my West Coast number."

Dana's phone pinged and there was a text notification, a smiling emoji staring at her. "Got it."

"So." It was clear that Laura hadn't thought any further ahead in this conversation, and Dana let her twist in the wind for a bit.

"So."

"I'll call you tomorrow?"

"Text me."

"Okay." A bit deflated, Laura's tone, but she took it. "I hope I get to see you. It was nice to hear your voice."

"All right. Bye, Laura." Dana hung up without waiting for any more conversation because her heart was hammering in her chest and she suddenly felt like she couldn't breathe fully. "Laura? Really? What the hell is happening?"

Not surprisingly, her empty office had no response.

❖

There was a knock on the door at the exact same time Sophie's phone rang from the coffee table. She snatched it up, saw the screen, and answered as she pulled the door to her penthouse open and let Andrew and Michaela in. Andrew had a large garment bag draped over his arm and Michaela carried her ever-present makeup kit, which looked like a small suitcase.

"Hi, Mom." There was a ton of sound in the background, lots of pounding and far-off voices. "Mom? How are you?" She pretended not to notice Andrew's slight eye roll or Michaela's knowing expression as they walked past her and into the penthouse.

"Hi there, sweetie. I'm good."

"How's the bathroom remodel going?" Sophie watched as Andrew hung the garment bag from the top of her coat closet door and unzipped it. Something glittery peeked out from inside.

"Well, that's why I'm calling," her mother said, and Sophie felt every cell in her body deflate. Of course it was.

"Costing more than you thought?" she asked quietly. She turned her back to her friends so she wouldn't see their sympathetic looks.

"A little bit, honey. I'm sorry. Can you help?" Her mother actually did sound sorry, and Sophie clung to that, until she heard noise in the background and then sound was muffled, like her mother had pressed the phone to her chest. "Sorry," she said after a minute. "The tile guy had a question. You'll send some?"

"Of course. I'll have Bradley send some more."

"Oh, thank you. You're the best."

"Hey, Mom, did you see me on *Sing It!* last week?"

"No, over there," Debbie ordered and it took Sophie a minute to realize her mom wasn't talking to her. "Yes. Right there. I'm sorry, honey. What?"

Sophie exhaled quietly as more noise echoed over the line. She raised her voice a bit. "I asked if you'd seen me judging on *Sing It!* last week. Didn't you get my text?"

"Your text? I don't think so…" A beat passed. Two. "Oh, there it is. Darn it, I must have missed it. I bet you were amazing, though. What did you sing?"

Sophie closed her eyes, her voice small. "I didn't sing. I was a judge. Never mind."

"Sweetie, I have to go before these guys *ruin my carpet* with their dirty work boots." She emphasized the three words, apparently for their benefit. "Don't forget to call Bradley."

"Bye," Sophie said softly, knowing her mother had already ended the call and she was speaking to dead air. She held the phone in her hand, stared at it.

"You okay?" Andrew asked quietly.

Sophie pressed her lips together and nodded. "I am. Yeah." She turned to her friends. "Okay, what have we got? Make me beautiful."

"You're already beautiful." Michaela smiled at her as Andrew uncovered the clothes in the garment bag and pulled them out.

"All right." Andrew separated the four dresses and held each one up. They were all gorgeous. Evening gown–like. Elegant. Sophie stared at them. Squinted. "What?" Andrew asked, squinting back at her. "What's that look for?"

Sophie felt her brow furrow as thoughts raced through her head. She gave one determined nod. "Okay, these?" She waved a hand over the dresses, encompassing all of them. "These are gorgeous."

"Good."

"But."

Andrew did a double take. "But?"

"I'd like to go less elegant and more…sexy." She caught her

bottom lip in her teeth and raised her eyebrows at him, waiting for a reaction. Most likely a protest.

"Sexy?" Michaela repeated, but her face held a hint of mischief.

"Sexy," Sophie confirmed.

"Yes!" Andrew held his fist toward Michaela, who bumped it with her own. "You have no idea how long we've been waiting for you to say that." He quickly zipped the dresses back into the bag, as Sophie blinked in shock at his words. Then he stood in front of Sophie, hands out like he was performing a main number in a Broadway show. "I have some fabulous ideas. What kind of sexy do you want?"

"There are different kinds?" Sophie asked, not hiding her surprise.

"Oh, God, yes," Michaela said, then looked at Andrew. "Vampy sexy."

"Right. Erotic sexy."

Michaela held up a finger. "Which is not to be confused with slutty sexy. They're different."

"Edgy sexy."

"Classy sexy."

"Educated sexy."

"Surprise sexy. The sexy librarian falls into both of those categories."

They went back and forth for a good three minutes, Sophie's gaze following them as if she was watching a ping-pong match.

"Do you have a preference?" Andrew finally asked her, and both he and Michaela looked at her in expectation.

"Since I had no idea there were so many levels of sexiness..." Sophie looked from one to the other. "I'm gonna need some help. Can you do that?"

Andrew looked at Michaela and the twin smiles that blossomed on their faces were almost comical. "We thought you'd never ask."

❖

The Almost Wee Hours—or just *Wee*, as it was known in the industry—was a late night talk show that had been on the air for almost ten years. The ratings were steady and it had survived the onslaught of probably a dozen or more other late night shows that had come and gone. Its host, Jeff Cruze, was a super likable guy, with his boy-next-door good looks and his self-proclaimed nerd status. He'd been on the air long enough to dictate some things to the network, one of which was who he wanted as guests. Some, he put the kibosh on the second a request came in. Others, he brought back over and over simply because he enjoyed them.

Sophie fell into that last category, Dana discovered when she'd sent a request to Cruze's people.

Arriving at the *Wee* studio a bit later than she'd meant to, Dana felt slightly rushed as she headed toward the dressing rooms. Laura's call had thrown her for a loop and she'd spent the rest of the afternoon trying to figure out what to make of it. She could already hear Anya's voice, a booming "Absolutely not!" echoing through the entire world in response to Dana asking if she should go to dinner with Laura. Which was why she hadn't called her immediately. Asked her right away.

Because part of Dana wanted to hear what Laura had to say. And another part of Dana had some things *she* wanted to say.

Reaching the dressing room she'd been directed to, Dana rapped on the door. "It's Dana," she said, then pushed her way in without waiting for a response. Inside, she closed the door behind her and asked, "How's it going?"

Andrew's back was to her. Michaela faced her, a makeup brush in her hand as she dabbed at what Dana had to assume was Sophie's face, even though Andrew was obscuring her view.

"Hey, Dana," Sophie said, and waved a hand without turning around.

Michaela pulled her brush back and surveyed her handiwork while Andrew fluffed the back of Sophie's hair. There was a beat of stillness before they both stepped away and Sophie glanced over her shoulder at Dana.

Whose heart skipped a beat in her chest. Maybe two beats. Might have been ten. It was entirely possible it just completely stopped altogether.

"Oh, my God," she said quietly before she could stop herself.

Stunningly sexy.

That was the best description Dana could come up with for how Sophie looked at that moment. Stunningly sexy and completely unexpected. And also, crazy sexy. *My God.* She wore black pants that were either leather or something close. Skintight, making her legs go on for days and hugging her ass like a lover. Three-inch heels at a minimum, and Sophie was tall anyway, so in those shoes, she was nothing short of statuesque. Above the waistband of her pants was skin. *Skin. Bare skin.* Sophie's bare stomach—toned and smooth-looking—

stared back at Dana, belly button and everything. Her black top, also skintight, didn't even begin until just under her breasts. It was ribbed, had a V-neck, and actually covered more than Dana originally thought. The capped sleeves left Sophie's arms bare, and several silver bangle bracelets jingled on her slim wrist. Her dark hair was pulled partway back, the rest hanging down, all of it in a thousand corkscrew curls. Her makeup was smoky but tasteful, and Dana marveled at how she somehow managed to stay on the right side of tastefully sexy.

"Wow," Dana said, seemingly unable to move her feet.

"Yeah?" Sophie held her arms out slightly.

"It's...you look...wow."

Andrew pointed at Dana. "*That* is the reaction we were going for." He reached around and high-fived Michaela.

A knock on the door sounded and a voice from the other side of it called, "Ms. James? Ten minutes."

"Thank you," Sophie called back.

"What...why..." Dana stopped and cleared her throat, tried to unscramble her brains that had been thrown into a blender by the vision of loveliness in front of her. "What happened?" was the question she finally managed to push out. Not exactly what she wanted to say, but it was the best she could do.

"What do you mean?" Sophie asked, grabbing a water bottle from the vanity and taking a sip.

Dana tried hard not to stare, wondered if she was failing. She waved a finger up and down in front of Sophie. "You...this isn't what people expect of you."

"Exactly."

Dana furrowed her brow as reality began to seep in and the details of her actual job filtered back into her head. "This isn't what *Miracle* expects of you."

For a fraction of a second, Dana could see Sophie's confidence slip just a hair. "I've decided to make a few changes." Dana was pretty sure Sophie had hoped to project a bit more firmness into that line, but her inflection went up at the end, as if she was asking a question.

"You're not singing tonight, Sophie. You're just sitting and talking to Jeff. Doing a bit of damage control as well as talking about your upcoming album. How are you going to do that if you don't look anything like your audience expects you to?"

Another knock on the door. "Five minutes, Ms. James."

"Thank you," Sophie called out. Turning to Dana, she stepped closer, so they were only a few inches apart, and Dana had to look up slightly to maintain eye contact. Sophie held her gaze, those dark eyes seeming to somehow grab onto Dana's and hold them, keep her from moving, from looking away. "How do I look, Dana?" she asked so softly, Dana knew she was the only one who heard.

She couldn't fake it. She couldn't lie. She knew this wasn't going to go over well with Davis Silverstein. Sophie James was sweet and innocent and *wholesome* and her demographic expected it. The drunk-in-public stuff had gotten her some backlash. She was supposed to be making it up to her audience. That's what her appearance on *Brooke Talk* was about. That's what *Sing It!* was supposed to help with. That's what tonight's appearance was for. Getting back to *wholesome*. Not skintight leather pants. Not sky-high heels. For God's sake, not acres of cleavage.

"You look absolutely beautiful," Dana said, and she'd never meant anything more honestly in her life.

The smile on Sophie's face then…the softening of her expression, the happiness that was so apparent it couldn't possibly be mistaken for anything else…those things meant everything. Dana had no idea how, but when Sophie lifted her hand and touched Dana's cheek with it, whispered, "Thank you, Dana," it didn't matter. Nothing mattered but how happy she looked.

A rap on the door and it opened this time. A woman wearing a headset and carrying a tablet smiled at the four of them. "Ready, Ms. James?"

Sophie gave a nod and slid her hand off Dana's cheek. "Lead the way."

Five minutes later, Sophie was being introduced and Dana was watching from the green room. Sophie's confidence seemed high as she crossed the stage in those killer heels and waved at the crowd, her smile wide, her eyes dancing.

"She looks amazing," someone else in the green room said. "What happened?"

"God, right? I had no idea she was that sexy," said another.

A sense of pride washed over Dana. She couldn't help it.

"Her voice is incredible," the first person was saying. "But she always seems a little…stuffy? Uppity? I don't know the right word."

"Maybe this is an image change," the other said. "Whatever it is, it's working. I will buy whatever she's selling. Take my money."

Their conversation stopped as the applause died down and Dana watched as Jeff Cruze, the host, made a comment about his eyes bugging out of his head. He was a terrific interviewer because he seemed like everybody's nice next-door neighbor, the boy who cuts the lawn without being asked to. He waited for Sophie to take a seat. She crossed her legs, got comfortable.

"I've known you for how long now?" he asked her.

Sophie scrunched up her face, obviously thinking. "Hmm. Six years? Seven?"

"That sounds about right. Long time."

Sophie nodded.

"I'm just gonna say it, then," he told her, as he glanced at the audience. "You look *incredible*."

The crowd erupted into hoots and whistles and applause and Dana could see Sophie blush through the TV screen, see her mouth her thanks even though it couldn't be heard over the crowd.

"It's…" Jeff squinted at her. "Not the Sophie James we're used to."

Sophie gave a gentle, one-shouldered shrug. "Change is good, right?"

"It is tonight." The audience laughed. "I'm not saying you didn't look incredible before, because you did," he said, once the audience quieted. "I mean, I asked you out."

"Years ago. You totally did."

The audience loved that.

"A story for another time," Jeff said to slight boos. "But I will say that Sophie here was very sweet and gentle when she turned me down."

Sophie's smile was charming. "I'm sure your new wife is very happy I did."

Sophie was nothing short of magnetic, and Dana cocked her head as she watched. The mix of the new, ultra-sexy look, the soft-spoken demeanor, the kind eyes. It worked like a charm and the audience ate it up.

So did Dana. She couldn't help it.

She was transfixed. Looking away would've been impossible. If she'd had any desire at all to actually look away. Which she did not.

"You've got a new album you're working on," Jeff said, segueing into the reason Sophie was there.

"I do. It's called *Unrequited* and I'm very excited about it." Sophie talked a bit about the album, what it was like getting back to work after losing somebody close to her, how she was feeling. She was heartfelt and, again, charming.

"I know you're not ready to perform yet," Jeff said, a twinkle in his eye. "But could you give us a tiny sample of something from the album?"

Uh-oh. Dana pressed her lips together in a straight line. What was he doing? Sophie wasn't there to sing yet. She'd made that clear when she set up the appearance. She waited for Sophie to politely turn him down.

"I'd love to," she said instead, and Dana's lips parted slightly as she realized this was not Jeff's doing, but Sophie's.

Jeff reached beneath his desk and pulled out a microphone, then pointed toward the wings. "Hit that clip Sophie sent over, Trey," he said to his DJ, and in the next second, a very sick beat rumbled through the studio. One Dana hadn't heard before.

Sophie stood from her chair, seeming like she was six feet tall in those pants and heels. She brought her hands together over her head and got the audience clapping to the beat as she moved her hips, looking for all the world like the sexiest woman Dana had ever seen in her life. She brought the microphone up and began to sing the lyrics to "Across the Room." But it wasn't the slow, dreamy ballad Dana had heard snippets of that first meeting. The words were the same. Dana remembered them because she'd found them moving. But this…this song was edgy and raw and full of want, desire. The theme was clear: I see you from across the room and want you. In my bed. Now.

Dana was instantly turned on.

The clip was done before Dana could take a breath and the audience lost its collective mind. Dana felt her phone buzzing in her back pocket and pulled it out, groaned when she saw Silverstein's name on the screen.

"Shit," she muttered as she left the green room and found an abandoned hallway. Hitting Answer, she pumped extra cheer into her voice. "Hey, Davis."

"What the fuck is she doing?" his voice boomed. "She looks like a tramp. She sounds nothing like she's supposed to. What the fuck is she doing, Dana?"

"The audience loves her." The words were out before Dana could catch them and she made a wincing face as soon as she realized it.

"This is not what we contract with her for."

"I know. She just…I didn't know she was doing this."

"How did you not know? You're her manager, Dana, and her publicist. You know everything she does. That's your job."

"I know." Dana started to sweat. "I know. I'm sorry."

"We have a ton of girls to sing this pop shit, all of them younger than her. We don't need another one. What we do need is for her to do what she's supposed to. She sings ballads for the Adult Contemporary crowd. Understood?"

"Yes."

"I'm trusting you, Dana."

"I know."

"This is why we put you on her."

"I know."

"Fix this. I mean it."

He cut off the call before Dana could say more. She held the phone against her forehead and closed her eyes. "Fuck," she muttered.

That was the moment Sophie came rushing backstage, looking all energized and flushed and gorgeous. "Hi," she said as her gaze landed on Dana and she reached out, laid a warm hand on Dana's arm.

Before Dana could say a thing, Jeff Cruze skidded up to them, having followed Sophie's trail. "Sophie!" he called, causing her to turn.

"Jeff, you've got, like, four minutes. Get back out there!" Sophie's grin was contagious as she playfully pushed at his shoulder, her rosy cheeks making her look ridiculously cheerful.

"I know, I know. I just wanted to tell you that was amazing. Tell your manager to set up another appearance as soon as the single drops, okay?"

Sophie turned to Dana. "Hear that?"

Dana nodded.

"Great." Jeff leaned in and kissed Sophie's cheek, then waved a finger up and down in front of her. "I like this new you." And he was gone, being whisked back toward the stage by a very frazzled-looking assistant whose head, Dana predicted, had been about fifteen seconds from exploding over how close he was cutting it.

"Oh, my God, you were incredible!" Andrew's voice boomed from inside the dressing room as Dana followed Sophie through the door. "I had no idea you were going to do that."

"Yeah, neither did I." Dana's voice was icy. She felt it herself, knew her expression matched it when Sophie turned to look at her and that cheerfulness of mere seconds ago dimmed significantly.

"It was kind of a last-minute thing, and I didn't even know if Jeff would go for it," Sophie said as she kicked off the heels. In her bare feet, she seemed instantly more vulnerable.

"You have to run these things by me," Dana said.

"You would've told me not to do it."

"That's right."

"So, why would I run it by you first?" Sophie's big, dark eyes held Dana's, blinked at her.

"I got a call. Davis Silverstein was not impressed."

"Did he not hear the audience?" Andrew asked, then visibly shrank as Dana sent him a withering glance.

"The Twitterverse is blowing up," Michaela said, commenting for the first time in a quiet voice. She looked up. "Both ways."

Dana pulled out her phone just as texts began arriving, some with links.

Michaela was right; they went both ways. Most were positive.

James Finds Her Inner Sexy

Where Has This Sophie James Been? And When Can We See Her Again?

And one that simply said, *Wow!*

Those, weren't the ones Davis sent, though. Those were from Anya. Davis's were from the other side.

From Class to Slut in One Night

Tasteless

Leather Pants and Crass

Where Have All the Good Girls Gone?

Davis's text, after the links, was made up of exactly two words: FIX THIS.

CHAPTER TEN

It was weird how you could tell it was cold outside just by looking out the window. There was no snow yet. It wasn't raining, so there were no pedestrians hurrying along, pulling their coats more tightly around them. It just...looked cold somehow. Sophie sat in her window seat, as always, notebook balanced on her knee, pen in hand, phone nearby. The windows in her penthouse were expensive. A million-paned glass or something ridiculous, meaning no draft came in. She was toasty warm, the gas fireplace glowing across the room. Dusk was falling on the city, earlier and earlier as fall slowly followed its path toward winter, lights coming on in bars and restaurants, on the streets.

Her phone pinged next to her thigh and she picked it up, another alert for a mention. She'd vowed long ago not to follow such things in order to keep herself from going insane. Ray's voice echoed in her head now.

Just do your job, Sophia. You're good at it. Don't worry about what others are saying about you.

Which was easy to say and hard to do and also not necessarily terrific advice for somebody in the field of entertaining others. While Sophie rarely enjoyed reading about herself online, she had also learned that it was smart to keep track of what her public was thinking, feeling about her work. It was Friday night, and it had been almost two weeks since her impromptu performance on *Wee*, and the comments were dying down a bit, but there was still buzz. Some called her new look refreshing. Some called it downright slutty. Some called it a publicity stunt by a has-been—that one stung, she wasn't gonna lie, because being considered a has-been at twenty-nine was just ridiculous.

Dana had not been happy about it.

Although...

Sophie felt a small smile form on her lips as she remembered the way Dana had looked at her when she'd first walked into the dressing room. She stopped dead, actually sort of stuttered to a stop. Her gorgeous blue eyes had gone wide at first, then ended up hooded as they raked over Sophie's body. Yes, raked. That's what they'd done. Sophie could almost feel them. She'd wondered then—and she still wondered now—if Dana had any idea or if it had happened without her knowledge. Oh, yes, Dana had liked the new Sophie. She'd liked her a lot.

But she wasn't happy about her, and Sophie also knew it was because Miracle wasn't happy about her. Which was not unexpected but was annoying. She'd gotten a call directly from Davis Silverstein himself—she was supposed to be impressed by that, she was pretty sure—speaking very kindly to her, but also very condescendingly. Clearly, he thought those two things went hand in hand.

"Sophie, sweetheart," he had said, and right there, he'd lost about two-thirds of her attention. "We here at Miracle know you're going through a rough time, having lost Ray. We know he handled the hard stuff for you and you're probably unfamiliar with how things are run, but there are methods and procedures and *contracts and expectations.*" He emphasized the last two and Sophie was irritated to feel a tiny sliver of insecurity seep into her veins. "We pay you a lot of money to give us a particular product and we all win. See?"

Sophie said nothing but, "Mm-hmm," angry with herself for not saying more, for not mentioning the reaction of the crowd, for not pointing out that there was as much positive feedback as there was negative, if not more. Instead, she just let him blather on and on.

"There are reasons for this. Different demographics demand different things and we fill those demands. Think of it like this: If the bakery started serving, say, steaks, the people who show up and pay money for a donut are going to be angry. Right?"

"Mm-hmm."

This went on for another eight or ten minutes until Silverstein was sure it was crystal clear that Sophie was to sing adult contemporary songs and dress like an adult contemporary singer and was absolutely not to change either of those things without the express permission of her record company. When he'd finally hung up, she'd immediately called Andrew and relayed the entire conversation.

"Jesus Christ on a cracker, seriously?" Andrew had said in utter disbelief. "Was he actually serious? Does he think you're ten years old?"

Now, as she sat alone, she felt a bit of guilt. Davis Silverstein calling her directly meant he'd cut Dana out of the discussion. Which meant she'd probably gotten in trouble, and Sophie felt bad about that. She hadn't seen Dana face-to-face since that night, but they'd talked on the phone and they'd emailed. Dana had been uncharacteristically distant, which was another clue she'd probably been reprimanded. Sophie would need to fix things. Somehow.

Davis told her he'd spoken with Brooks and Kettle. Sophie hadn't contacted them yet but would see them tomorrow during a recording session, so she'd talk to them then.

A big sigh left her lungs slowly and she turned her focus to the notebook on her lap.

It's hard to explain, 'cuz they're handsome and kind
People might think that I'm out of my mind
But something keeps me from reaching out to them

She added the second verse that had come to her in the shower a little bit ago. Erased, rewrote, tweaked.

Whenever you're near, can't remember my name
Feels like I might be going insane
You keep me from reaching out to them

She had no idea where this song was going, or any of the others she'd been cobbling together lately, but she was compelled. They compelled her to write them down. Painfully slowly. A word here. A line there. Different rhythms, but all the same theme: love, desire, confusion. But they wouldn't let her go. She felt like she was supposed to stay with them, and that was…weird at best. Another fifteen or twenty minutes of staring out the window and then she turned back to the paper. The words were important. She needed to find the words.

And the whole time, in the back of her mind, she wondered what Dana was doing tonight.

❖

"I would like to state for the record, one more time, that I think this is a bad idea." Anya's voice over the speaker on her phone was a bit louder than usual, which told Dana that she was annoyed. "No. Scratch that. It's a terrible idea. Terrible. One of the worst you've had in all the years I've known you."

"Seriously?" Dana said, cocking her head. "Worse than the bangs?"

"*Worse than the bangs, Dana.* That's how terrible. This isn't a bad haircut. This is dinner with the ex who smashed your heart into a million tiny pieces. A million pieces I had to help pick up and glue back together. No, this is a terrible, horrible, no good, very bad idea."

"Your opinion is noted." Dana surveyed herself in the full-length mirror of her bedroom. Dark designer jeans, heels, a light yellow top, and a dark blazer, sleeves rolled up. She had tried to walk the line between a casual "this dinner means nothing" outfit and a more "this dinner means nothing, but I'm certainly going to look hot while I eat it" outfit. Not sure exactly where she'd fallen, she turned one way, then the other, examining all angles as Anya went on.

"Don't you dare bring her home. Don't you *dare* sleep with her. *Don't you dare.* If you do, so help me, I will personally drive my ass over to your place and kill you dead. Mark my words."

"You have a lot of feelings on this."

"*I have so many feelings on this, Dana.*"

"I know." Dana said it softly.

There was silence on the line for a beat. "I'm worried." Anya's voice had quieted as well.

"I know."

"You were a mess after she left you. And I know. I had to pick you up. With a broom and a dustpan."

"And I will be forever grateful." Dana fastened an earring.

"I'm not telling you so you'll thank me. I'm telling you so you'll remember what happened the last time you gave that woman your heart to play with."

"It's just dinner, An. I promise." Exactly the same words Laura had spoken to Dana, Dana now said to Anya. And she loved Anya's concern. She loved having a friend who cared that much. The truth was, Dana *was* nervous. She'd almost texted Laura on six separate occasions to cancel, but she didn't want to give her the satisfaction of knowing that this was at all a big deal, that it had taken up more than an ounce of her attention. At all.

But Laura promised no strings. *It's just dinner.*

"It had better be," Anya said, but her tone had lost its edge. "Text me when you get home, okay? So I know you're all right?"

"I will."

They hung up and Dana surveyed herself in the mirror one more time.

"Not bad for almost forty," she whispered into the empty room. "Not bad at all."

❖

Dana had done a good job hanging on to most of the control in the situation with Laura. For one, she'd picked the restaurant. Arago was a somewhat new, trendy restaurant that Dana visited often. She was comfortable there, and that's why she'd chosen it. It was close to being on her own turf, an advantage she thought she could use, given she was about to see the only woman she'd ever been in love with for the first time in over a year. Secondly, she'd also insisted they meet, rather than having Laura pick her up. Frankly, she didn't want Laura in the apartment again, didn't want her crossing the boundaries of Dana's sanctuary, tainting it with their history. No, Dana decided they'd meet at Arago at eight and her place would remain clean.

"Ms. Landon, welcome." Marina was the hostess tonight, and she led Dana through the crowd as if she floated rather than walked on what had to be four-inch heels. Dana nodded to a few familiar faces and then Marina showed her a table for two, asked if it was to her liking.

"It's perfect." And it was. Not set in a romantic corner. Not tucked away from other eyes. The small, round table was pretty much in the thick of things. Perfect for…whatever this was going to be. Dana took her seat and focused on the wine list Marina left with her. She wanted to keep a clear head for this dinner. She also wanted a goddamn drink.

She saw Laura coming over the top of the wine list and tried hard not to watch her approach. Failed. Spectacularly. Because Laura may have crushed her, might have squeezed the life out of her heart, might have destroyed Dana's carefully constructed walls, but she still looked amazing. Damn her.

She wasn't tall, but her confidence and self-assurance were palpable and that made her seem almost larger than life. Her hair was a chestnut brown/blond highlights combination that could look alarmingly artificial on some women but seemed perfectly natural on Laura, like she made no effort at all—though Dana happened to know that Laura had gone gray early and paid a stylist a disturbing amount of money every four weeks like clockwork to make her hair look that natural. Not one to dress down, like, ever, she wore black dress pants, heels that probably cost upward of three hundred dollars, a long-sleeve top in a geometric pattern of black and red, and a long, black trench. Laura looked like she'd just stepped out of a Michael Kors catalog and Dana's loudest thought was how some things never change.

Smile wide, attention fixed on Dana, seemingly not noticing the heads she turned as she passed, Laura arrived at the table, came right around, leaned over, and kissed Dana on the cheek. Her warm hand on Dana's shoulder felt both heavy and light, wanted and dreaded, like home and completely foreign.

"My God, you look gorgeous," Laura said, with her signature smile, dimples prominently displayed, as she used her thumb to stroke off the lipstick print she'd left on Dana's face. She took a seat and smiled across the small table. "Hi."

"Hi." Dana wasn't sure where to look. She wasn't sure what to say. The situation was way weirder and less comfortable than she'd predicted. And she was not about to tell Laura how good she looked, no matter how many compliments she paid Dana. No way. "You look great, too."

Goddamn it.

Dana was reasonably sure Laura was now blushing, but she was not about to dwell on that. Thank God the waiter showed up and took their drink orders. Deciding that ordering a bottle of wine would keep her there longer, she chose a glass of Cabernet and handed the list over to Laura. Who didn't open it, just ordered the same as Dana.

"Should we just order a bottle?" Laura asked and without waiting for Dana's response, did just that. The waiter hurried off.

Again, Dana marveled at how some things never change.

"So, how are you? How's work?" Laura asked, folding her hands on the table and staring intently at Dana with those green eyes she used to know so well. "Catch me up."

"Work is good. Busy. I just took on managing Sophie James a few weeks ago."

"Sophie James? Really? Wow. Is she a diva? I've heard stories."

The instant desire to leap to Sophie's defense was not something Dana was happy to feel, and she did her best to tamp it down. "No, she's not a diva at all."

The waiter arrived with the wine and, of course, all his attention was on Laura even though Dana had chosen the wine first. He went through the ritual of showing her the label, opening the bottle, letting her taste it before filling the glasses.

"What was the deal with that new look on *Wee*? She went from demure to crazy sexy. And that song she sang a snippet of? So not her usual thing. Was that your idea?"

Dana snorted a bitter laugh before she was able to catch it, and that meant she had to tell the truth. "No. Not my idea at all. Total surprise, actually."

Laura's eyes went wide. "Oh," she said, drawing the word out a bit, and something about the tone of it set Dana's teeth on edge.

"Listen, Laura." Dana took a healthy sip of her wine before diving into Blunt Lake headfirst. "What are we doing here?"

Laura blinked several times, doing her best to look confused by the question. But she was too smart to fool Dana with that. "We're having a nice dinner."

Again, with perfect timing, the waiter arrived and took their dinner orders.

"You know what I mean," Dana said the second he was gone, keeping her voice low even as she leaned over the table a bit. "We have had zero contact in over a year. Zero. All of a sudden, out of the blue, you show back up and invite me to dinner? Act like the past year never happened?"

Laura had the good sense to look slightly chagrined…but only slightly. She reached across the table and grasped Dana's hand before she could avoid it. Her green-eyed gaze snagged Dana's, and just like old times, Dana had trouble looking away.

"I have been the biggest fool, Dana." Laura's voice was soft. Quiet. Alarmingly sincere. "I got so blinded by my work, by opportunity, by money, that I couldn't see what wonderful things were right in front of my face. Right in my own hands."

Dana didn't want to listen to this but wanted to hear every word. Didn't like where it was going but knew she was along for the ride anyway. Was both angry and curious. Both heartened and hesitant. God, Laura always made her feel such conflicting things.

"I was so unhappy in California." For the first time since she'd started explaining, Laura let her gaze wander around the restaurant, seemed suddenly less certain. "I kept waiting to like my job. I mean, I uprooted my life, made some hasty decisions because I was sure it was the chance of a lifetime." She looked at their hands, hers still holding

Dana's, Dana too polite to pull hers away. "I kept waiting for it to get better, and it didn't. And after about four months, I was just miserable."

"Why didn't you call me?" Dana asked, her voice barely above a whisper.

Laura inhaled, then let the air out gradually as she shook her head slowly from one side to the other. "I couldn't. I just couldn't. I was so embarrassed and I couldn't admit that I'd made a huge mistake." She grimaced. "You know me and my pride."

Dana barked a quick laugh. "Oh, yes."

"Plus, you blocked me on all social media."

"I had to." Dana narrowed her eyes at her ex. "I *had* to. I didn't want to see your awesome new life in California every time I opened up Facebook."

Laura's eyes cast downward and she seemed to study the tablecloth for a moment. "Fair enough," she said with a nod. She wet her lips and returned her gaze to Dana. "So, when the opportunity for this job with the Carrington came up, I jumped at it."

The waiter arrived with their dishes, and Dana silently sent a thank-you up to the heavens for allowing her to retrieve her hand without incident. She had let herself start to feel connected to Laura again—it was that easy—but now, she sat back in her chair, picked up her fork. "Were you looking for something at that point?"

"No, I was contacted by a headhunter."

"Wow. They came looking for you, huh?"

Laura took a bite of her fish, chewed, grinned. "Not gonna lie, that felt pretty good."

"I can imagine." Dana knew from experience that the chicken Marsala she'd ordered was beyond delicious…that it could change lives. But in that moment, sitting with Laura, listening to her lament her life in California, express what a mistake she'd made leaving, she barely tasted it. The bite she swallowed hit her stomach like a rock and sat there.

"So," Laura went on, because Dana couldn't find the words, a reason, to stop her, "I interviewed over the phone. Then on Skype. Then they flew me here for a series of interviews. I got back to California and the next day, got an email with an offer that was *way* too good to pass up."

"Wow."

"It was kind of nuts." Laura laughed then, and the sound instantly shot Dana back in time, back to when she loved that sound. Lived for it. Then her face grew serious. "And I couldn't pass it up. The chance. The job, yes. But being back in the city more. Being near you."

Dana set down her fork and stared at her food, took a moment to compose herself. Or at least attempt to. She felt so many things right then, so many conflicting feelings, though most of them were under the very large umbrella of anger. When she finally looked up at Laura, she knew her eyes were flashing blue fire. "What are you doing, Laura? What exactly are you doing?"

Laura looked like she'd been pushed just a bit off balance, like a person who didn't realize she was drunk until she stood up. "Um…I just wanted to see you. To talk to you. To apologize."

Dana felt her eyebrows climb up toward her hairline. "Apologize? Seriously?"

Laura nodded, eyes wide with…what? Surprise? Fear? Dana couldn't tell. "And also, to see if maybe we could…reconnect?"

Dana was dumbfounded. Seriously, taken so off guard that she simply sat there for what felt like years, blinking at Laura as she tried to comprehend the words. "You want to reconnect? Like, this?" She waved a finger in the space between them.

Laura nodded again, her eyes never leaving Dana's.

"You broke my heart. You know that, right?"

She saw Laura swallow before she nodded again. "I know. I'm so sorry, Dana. I'm so very sorry. It's the biggest regret of my life."

"I don't…" Dana shook her head. "I can't…I don't even know what to do with this right now."

"Just think about it. Can you do that? Can you think about it?"

Don't look in her eyes. The warning shot through her head, but she couldn't help herself. Dana never could. Laura's eyes were incredible, and somehow, looking at them could sway Dana in almost any case. It was like they were hypnotic. Dana looked. Laura's gaze held hers, her eyebrows raised in gentle expectation, her expression softened.

"Fine," Dana said, defeated. "But thinking about it is all I'm doing."

Laura's face lit up then like the sky during a July Fourth fireworks display, and for a split second, Dana let herself see it. Let herself feel how wonderful it always was to make Laura happy. Almost immediately, though, her brain tossed her a shot of herself in the fetal position on her bed, sobbing like a child, for days. Weeks. Heartsick. Broken.

"That's all I'm asking," Laura said. "Just think about it." She paused, studied Dana, who had to work hard not to squirm under the scrutiny. "We were good together once. You know we were."

❖

"She did not say that." Anya's tone was incredulous.

"She did." Dana donned an old Nike T-shirt and panties and slipped beneath the covers of her king-size bed.

"'We were good together once. You know we were'? She said those exact words?"

"Exactly those." There was such indescribable relief for Dana to slide into bed at the end of the day. Her entire body relaxed. Her brain let go of most of the things it had a death grip on all day. It was heaven to her. She picked up the remote, clicked the television on, and hit mute, as she had Anya on speaker.

"That woman has got a set of titanium balls, I'll give her that."

"God, right?" Dana had left the restaurant feeling such an overwhelming mix of things that she ended up angry at Laura. It was the only way to keep herself sane in the moment and, maddeningly, Laura seemed to get that. Dana had gotten into her Uber with barely a backward glance at Laura—which was very rude of her since Laura paid for dinner…she could've thanked her at the very least—and the car pulled away to Laura's voice saying, "I'll call you!" loudly into the New York City night.

"You don't really need to think about it, though. Right?" There was just enough veiled uncertainty in Anya's voice for Dana to understand that her friend was worried.

"I'm too tired to think about anything right now." It was a lie, but it worked because Anya let her go with a promise that they'd talk again soon. She hung up the phone and pressed the channel button, fully intending to watch *The Almost Wee Hours*. But when she hit *You've Got Mail*, right in the middle, her finger paused as if it had decision-making abilities of its own and she set the remote down. She'd only seen the film two or three dozen times, but she snuggled down into her covers and let herself get lost in Tom and Meg.

We were good together once. You know we were.

The worst part of Laura's words?

They were true.

CHAPTER ELEVEN

*C*offee Chats was a much different show than *Brooke Talk*, and for that, Sophie was grateful. The interview was fun, informal, five people sitting around a table and, as the show's title proclaimed, chatting. Having four different hosts was also interesting. Two women, two men, many different angles, but pretty harmless and casual. Sophie actually enjoyed herself, which was rarely the case with a talk show.

She said her goodbyes to the audience, making way for the next guest, and when they cut to commercial and the thunderous applause died down, she was free to go. Suspecting Dana was probably in the wings or the green room waiting for her, Sophie felt a little flutter in her stomach...something she tried hard not to dwell on, while at the same time understanding it was becoming a regular occurrence. She liked that Dana came to her appearances. She didn't have to. Many managers didn't. There was no need. Dana didn't do anything while there but stand and watch, but she seemed to enjoy it, and Sophie wasn't about to deter her in any way.

Sophie made her way through the wings, nodding at the barrage of "nice job" and "hi, Ms. James" before she caught sight of Dana. She was very enjoyable to look at, a fact Sophie had realized pretty early on. Today, she wore a pantsuit. Navy blue slacks and blazer and a blue-and-white-striped shirt underneath. The sleeves of the blazer were pushed up to her elbows and something about that made her seem almost... sexy? Sophie didn't like that the word popped into her head, but it was true, and she might as well admit it, at least to herself. Dana's hair was down, hanging in soft waves around her shoulders, and her heels added a good three inches to her height—which still didn't make her as tall as Sophie in her heels, but she was closer.

Their eyes met and Sophie felt the flutter kick into high gear. *What is that?* Dana smiled at her, but there was something a little...*uneasy* was the only word that came to mind. Sophie furrowed her brow just as Dana stepped aside to reveal another woman standing behind her.

"Oh, my God," the woman said, her smile huge as she held out a hand. "Sophie James. I'm such a huge fan of yours."

Sophie took the hand, shook it, turned her questioning eyes to Dana, who looked just the tiniest bit embarrassed.

"Calm down, crazy pants," Dana said to the woman, then turned to Sophie. "I'm very sorry. Don't mind her."

There was an underlying sense of familiarity between the two women, and Sophie found herself feeling oddly excluded. She looked back to the woman, who was very pretty, smaller than both her and Dana, with stunning green eyes and dimples you could dive into. "And you are?"

"Oh, God, I'm such a dork. Laura. Sorry. Clarkson. Laura Clarkson."

Sophie squinted, wondering where she'd heard the name before.

"I'm Dana's—"

"Ex," Dana said quickly. "She's my ex."

"Something I'm hoping to change," Laura said, leaning in and lowering her voice as if she was sharing a secret with Sophie.

"Terrific job out there," Dana said, obviously trying to change the subject. "You were warm and charming. The audience loved you."

Sophie nodded her thanks even as it felt like wind was rushing in her ears, the whooshing sound coming from inside her own head. She forced herself to focus on Dana's comments. She'd decided not to veer too far from the image Miracle Records expected her to play, at least not today. Morning show audiences skewed a bit older than late night, so she'd had Andrew dress her somewhat conservatively. He hadn't been thrilled about that, which Sophie found amusing.

"She's right," Laura chimed in. "You were amazing." Her smile was so wide that for a second, Sophie could almost picture her as the deranged killer in a teen slasher film. Finally dialing it down a notch, she said, "Okay, I've got to run. It was so nice to meet you, Sophie." Laura turned to Dana. "Call you later?"

"Fine," Dana replied and before she could say anything else, Laura gave her a quick peck on the lips.

"Bye, babe."

Sophie's gaze shifted back and forth, from Laura's retreating form, to Dana's carefully expressionless face—which she didn't turn to Sophie for what felt like a long while. "So," Sophie said, and waited until Dana finally did look at her. "The ex, huh?"

Dana sighed, scratched her head.

"I thought she lived in California."

"She did. She just moved back."

"Wow."

"Yeah." Dana seemed incredibly uncomfortable with this whole topic of conversation.

"You guys getting back together?" The question was out before Sophie even knew she was thinking it. She felt herself grimace, felt like she had a bad taste in her mouth. Because she did.

Dana shook her head but was saved from verbally answering by the producer of *Coffee Chats*, who walked up to them then and held out a hand to Sophie, thanking her for her appearance.

Sophie smiled, nodded, pretended to listen raptly as the man heaped praise on her, mentioned having her back in the near future, once the album dropped next month. But the whole time, her brain was playing make-believe clips of Dana and Laura together. Sitting in the audience at a Broadway show. Sitting under a shared blanket in a horse-drawn carriage as it rolled past the Ritz. Strolling through Central Park. Her jaw began to ache, and she realized she was clenching it like crazy. By the time the producer bid her thanks one more time and walked away, Sophie was pretty sure she was about to crack a molar.

"You're going to the studio from here, yes?" Dana asked.

Sophie nodded, taking note of the fact that Dana had smoothly changed the subject. "Yeah, the guys are ready to record. You gonna stop in?"

Dana shook her head. "I've got to get back to my office. Meeting with a new client."

"Oh." Sophie tried to hide the disappointment in her voice. Failed. "Okay."

Dana donned a long, gray trench coat that only made her look classier. "I'll touch base with you later?"

"Sure."

Sophie watched as Dana hurried away, noting that the only way she'd move any faster was if she broke into a run. She waited until Dana was completely out of sight before forcing her legs to move, to carry her back to the dressing room so she could change into something more comfortable for hanging out in the studio. It bothered her that she was disappointed to find out Dana wasn't coming to listen to her record, and she tried to shake it off, but it must've been clear on her face.

"Uh-oh, what happened?" Andrew asked when Sophie entered the dressing room. He was packing up some of his things, an open garment bag hanging on a door, waiting to enclose the outfit Sophie had on.

"Nothing happened." Sophie shrugged and began to undress. Somebody else might have raised an eyebrow at how easily she did it, but she'd never had any qualms about stripping down to her underwear in front of Andrew. Ever. He barely batted an eye.

"Then why do you look like somebody just told you there's no Santa?"

"I'm just tired, I guess." The yoga pants and tunic top she'd packed for the studio were waiting for her on a table, so she started to dress while Andrew hung her outfit up, smoothed the wrinkles.

"God, did you see that woman with Dana?"

Sophie stopped with one foot halfway into her yoga pants, cleared her throat. "Um, yeah. Her ex."

"Really? Wow. She was gorgeous."

Sophie made no comment, pulled up her pants and turned to look at him. He was staring knowingly at her. "What?"

"Is that what has you feeling 'tired'?" he asked, making air quotes. "The ex?"

Sophie's scoff sounded forced. Probably because it was. "I don't know what that means."

Andrew narrowed his eyes at her, and it took every ounce of energy Sophie had to keep from squirming under the weight of his gaze. Even when she was able to finally turn away, she could feel his eyes on her. Eventually, he turned back to his things and said simply, "Mm-hmm."

Sophie whirled on him, her voice snarkier than she intended as she said, "What does *that* mean?"

Andrew knew her well. They'd worked together for many years and he was the closest thing to a best friend she had. That meant he also knew when to back the hell off, so he did, hands up, palms toward her. "Nothing. Doesn't mean a thing."

They finished what they were doing in silence. Finally, Sophie turned to him and said, "I'm sorry, Andrew. I'm just not feeling like me today. I shouldn't have snapped at you."

He lifted a shoulder in a half shrug, told her it was fine, but she knew she'd hurt his feelings. So she walked right into his space and wrapped her arms around his tall, lanky frame.

"Oh, God, are you forcing a hug on me?" he asked with distaste. "Are you force-hugging me?" But she felt his arms go around her back and Sophie knew then that she was forgiven.

"Shut up, you love my hugs."

"Yeah, yeah. Whatever you need to tell yourself." But his arms tightened and Sophie was shocked at how much better she felt.

"Okay," she said, letting him go. "Gotta go sing so I can pay you." Andrew made shooing motions. "Go. Hurry."

Sophie's car and driver were waiting for her outside, and she was suddenly very grateful for that when a blast of almost-winter air assaulted her during the short walk from the building to the back seat. Once inside and warm, she tried to shake the weird feeling she'd gotten from meeting Laura Clarkson. Sophie had no reason not to like her. She was kind and charming, if a tiny bit fangirly, but Sophie had felt instantly uncomfortable. And she'd felt a little bit of something else that she didn't want to dwell on, even though she was disturbingly clear on what it was.

Possessive.

❖

Dana's day had been busy. Thank God, because if she'd been left to her own thoughts, she might have jumped out her very high office window.

Okay, not really, but there was definitely stuff going on in her head. Too much stuff, especially after this morning.

Her thoughts were interrupted by the ringing of her cell. When she saw Anya's name on the screen, she snatched it up, eager to talk to somebody who was currently *not* causing her any stress.

"Hey, baby. How's life?" Anya asked.

"Let me just say, it's wonderful to hear your voice."

"Uh-oh. What's going on? You okay? Talk to Auntie Anya."

Dana smiled at the warmth of her friend's tone, the slight concern coupled with openness. "Laura showed up at the studio for *Coffee Chats* without giving me a heads-up."

"What? How did she manage that?"

"I guess she knows one of the producers, and when I told her that I'd be there watching Sophie's appearance, she took it upon herself to contact him. Got him to let her in."

"Wow. Ballsy. Also, resourceful." Anya paused, and Dana could almost hear the wheels turning. "And how did you feel about that? About her just showing up out of the blue?"

"Seems to be her MO now, doesn't it?" Dana sighed.

"Showing up out of the blue? Sure does."

"I think she wanted to meet Sophie. She's a big fan."

"Really? That's what you think?" Anya's voice held no inflection.

"I can see the look you're giving me right now," Dana said, with a small laugh. "One eyebrow arched, chin down, grimacing at me." Her phone beeped in her hand, indicating a text, and she opened a selfie of Anya making the exact face she described. Dana laughed harder. "See how well I know you?"

"And I know you, my sweet. What are you doing with Laura?"

Dana's laughter faded a bit. "What do you mean?"

"I mean, what's the deal? What do you want to come of this... *return* of hers?"

Dana let out a breath and shook her head. "I don't know, Anya."

"Sure you do."

Dana didn't respond, and Anya went on.

"Do you want to get back together with her?"

"I didn't at first..." Dana let the words hang in the air.

"And now?"

"I don't know."

"Can I point out some facts?" Anya's tone was gentle, and Dana knew her well enough to know she was treading carefully.

"Go ahead."

"She only steps up when she's losing you. Remember that fight you guys had about her ridiculous hours? And you told her you needed some time away? To think about things?"

"I remember."

"And all of a sudden, she was doing everything you'd ever asked of her. Texting more often. Checking her schedule against yours so you'd have more time together."

"Mm-hmm." It was true. Faced with the possibility of losing Dana, Laura had made an extra effort.

"And then you came back and what happened?"

"We were good for a month and then she went right back to her old ways and I ended up in the same boat."

"Exactly. She was perfectly okay leaving you behind without a backward glance when it was what she wanted. Remember that. And now she's back and wants you again, so she's on her best behavior.

Except she's making sure she's the one in control by calling you at work, showing up unannounced at your client's television appearance. She's running the show. Don't let her."

Dana was quiet for a moment, letting the words sink in. She remembered the way she'd felt when Laura had magically appeared next to her in the green room that morning. There had been surprise, a momentary sliver of happiness, but mostly irritation at Laura just showing up at her job without asking first. "Okay."

"I'm only looking out for you, babe." Anya's tone held a hint of hesitation, and Dana immediately felt bad.

"I know you are. And I appreciate it. I do. I promise." Searching for some levity, she added wryly, "I don't think Sophie was impressed by her."

"No?"

"No." Dana chuckled. "I mean, she was nice. Sophie's always nice. But the look on her face was..." Dana sat back in her chair and looked up at the ceiling, searching for the right description. She recalled Sophie's face, excitedly flushed from a successful appearance, her smile then freezing as Laura stuck a hand out at her, rather demandingly. "I don't know. She just wasn't prepared and I didn't help matters. I just let Laura ooze all over her." She groaned. "Very professional of me."

"Well, we both know Laura can be kind of a bulldozer."

"Very true."

"And it sounds like Ms. James can handle herself just fine."

"Oh, she absolutely can." Despite the deer-in-the-headlights look Sophie'd had for a moment, she *had* actually handled Laura very well. Calmly. Kindly.

"Don't beat yourself up. Just take your power back. You're the boss here."

Anya was always great for a pep talk. She was fantastic at making Dana feel better about herself when something got her down. Dana wasn't a pushover by any means, but with Laura? She always seemed to drop down a few pegs on the Assertive Woman scale and she didn't like that.

"I will. Thanks, oh BFF of mine." Dana felt a bit better. "I feel the need to apologize to Sophie. Is that weird?"

She could almost hear Anya shrug. "I don't think it's necessary, but if it makes you feel better..."

"It would. She's recording today. I could stop by the studio later, say I came by to listen, and then tell her I'm sorry about this morning."

"You do you, babe. Tell her I said hey."

Dana laughed. "She doesn't know who you are."

"Then tell her. And don't forget to let her know how awesome I am. And tell her I think she sings like a fucking angel."

"I'll get right on that," Dana said, still laughing. When she hung up, she felt better. It wasn't unusual for Laura to throw things off-kilter for Dana. That's what she did, what she was best at. But Dana was different now. The past year had changed her and maybe Laura needed to know that.

Chapter Twelve

"Ugh." Sophie made a slashing motion across her throat and looked up at the window of the studio where Tim and Damon sat. "I'm sorry, guys. I think I'm done for the day. My voice is fried."

Tim gave one nod as he hit the button for his mic so Sophie could hear him. "No worries at all. We'll call it a day. We got some incredible stuff. I can't wait to play with it. Now go drink some tea with honey and get some rest. You did great."

It was yet another thing Sophie found she loved about working with Brooks and Kettle: They *got* her. They got what it meant to be a singer. They pushed a little but also knew that if she told them her voice was shot, it was shot. Sophie recalled another solo singer she'd met many years ago. Her producers had pushed her well beyond the point of her feeling like she needed to rest her vocal cords, and being new and not wanting to rock the boat, she'd kept singing. A week later, she'd ended up in the hospital with nodules on her vocal cords and had to have surgery. Her voice was never the same.

"That will never happen to me," she'd said to Ray at the time.

"No, it won't," he'd agreed, and he'd made sure to be at her recording sessions—every one of them—to make sure she wasn't pushed beyond her limits.

Sophie gathered up her music, her water, her notes, and headed out the door of the studio and into the area where the controls were, then through another door to the common area with the couches and food. She stopped in her tracks when she saw Dana. She was sitting comfortably, the view allowing her to look through the control room and into the actual studio. Sophie hadn't seen her, hadn't realized she was there.

"Hey," she said, sure her surprise was clear in her voice.

"Hi," Dana said, and her smile seemed slightly...hesitant? Unsure? Sophie couldn't put her finger on it, but it wasn't Dana's usual smile. "You sounded terrific."

"Thanks." Sophie went to the kitchen area and picked a mug out of a cupboard. "I didn't realize you were here." She filled it with water, popped in a tea bag, and put it in the small microwave on the counter.

Dana sat forward on the couch and braced her elbows on her knees, clasped her hands. It was an interesting posture, not one Sophie had seen of her yet. "Yeah, I didn't want to...I don't know. Make you nervous? Put pressure on you? Whatever might happen when you've got extra eyes on you that you weren't expecting."

Sophie felt the small grin appear on her face as she had her back to Dana. It was a lame excuse, and Sophie was pretty sure they both knew it; people came and went from recording studios all the time. Dana's appearance wouldn't have registered as anything odd to Sophie. But she let it sit and instead replied with, "That's very sweet of you, but you don't have to worry. You won't distract me." When she turned to face Dana, her brain amended that to *or maybe you would...*

Dana still looked gorgeous, the navy blue suit and striped shirt looking as crisp as if she'd just put them on, and those damn heels that were starting to give her a little something extra lately. To Sophie, anyway. Her hair was a little more tousled than it had been earlier, and there was something about her posture that was... Sophie mentally shook her head.

"Oh," Dana said, and sat up. "Good. Maybe I'll continue to pop in, then." This time, her smile was more genuine. More...Dana.

"I'd like that," Sophie said, and it was true. The microwave beeped and she removed her tea, doctored it with honey and avoided the cream she loved so much, as dairy tended to coat the vocal cords and create phlegm.

"Listen, Sophie." Dana stood up, wet her lips, her blue eyes catching Sophie's. "I wanted to apologize about Laura this morning."

Well. *That* was a surprise. She furrowed her brow.

"She was a little bit...over the top." Dana rolled her eyes to punctuate the statement. "She's a big fan and got a little carried away. I'm sorry about that."

Sophie waved a dismissive hand. "Please. No need." She paused, took a sip of her tea, which was much too hot for sipping yet, but she needed an activity so she didn't just stand there. "So...she seems nice." God, it almost killed her to say it, but she managed to force the words out. Hopefully, her smile looked like an actual smile and not like she'd just smelled a fart.

"Yeah," Dana said, vaguely, and her gaze moved around the room, as if she wanted to look at anything but Sophie's eyes.

"Dana, are you okay?" Sophie squinted at her. "You seem a little… jumpy. You have since this morning."

Dana flopped back down onto the couch and Sophie took the opportunity to sit across from her, study her expression, which seemed…uncertain. "Yeah, I'm fine. It's just…she's a lot. Laura is." Dana met Sophie's gaze. "There's never any warning with her. She just shows up with a goal and she usually accomplishes it."

"Like, getting you back." Sophie had figured from Laura's words earlier that that's what she'd meant.

Dana blew out a big breath. "Like that. Yes."

"Do you want to get back with her?"

Dana's head shook slowly from side to side as she spoke. "No. She's terrible for me. She always was. I lose myself when I'm with her, and not in a good way."

"Then don't." Sophie shrugged, as it seemed pretty simple to her.

Dana's scoff said it wasn't. "She's doing and saying all the right things right now and…" She swallowed audibly.

"It's hard to resist," Sophie finished.

"Yeah."

They sat quietly. The guys were still in the control room, probably working through some ideas and remixing stuff they'd recorded. Sophie could hear music start and stop, start and stop. The weird thing was, it wasn't uncomfortable to be there in silence with Dana. In fact, it was the opposite, and it was the second time she'd realized it.

"Do you spend Thanksgiving with your mother?" Dana asked, her voice startling Sophie just a touch. Dana seemed to realize it and smiled in apology. "It just occurred to me that it's next week."

She grimaced. "No. She's going on a cruise this year. One that I paid for, of course." She immediately wrinkled her nose. "You know what? That wasn't nice. I take it back. She deserves a cruise. I guess." Having gone from comfortable to very uncomfortable in about three seconds flat, she scrambled to put the focus elsewhere. "What about you?"

Dana nodded and a gentle smile formed on her smooth face. "I go home to my parents' place. My brother and sister and their families come."

"Do they both have kids?"

"Yep. My sister has two and my brother has one. Two nephews and a niece."

"One of the bummers of being an only child. No nieces or nephews."

"So, what will you do on Thanksgiving?"

"It'll be weird with Ray gone. My first holiday without him." Sophie shrugged sadly. Andrew would go to his parents' and Michaela would go to her in-laws'. "I have no idea what I'll do. Order a pizza and watch Netflix all day?"

"Oh, no." Dana looked like she'd been slapped. "No, you will not. You're coming home with me."

Sophie felt her own eyebrows shoot up. "What?"

"You come home to my parents' house with me."

"Oh, Dana, that's really nice, but I don't want to impose." Sophie was trying her best not to picture it. The possible wonderfulness *or* the possible awkwardness. Because it really could go either way.

Dana made a *pfft* sound and said, "Are you kidding me? My parents would love it. The more, the merrier."

"I don't know, Dana…" God, so much ran through her head then. How nice it would be, not only to be with a family for the holiday but to get a glimpse of where Dana came from, where she grew up. Even though Sophie didn't want to admit that to herself because then she'd have to think about other things like why she thought that glimpse would be so nice. Also, though, it could just be awful. Awkward. Uncomfortable. And she'd be stuck, unable to escape and get away if she needed to.

Dana got up and moved from her couch to sit on Sophie's next to her. She put her warm hand on Sophie's thigh…Sophie could feel the heat through her yoga pants. "Just think about it, okay? Nobody should be alone on a holiday, especially not if they have someplace to go. No pressure, just come and enjoy some downtime. I promise my family is nothing like Laura. They will not fawn all over you." She held up a hand. "Well. My niece might. She's a fan, not gonna lie. But I can rein her in."

The smile Dana shot her then, sitting so close to Sophie, was sweet and inviting and somehow intimate. All the things. Sophie knew right then, even as she told Dana she'd think about it, that she was going to go. It was as if she didn't have a choice or any say in the matter.

Weirder, still? She didn't mind.

❖

"What are you doing, Dana?"

Anya's chin was propped in her hand, her elbow on the bar of Grape, a cute little wine bar smack-dab in between their respective offices, and studied her. Dana felt no sarcasm. No animosity. Not a blip of judgment. Only curiosity and maybe the tiniest sliver of concern.

"What do you mean?" Dana, of course, knew exactly what she meant. Despite the clear lack of confrontation, she was stalling anyway.

Anya knew it too, judging from the way she simply cocked her head slightly and raised one eyebrow.

Dana sighed as she picked up her Merlot, took a sip.

"You ever taken a client home for the holidays before?" Anya asked.

"She's going to be all by herself. The person she spends the holidays with died recently. I couldn't stand the thought of her spending her first holiday without him alone." It was the truth. For the most part.

"I get that. I absolutely do." Anya sat up straighter, her arm draped on the bar, her hand around her water glass. "Look, I am the last person to judge anybody for their choices. Lord knows, I've made my share of stupid ones." She held up a hand quickly as Dana opened her mouth to retort. "Not that I'm saying yours is stupid. I'm not saying that at all. I'm just taking your pulse, making sure you're okay with this."

"Why wouldn't I be okay?"

Again, with the raised eyebrow look.

"Jesus, would you stop that?"

"Stop what? Knowing you so well? Sorry. Can't."

Dana chuckled. She couldn't help it. "Yes. That."

"All I'm asking is that you step carefully. You've got the Laura thing. Now you've got"—she paused for a moment, as if looking for the right word—"a guest. For the holiday. A pretty well-known one. There could easily be complications. I mean, it might also be an awesome time. Who knows? Just…step carefully. Okay?"

"I will. I promise." They sat quietly for a beat, Dana sipping her wine, Anya sipping her water— Dana's eyes flew open wide as her head snapped around to face Anya. "You're drinking water."

"I am." Anya tried to hold a straight face, but that only lasted a few seconds before a smile exploded onto her face.

"You're pregnant?" Dana nearly shouted.

"I am." Anya's expression was the most gorgeous thing Dana had ever seen. "Not very far along, so we're not telling anybody."

Dana nodded vigorously. "That makes sense." She looked around Grape, at the small crowd of patrons. "Do you know anybody here?"

Brow furrowed, Anya glanced around. "No. Why?"

"I'm gonna be an aunt!" Dana shouted and several patrons lifted their glasses in salute or clapped in support. Then Dana threw her arms around Anya and crushed her in a hug, whispered, "I'm so happy for you."

Later that night, when she was alone in her apartment and finally coming down off the high of the big announcement, Dana thought about Anya's words, not only the ones she'd said, but the ones she hadn't. Oddly, she hadn't told Dana not to do this, not to bring a celebrity client home for Thanksgiving. Dana had literally braced herself for a flagellation that never came.

I mean, it might be an awesome time. Who knows?

Recalling that line brought a smile to Dana's face she wasn't expecting as she stepped gingerly into her garden tub and sank down into the steaming water. It hadn't really been something she'd thought about. She'd been telling the truth when she'd explained to Anya why she'd invited Sophie home for Thanksgiving. She really hadn't thought it through, hadn't entertained anything other than her belief that people shouldn't be alone for the holidays. Her mother would have extended the same invitation. Once she'd left the studio and had been in an Uber on her way home, a tiny sliver of worry crept in. What if it was weird? Awkward? The reality was, they didn't really know each other all that well, she and Sophie. What if, outside of work, they butted heads? Hated each other? It could happen.

"Oh, my God, relax," she whispered into the empty bathroom, the air scented with lavender and vanilla. "She seems really happy to be coming. A little nervous, even. Cutely so."

That was completely accurate. Sophie had turned to her yesterday as they were calling it a day and said, "Hey, if the offer still stands, I'd like to spend Thanksgiving with you and your family." Before Dana could even take a breath to reply, Sophie hurried immediately into, "Unless you've changed your mind. Which is totally fine. No worries at all. No big deal. I'll be fine."

Dana had stopped her with a hand on her arm, and she could feel the giant smile on her own face. "The offer does still stand. I'd love for you to come home with me." She felt the intimate weight of the words the second they were out of her mouth and hoped Sophie didn't see the surprise in her eyes. If she did, she stayed quiet about it.

Dana dried her hands on a nearby towel, put her earbuds in, and dialed her phone. It was picked up on the second ring.

"Well, hello there, Pickle," Carter Landon answered, voice jovial as always. Dana could call him at three in the morning, and he'd still sound like that: cheerful and happy to hear from her.

"Hi, Dad. How's life? Are you helping Mom get ready for Thursday? How many times has she sent you to the store?"

"Only seventeen so far. A record. Gotta be."

Dana laughed. "Hey, listen, I'm going to be bringing somebody home with me tomorrow."

"What?" Dana could envision her father's white brows shooting upward toward where his hairline used to be. "Honey, come here," he said, and Dana could tell by the rustling and change in sound that he was talking to her mother and not her. "Dana's bringing somebody home with her tomorrow."

A clattering sound happened and then Connie Landon was on the extension. "You're bringing a girl home?" she asked, the hope in her voice glaringly apparent.

Dana rolled her eyes. She loved her parents so much and knew they just wanted her to find a nice girl and settle down. They'd been crushed when she and Laura had split but had jumped in to help her heal. "Don't get excited, Mom. She's not a date. She's a client."

There was a pause, her parents probably exchanging a glance from different rooms. "A client, you say?" her father asked, and it sounded like he was trying not to seem puzzled by this information, even though he was.

"Yeah." Dana didn't mention Sophie's name but told the story of how she'd lost somebody recently—the person she'd normally spend the holiday with—and Dana didn't want her to be alone.

"You're absolutely right, sweetie," her mother said, her voice kind. "Nobody should be alone on Thanksgiving. I'm happy to set another place at the table."

"Who is it?" her father asked. "Anybody we know?"

Dana didn't make it a habit to brag very often about her clients. She repped some big names. She repped some unknowns. She repped people who were neither of those things. But Sophie was pretty high up on the list of well-known clients. Dana cleared her throat. "It's Sophie James."

She waited for a beat of silence.

Two.

Three.

"Oh, my God," her mother said loudly, suddenly.

And there it is, Dana thought with a grin.

"You're bringing Sophie James home for Thanksgiving?"

"Yes, Mom."

"*The* Sophie James?"

"The very one."

"To *my* house?"

"To your house, yes."

"Oh, my God. What? Oh, my God, this is going to have to be *the best* turkey I've ever made in my entire life." Connie said it sort of out loud and almost a little bit under her breath, and Dana wasn't quite sure if she was talking to her daughter or herself. Which made her laugh.

"Relax, Mom. Sophie's very down-to-earth. You're going to really like her." It was true. She was sure of it.

"Are you friends or is she a client?"

That gave Dana pause, caught her slightly off guard, and she took a moment to think about it—to remember the pizza in Sophie's penthouse and the way she'd squeezed Dana's hand while she got a tattoo—before answering truthfully. "She's a client, but…we've become friends."

"That girl sings like an angel," her father said. "I watched her Christmas special on television last year."

"I remember it," Dana said. Sophie had sung holiday standards as well as a few more religious selections. The show itself had been a little hokey, almost reminiscent of the old variety specials of the 70s and 80s, but Sophie had nailed every number. Easily. The show had essentially been a plug for Sophie's Christmas album from last year. Dana had downloaded it and played it many times throughout the month of December.

"Her version of 'O Holy Night' is a standout," Carter commented.

Dana agreed wholeheartedly. Sophie's voice, especially on that particular song…you could *feel* it. Deep down in your soul, you could actually feel her singing. She remembered thinking that same thing when she'd been in the studio last week, listening to her record. *I can feel her voice in the depths of my soul.*

Shaking herself back to the present, Dana tuned back in to her mother's rambling list of all the things she had to get done now that she was going to have an international superstar sitting at her dining room table. Dana held back her chuckle, refrained from pointing out that Connie would do all the same things anyway, regardless of whether or not Sophie would be there.

"What time do you land, Pickle?" her father asked, finally—thankfully—interrupting his wife's babbling.

"Three thirty, barring any delays. But don't worry, we'll take an Uber from the airport to the house."

"You'll do no such thing. I'll come get you." Her father insisted on picking her up from the airport, regardless of time or weather. "Just text me if you're on time."

Dana knew better than to argue. "Okay. See you tomorrow, Dad. Bye, Mom. Love you both."

Her bath water had become tepid, so Dana hit the drain and stood, letting the water drip for a moment before grabbing a towel.

It would begin tomorrow, the odd mixing of business and pleasure, something she did very rarely. She would be with Sophie nonstop from tomorrow afternoon until their flight back to the city on Friday evening.

Holding the towel over the lower part of her face, Dana stared at her eyes in her reflection in the mirror across from the tub.

If nothing else, Thanksgiving would be interesting.

God, she hoped she knew what she was doing.

Chapter Thirteen

Sophie was pretty sure Dana made a more-than-decent living as an entertainment manager, so it came as a bit of a surprise that she'd never flown first class before.

"How is that possible?" she asked, as they prepared to board the plane before the majority of the other passengers. "Never?" Sophie was wearing simple clothing—jeans and a New York Yankees sweatshirt—had very little makeup on, her hair tucked up in a navy blue ball cap with a white Nike swish on the front, but the guy who scanned her boarding pass did a double take when he saw her name.

"Welcome aboard, Ms. James," he said, obviously trying to keep his cool. And doing a decent job of it for the most part.

"It's just never been something I thought about," Dana said with a shrug, and for a second or two, Sophie wondered if she'd offended her. "And you didn't have to do that, you know." She lowered her voice to a whisper. "I could've paid for my own ticket."

"I know that. It's the least I could do for you taking me home with you." She smiled over her shoulder. "I think you're going to enjoy this." The truth was, Sophie was more than happy to pay for the plane tickets, and it gave her an odd sense of happiness to know when Dana flew first class for the first time, it would be with her.

Since their stay was only two nights, they'd both opted for carry-ons, so Sophie stowed hers above their seats, then took Dana's from her and tucked it next to her own. Turning to Dana, she asked, "Window or aisle?"

"I'll take the aisle. I have no desire to look out the window and see how high we are."

Sophie scooted in and sat. "You afraid of heights?"

Dana nodded, sat, and made a show of not looking at the window.

Sophie grinned. "We're not even moving yet. You can look." Dana's cheeks blossomed with pink, and she smiled sheepishly, then turned to Sophie. "Oh, well, hello there."

"Hi, smart-ass," Dana said, her own grin forming on her face.

"Can I get you ladies something to drink?" the flight attendant asked. She was a pretty blond, her hair in a ponytail, her big eyes hazel and expressive. They widened when her gaze landed on Sophie. "Ms. James. Wow. Hi there. I'm a big fan."

Sophie gave a nod and smiled at her. "Thank you so much. I appreciate that. Can we each get a glass of champagne?"

Dana's eyes widened as she turned to Sophie. "Really?"

"Why not? We're on vacation. Plus, the flight's barely an hour, so we should take advantage."

Dana seemed to not have an argument to that. The flight attendant nodded and zipped away to get their bubbly. "So much for your dressed-down disguise," Dana said with amusement.

"Right?" Sophie chuckled, but what had caught her eye was how Dana was also dressed much more casually than usual. She wore jeans, cute black ankle boots, and a long-sleeved black T-shirt accented by a black-and-green-striped scarf. But instead of blending in, she stood out. Sophie knew that, even if they were completely unacquainted, Dana would turn Sophie's head in any venue. She'd turn, look, watch for as long as she could. Dana just…drew her somehow. She had from the beginning. Magnet to steel. Moth to flame. All those corny clichés. And while she'd been trying really hard to ignore it, these next couple of days were going to make that impossible.

The flight attendant returned with two flutes of champagne. "Let me know what else I can get for you," she said, then moved to the seats behind them.

Sophie held up her glass. "To Thanksgiving with family and friends. Thank you, Dana," she said sincerely, and Dana's soft smile told her it resonated.

"I'll drink to that." They clinked and sipped. "Oh, my God, that's good. I didn't expect a plane to have decent champagne."

"It's first class, baby," Sophie said.

They sat back and relaxed in the big, buttery-soft seats, and Sophie felt almost…content. It was the first time since Ray's death that she didn't feel burdened or depressed or just downright sad. She still missed him terribly, and though she was putting on a happy face, the holidays without him were going to be tough. Part of why she took Dana up on her invitation was that she thought, maybe, being around a bunch of other people might take her mind off how much she'd be missing Ray. The other part—the part she didn't like to dwell on—was that the idea of spending uninterrupted time with Dana was…very appealing.

Yeah, she was going to have to explore that feeling at some point.

She looked into her champagne. Held it up a bit and turned the flute so it caught the afternoon light from the window. Watched the small bubbles appear from nowhere and float up to the top of the liquid like they had someplace important to be.

But I don't have to explore it right now, she thought. A glance at Dana showed her sipping her own champagne and watching as people shuffled down the aisle, mostly harried and exhausted and hoping to get where they needed to be by tomorrow. She was so beautiful. Blond hair falling in waves, blue eyes large and expressive. Sophie swallowed hard as a pang hit her low in her belly, and she turned back toward the window. *Not right now.*

❖

"There he is." Dana saw her father immediately, standing near baggage claim, silver hair precise (what was left of it), flannel shirt tucked neatly into his jeans, gentle blue eyes scanning the crowd for her through his wire-rimmed glasses.

She waved, caught his eye, and picked up the pace. Oddly, she could feel Sophie behind her, so wasn't worried about losing her as she hurried toward her dad and walked straight into his open arms.

"There's my Pickle," he said, wrapping her up tightly. She felt him press a kiss to the top of her head.

"Hi, Daddy," she muttered against his chest. She allowed herself a moment to just feel his strength, his love, smell his Old Spice. Finally taking a step back, she turned to Sophie. "Dad, this is Sophie James. Sophie, my father, Carter Landon."

Sophie held out a hand, her smile wide and open as Carter took it and shook it firmly. "It's so nice to meet you, Mr. Landon. Thank you for having me." Sophie was amazing at meeting people; it was something that really impressed Dana, given all the strangers who forced their presence on her. Sophie never acted put out or imposed upon. She always made eye contact. Always smiled.

"And it's so lovely to meet you," Carter said, eyes bright as he closed his other hand over Sophie's. "And please, call me Carter."

Sophie gave one nod, then shot a sideways glance toward Dana before adding, "And Pickle?" Her eyebrows went up as Dana closed her own eyes and shook her head with a smile.

"Oh, you don't know that story?" Carter said as he turned and led the way out the door of the small airport.

"I do not. Please, enlighten me." Sophie smiled wider and Dana groaned.

The double doors slid open as Carter led the way through and out into the November air, much crisper than it had been in the city, the smell of impending snow floating around them. "When Dana here was about four, she went through a phase. She wouldn't eat a single bite of a single meal unless we gave her a dill pickle to go along with it. Even breakfast."

"A pickle with breakfast?" Sophie shot her a look. "What a weirdo."

Dana bumped her with a shoulder. "Shut up. I was four."

"She'd be sitting there with her Cheerios and a big dill pickle." Carter turned and wrapped his arm around Dana's shoulders. "I started calling her Pickle and the name stuck."

"I'm almost forty, Dad."

Sophie shrugged. "I think that makes it even cuter."

Dana caught her gaze and held it and something passed between them. Something electric. With a sizzle. *Oh, boy.*

"Might get some snow tomorrow," Carter said, once they were in his SUV and headed out of the parking lot.

"Really?" Sophie asked, and there was a sweet, childlike quality to her voice that made Dana turn from the passenger seat and smile back at her.

"Temperature's gonna drop after midnight. We'll see."

They drove onto the on-ramp for the expressway and were zipping along at a good clip when Sophie commented, almost to herself, "There's hardly any traffic."

"You're used to New York City," Dana said. "Upstate is… different."

"I've been up this way for shows, but never spent much time. It's pretty."

Dana chuckled. "It's much prettier in the spring and summer when the trees aren't naked and everything isn't brown."

"You been a lot of places to do shows, I bet, huh?" Carter asked, glancing at Sophie in the rearview mirror.

"I'm embarrassed to say almost too many. I think I've actually forgotten a lot of them."

Dana was still turned in her seat, watching Sophie as she spoke, and her shame really did seem genuine. "Well, you started touring at, what? Sixteen?"

Sophie nodded.

"You can't possibly be expected to remember every place you've been over the past..." She did the math in her head. "Thirteen years?"

"I think I remember most, though." Sophie watched out the window as they traveled a route that was second nature to Dana. She'd been living in New York for nearly twelve years now, but the way home never left her memory.

"Oh, that's pretty," Sophie said quietly as they passed St. Mark's Cathedral, an old stone church with gorgeous nighttime lighting.

"My wife and I got married there," Carter said.

"I bet the inside is beautiful," Sophie breathed. "How long have you been married?"

"Fifty-five years in February," he said, and Dana felt herself smile at the pride in his voice.

"Wow. That's amazing." Sophie said it like she couldn't even imagine such a thing.

"*She's* amazing," Carter said. "I just got lucky."

"You're both amazing," Dana said, squeezing her father's arm. "And you both got lucky." *I only hope I can be as lucky one day.* The thought came out of nowhere and was sobering, to say the least. Dana felt a light sadness fall over her like a blanket, and turned to look out her window. When she shifted her gaze to the side mirror, Sophie's face was reflected back, looking at her.

"And here we are," Carter said, pulling Dana back to the present and away from the intensity of Sophie's gaze.

"Oh, this is lovely," Sophie said, and Dana tried to see it through her eyes, the eyes of somebody who'd never been there before.

It was an old but updated farmhouse set on two acres. Still part of a neighborhood, but one where the houses were spaced out enough to allow privacy and a feeling of roominess. White siding and an open front porch across the front gave Dana's mother ample space for decorating, be it Christmas, Easter, or Halloween. Currently, the black front door sported a very fall-ish wreath, all orange and red leaves and pinecones. Two enormous pots of mums still held on to their bright yellow color, despite the cold temperatures. There were two other cars in the driveway.

"Sean's here already?" Dana asked, recognizing one of the cars as her brother's.

Carter shifted into Park. "They got here this morning. They're going to stay overnight so they don't have to drive in the morning and Jeanine can help your mother." He punctuated that with a scoff that made Dana laugh.

"Jeanine is a god-awful cook," Dana said, explaining to Sophie. "Every holiday, she wants to 'watch and help' my mother." She made air quotes with her fingers.

"And after eleven holidays, she hasn't learned a damn thing." Carter pushed himself out of the car, leaving Dana laughing and Sophie smiling widely.

"Dad!" Dana scolded, and he gave her a wink.

They got their bags out of the back and headed up the front stairs of the house and in.

It was instant. Dana never could explain it, but the very second she walked into her parents' house, everything inside her simply relaxed. Her shoulders dropped, she let out a huge lungful of air and just felt... content.

"You're here!" came a shout from the back of the house, and Dana's mother shot out of the kitchen like a cannonball, barreling straight to the door and into Dana's arms. She held her daughter tightly, rocking back and forth like mothers do, and kissed her loudly on the cheek once, twice, three times.

"Okay, okay, Mom." But Dana was laughing because her mother was her favorite person on the planet. Once she was able to step back an inch or two, she turned and held out a hand. "Mom, this is Sophie James. Sophie, my mother Connie."

"It's so nice to meet you." Sophie held out her hand to shake and Dana almost snorted because she knew how that would go. Connie made a *pfft* sound, pushed Sophie's hand aside, and embraced her. Sophie's eyes went wide for a split second as she looked over Connie's shoulder at Dana for help, but in no time, she sank into the hug. Dana saw her arms tighten and her eyes close. That was the Connie Effect. When they parted, finally, Sophie said softly, "Thank you for letting me crash your Thanksgiving. I hope it's not an imposition."

Connie waved a dismissive hand. "Are you kidding? The more the merrier. Let me take your coat." She hung it in the nearby closet and headed back toward the dining room table.

"Aunt Dana!"

It was a voice Dana knew and loved, and she turned around just in time to catch her nine-year-old nephew, Matthew, as he launched himself at her. "One of these days, you're going to do that and I'm not going to be ready."

"You always say that," Matthew laughed, his face buried in Dana's shoulder. He smelled wonderful, like peanut butter and the outdoors and little boy.

"You're getting so big. What happens when you're too big for me to catch you?"

"Then I'll catch you."

Dana felt her eyes well up, and pulled him in for another hug as her gaze landed on her brother coming from the living room. "How did such a sweet boy come from your genes?" she asked Sean, who shrugged.

"Don't ask me. I have no idea." He tapped his son's shoulder. "Hey, let your old man in." When Matthew moved, Sean wrapped Dana in a hug and picked her up off the ground like he always did, given that he was six three and she was not.

"Sean," Dana said, once he put her feet back onto the floor. "This is Sophie. Sophie, my brother Sean." Her hand on Matthew's head, she added, "And my nephew, Matthew."

Sophie shook hands with both of them as Sean said, "Wow. A real-life celebrity for Thanksgiving. Dana never shares her famous clients with us."

Dana socked him on the arm just as her mother called, "Come on in here and sit. There's wine, cheese, snacks."

Everybody filtered toward the dining room and Dana glanced back at Sophie. "You doing okay?" she asked quietly.

"Are you kidding? This is amazing." Her dark eyes were bright, her smile wide.

"Good, 'cause there's more to come." Dana put a hand on the small of Sophie's back and let her walk ahead, into the noise and warmth of happy hour with the Landons.

CHAPTER FOURTEEN

"Wine, Sophie?" Connie asked, holding up an empty crystal wine glass.

Sophie nodded. "Yes, please."

"Mom, Sophie knows wine," Dana said. "Give her the good stuff, not the cheap crap."

Connie gasped, feigned insult. "How dare you?" she said to her daughter. "My cheap crap wine is very good, I'll have you know."

"I'm not picky," Sophie said, watching the exchange with amusement. "Anything red. Surprise me."

"Oh, she'll surprise you, all right," Dana muttered, and Sophie playfully poked at her.

"Stop that," she said quietly. "Your mom's amazing."

Dana nodded, her blue eyes fixed on Sophie's as she nodded. "True."

The dining room was not large, but there were somehow nine chairs crammed around the table, the top of which was covered in food. Covered. Sophie had been to endless spreads of hors d'oeuvres, both at her concerts and at shows and events where she'd been a guest. But this was different. Those fancy settings had all been…cold, somehow? A bit sterile in comparison to the Landon table. There was a huge plate of what looked to be homemade cookies, a giant platter with a good five or six different kinds of cheese, bowls of nuts, a bread bowl filled with some kind of dip, pieces of bread scattered around it, a huge plate of cold cuts, cheese, and rolls for sandwiches, and more. Sophie wasn't exactly sure how it all felt wonderfully overwhelming, but it did. She took a seat next to Dana just as Connie handed her a glass of red wine.

"There you go, sweetie," she said, and rubbed her hand along Sophie's shoulder as she moved on to fill other glasses.

Another woman exited the kitchen. She was petite, with chestnut hair and kind green eyes. She immediately held her hand out to Sophie from across the table. "You must be Sophie. I'm Jeanine, Sean's wife."

"And my mom," Matthew chimed in.

They shook hands and Jeanine flitted around the table like a hummingbird, adjusting plates and refilling anything that needed it. Sophie decided she was one of those women with endless energy.

Watching Dana with her family was so many things for Sophie, and she had trouble staying with one emotion. She'd never had this kind of a holiday gathering. It had always just been her and her mom, and her mom was not exactly the sentimental type. One of the first things she'd noticed about the Landons was how physical they were. Tactile. There was a lot of touching and hugging, and it was almost foreign to Sophie…though not unpleasantly so. The second thing was how different Dana looked from the rest of them. While both Carter and Connie had gone gray, their skin was fairly pale, creamy, and Connie had freckles on her face and forearms. Sean was a redhead, as was Matthew, and they both shared the same pale skin and green eyes. Dana was not only blond, but her skin was a lighter shade of olive. Sophie bet she got a beautiful tan in the summer.

"What are you grinning at?" Dana asked quietly, as she leaned close to Sophie.

"Skin tones," Sophie answered honestly.

"One of the perks of being adopted," Dana said with a grin.

Sean scoffed, obviously having overheard, and pointed at Dana. "When we were kids, that one would become a bronze goddess in about an hour while the rest of us were slathered in SPF 50 and still burned as red as lobsters."

As Carter chuckled along at his kids, Sophie said to him, "So, you'd have two lobsters and a pickle on your hands."

Carter's chuckle turned into a belly laugh, a sound Sophie instantly loved and found contagious. "Exactly that."

Dana shook her head. "I am never living that down."

"Nope," Sophie said. "Never."

The front door opened then. Sophie felt it more than heard it, felt the rush of cold air seep in before a woman's voice called out, "Happy Thanksgiving!"

Two more people entered the dining room, a man and a woman. The woman's red hair told Sophie right away that this was Dana's sister. She looked to be around fifty, her hair in a French braid that ended between her shoulder blades. She had soft green eyes and wore very little makeup, so her freckles were prominent on her smooth face.

Dana stood from the table and hugged both of them, holding on to the woman as she turned to the table and said, "Sophie, this is my sister, Bethany, and her husband Kyle."

"Wow," Bethany said, shaking Sophie's hand. "You're even more gorgeous in person."

Sophie felt herself blush as Sean said loudly, "Right? I thought the same thing, but didn't want to say it and sound like a creeper."

"Same," Jeanine piped in.

"Oh my God, you guys," Dana said, covering her eyes with a hand as Sophie shook Kyle's hand. "Stop it. You're embarrassing her."

Sophie grinned and tugged Dana back to her seat by an arm. "It's fine. Thank you all. You're very kind."

"Where are the kids?" Connie asked as Bethany and Kyle made their way into the room and wine was poured for them as they found chairs. Kyle stayed standing and immediately made himself a roast beef sandwich.

"Lydia just drove back from school today and she's 'exhausted.'" Bethany made air quotes. "So, she and Micah are staying at the house tonight and then they'll drive here in the morning."

Dana leaned close to Sophie again, and Sophie tried to ignore how much she liked the feel of it, the inviting smell of her. "Lydia is twenty and in college about three hours away. Micah is eighteen and in his senior year of high school."

Sophie nodded. So many people to keep track of, and it wasn't even that big a family. It was all so new to her.

"Sophie, sweetheart, help yourself to anything," Connie said, making eye contact with her across the table. "Don't be shy. We're very informal here."

Sean leaned toward her. "Mom's worrying that you've been sitting for seven minutes and haven't eaten."

Sophie grinned as he went on, holding out an arm toward his brother-in-law in introduction.

"You'll notice Kyle here started in on the food before he even sat down."

Kyle held up his sandwich in a toast, nodding and chewing a large bite.

Sophie laughed. "Your family is great," she said to Dana.

"Yeah, yeah. They're okay, I guess."

"Beggars can't be choosers, Dana," Bethany said with a wink.

Dana tossed a grape at her. "Adoption jokes are not funny."

"They're kind of funny," Sean said.

"I laughed," Carter added.

"Me, too," said Connie.

"I hate you all," Dana told them.

"Lies," Bethany said, reaching for a roll.

Sophie sipped her wine, perfectly content to sit back and watch the banter, the joking, the love that was so apparent in the Landon family. It was true that she'd hesitated in accepting Dana's invitation. She was good with strangers, could hold her own in a conversation filled with small talk—she did it all the time on talk shows. But this was a holiday, and it was only natural that she'd feel a bit like she was intruding on family time. She didn't feel that way at all now. The Landons were the nicest, most welcoming people she'd ever met. Even their quick moments of being a little starstruck by her were sweet and heartwarming. And then over, just like that.

Sophie shifted her legs, crossed them the other way, and her foot touched Dana's under the table. Dana never looked at her, but also didn't move her foot. In fact, did she wiggle it a bit? To let Sophie know she felt it? Could be her imagination, but Sophie made no effort to move again. She kept her foot against Dana's, ate delicious food, sipped a wine that was damn good regardless of its price, and had a better time than she'd remembered having in…too long to think about. And it might have been odd, a little strange, but there was a sliver of her that felt as if she was a part of the Landon family. Like this was her seat during holidays and family gatherings. Like they'd always welcome her, from here on out. As if she'd become indoctrinated into a club of sorts. A club filled with laughter and humor and love. She turned to look at Dana as she laughed at something Sean said. Her face was flushed, her blue eyes bright, and Sophie couldn't remember ever seeing her look so perfectly comfortable as she did right in that moment.

It was a beautiful sight.

❖

It was after midnight by the time the Landon crew decided to call it a night. Much wine had been drunk by all, Matthew had crashed on the couch more than two hours before, and the dishwasher had been filled and turned on.

"I have you two in your room in the attic," Dana's mother said to her as they grabbed their bags from near the front door.

Dana felt her own eyes widen slightly as she lowered her voice so only Connie could hear. "Both of us? I thought we'd have our own rooms."

Connie shrugged. "Sweetie, there are too many people. I didn't know Bethany and Kyle were coming overnight until the last minute." She dropped her voice to just below a whisper and shifted her gaze toward Sophie, who was laughing with Sean. "Will she be upset? I mean, the cot is up there. It's no five-star hotel, but..."

Dana had embarrassed her mother and now she felt awful, needed to erase the line of concern that suddenly creased Connie's forehead. "No, Mom." She laid a hand on Connie's arm and gave her a warm smile. "It's fine. We'll figure it out. No worries." Sophie turned her dark gaze Dana's way and Dana didn't have to force a smile. It just appeared on her face; she could feel it. "Ready?"

"Absolutely," Sophie said, hefting her bag. "I'm beat." Turning to Connie, Sophie's face lit up as she held out a hand and squeezed Connie's forearm. "Thank you for a lovely evening, Mrs. Landon. I'm already looking forward to tomorrow."

"You are the most pleasant and polite celebrity I've ever had in my home," Connie said.

"She's the only celebrity you've ever had in your home, Mom," Dana said, shaking her head.

Connie playfully slapped at her. "Do you have to spoil all my fun?"

Dana led Sophie up the narrow stairs. In the upstairs hallway, she turned to her and said, "Okay, we're in the attic. It's my old room."

"Ooh, that sounds fun. Lead the way."

Quietly, Dana took a deep breath, opened a door, and headed up a second flight of stairs. Why it hadn't crossed her mind that she and Sophie might end up sharing a bedroom, she had no idea. And she was annoyed at herself for not planning for the possibility. For not preparing Sophie ahead of time. At the top of the stairs, the room opened up into the place that was Dana's sanctuary growing up.

"Wow," Sophie breathed, her dark eyes wide as she looked around.

It was a fantastic room, there was no doubt about that. Dana's school friends loved coming over to hang in her space. Beamed high ceiling, a skylight her father had installed for her when she was a teenager, hardwood flooring with two thick braided area rugs, two dressers, a homemade closet she and her father had built together, a double bed with slatted head- and footboards in black. The only thing that had changed since Dana's last visit at Easter was the appearance of a twin-size foldout cot jutting out from one wall. Her mother had made it up nicely in sea-foam green sheets and a green-and-yellow quilt, but it was still a very old cot.

"This is amazing," Sophie said, her voice still breathy, almost a whisper.

"Thanks. It was Bethany's first, but when she went to college, I got to move up here. My dad and I did a lot of the work, redid stuff, added things. We built the closet. I helped him put in the skylight for my sixteenth birthday. It's much cooler now than when it was Bethany's room." Dana wrinkled her nose and grinned.

"Well." Sophie set her bag down. "You were a lucky kid. I can't imagine having a room this big."

"You didn't?"

Sophie's scoff seemed partly sarcastic, partly sad. "We lived in a trailer. My room was about as big as that closet you built. And then once I started touring, I didn't really have a place to settle into at all. Not as a teenager, anyway."

"You must've been lonely." Dana said the words without thinking about it. For a split second, she wanted to take them back, but then changed her mind because Sophie's smile was sad and warm and grateful all at once.

"I was. Most people don't get that right away. Point to you."

There was a moment then, the two of them standing a foot apart, eye contact galore, warmth surrounding them. It held.

Dana finally cleared her throat, breaking the spell. "Okay. I will take the cot. You get the bed."

Sophie's brows went up. "What? No. No, Dana, this is your room. Your bed. I can sleep on the cot."

"Absolutely not. First, you're the guest. You get the bed. Second, my mother would kill me if she knew I put a 'celebrity' on the cot." She made the air quotes and filled the word with playful sarcasm.

Sophie gasped in mock-insult. "How dare you call me that?" While they laughed together, she added, "Whoever gets there first…"

The next forty-five seconds seemed to happen in slow motion. Both women glanced at each other, a silent acknowledgment of a challenge accepted, and then it was on. They each pushed off and ran the eight feet, launching themselves onto the nearly ancient metal-framed cot. They landed together, limbs tangling, laughter permeating the air, a perfect tie.

That was when the nearly ancient metal-framed cot decided it had had enough and gave up, the metal frame bending and then completely collapsing in the middle, sending its occupants down to the floor with a loud crash. The ends went up, as if it was trying to fold itself in half one last time, but the bodies in the center prevented it.

Thundering footsteps sounded and Sean skidded to a stop in the doorway in about three seconds. Dana didn't have time to marvel at his speed because she and Sophie were way too busy all tangled in each other and utterly cracking up like schoolgirls.

"What happened?" Sean asked excitedly. "Is everybody okay?" He took in the scene before him, eyes wide. "Oh, my God, you broke the cot? The cot that was around before any of us were born? I can't believe it." He turned on his heel to go but looked back at them, pointed a finger. "You guys are in so much trouble." He made eye contact with Dana for a moment, and the joking faded slightly for brother and sister. Then he was gone and the door at the bottom of the stairs clicked shut, voices muffled through the wood.

Sophie was practically in her lap, still laughing, and Dana took a moment to let herself feel it. Just feel it. Feel the tall, lithe, soft body against hers, smell the mixed scents of wine and cinnamon and warmth that seemed to radiate from her, absorb the heat from her skin where their arms touched.

As the laughter died down, the air suddenly seemed a bit charged, electrified somehow, as if they each suddenly realized how close they actually were and tried to be subtle about getting up quickly. Once on their feet, they stood looking down at the broken cot.

"Well." Dana pursed her lips.

"I guess it's the bed for both of us, then," Sophie said, though she didn't make eye contact.

"I mean, if you're okay with that..." Dana nibbled on the inside of her cheek as she looked at her old bed. Not a king-size. Not even a queen. A simple double that suddenly seemed so much smaller than every other bed she'd ever slept in in her entire life.

"I am if you are." This time when Dana turned to face Sophie, she was looking right at her, a gentle smile on her face.

It was going on one a.m.—much too late to try to come up with some other arrangements, and frankly, Dana was exhausted. Judging by the sleepy look on her face, Sophie was in the same boat.

"All right. Why don't you do what you need to do in the bathroom. Then you can change while I'm down there." With a nod, Sophie unzipped her bag, got her toiletries out, and headed downstairs without a word.

The attic room might have been fun to look at and hang in, but it could get cold in the winter. Her father had done some fancy thing with ductwork to install a heat run, but the lack of good insulation didn't help with the drafts that could seep in. She quickly grabbed the quilt off the dead cot and spread it out on top of the comforter on the bed, smoothing the wrinkles. She also snagged the pillow from the cot, not knowing what kind Sophie might prefer or if she wanted more than one.

Sophie's footsteps coming up the stairs were soft, but Dana knew the staircase well, knew exactly which step she was on by the pitch of the wood's squeak. Sophie appeared, all natural and shiny, her face scrubbed free of what little makeup she'd had on. *Radiant* was the only word Dana could come up with. With a forced grin and a hard swallow, she grabbed her own pajamas and toiletries. "Be right back," she said, and escaped to the bathroom.

Once safely locked inside, the small of her back against the counter, she covered her face with her hands.

Why was she so freaked out about this? She and Sophie were two grown women who were going to spend two nights in the same bed. A slumber party for adults. It wasn't like there was anything between them. Really. Sophie was straight. Wasn't she? Dana's mind took that opportunity to remind her what it felt like when Sophie pressed her foot to Dana's under the dining room table and kept it there. Reminded Dana how she didn't subtly move her own foot away. Or even not subtly. She kept her own foot in contact with Sophie's as long as she was able.

"It felt nice. So, sue me," she hissed at her reflection. With an annoyed sigh, she washed her face, brushed her teeth, and changed into soft gray gym shorts and a dark blue T-shirt so worn, it was almost see-through in spots. When she was finished, Dana braced her hands on the vanity, blew out a long, slow breath, and stared at herself in the mirror. "You are an adult," she whispered. "Get your shit together."

A sudden knocking on the door made her jump and let out a tiny yelp.

"Come on, Dana." Bethany's voice was low. "Other people need to pee, too."

"Fine." Dana pulled the door open. "All yours." She could feel her sister's eyes on her as she pushed past her and headed for the attic stairs, but she didn't look back. Instead, she shut the door behind her and headed up.

CHAPTER FIFTEEN

Sophie wasn't sure what woke her. A sound outside maybe? Somebody moving around downstairs on a—she opened her eyes, her head already facing the clock on the nightstand—3:30 a.m. trip to the bathroom? The weight on her body that was keeping her warm and pinned to the bed? She couldn't pinpoint one specific thing, but she was awake. She closed her eyes again in an attempt to drift back to sleep…

Wait.

The weight on her body?

Sophie's eyes popped back open and she swallowed hard. Without moving, she took stock of her position. Of Dana's. Sophie was on her back and exceedingly comfortable, so she had no desire to move. Which was good because she couldn't have, as Dana was sleeping soundly while covering her like a blanket. Her head was on Sophie's shoulder, tucked under Sophie's chin. Her arm was draped over Sophie's middle, her hand tucked around and under Sophie's side. Her leg was tossed over Sophie's, her knee dangerously close to Sophie's center—which was suddenly *very* awake and *very* sensitive.

Why aren't I freaking out right now?

That was the big question in her head. Because the truth was: She wasn't. At all. Shouldn't she be? The fact was, she couldn't remember the last time anything had felt this…right. This perfect. With a slow turn of her head, her eyes now adjusted to the dark, she looked at Dana's sleeping face. Relaxed, her brow smooth rather than furrowed like it so often was. Blond hair tousled, a hunk hanging over her ear. Full lips parted just slightly as she breathed, deep and even. Sophie couldn't see a lot more than that, as the blankets were all the way up over Dana's shoulder. The attic had gotten cold in the wee hours, but Sophie was warm. She moved the hand by her side, found Dana's bare knee with it, slid it over the impossibly soft skin of her thigh, let herself feel it…the velvety smoothness, the warmth, the—

Her thoughts came to a screeching halt.

Dana's breathing had changed.

Sophie swallowed again, shifted her gaze to Dana's face, found those blue eyes open, blinking back at her, so incredibly dark and full of desire that Sophie felt a tangible surge of arousal flood her body. Dana pushed herself up onto her elbow and stayed that way, looking down at Sophie's face, seemingly searching for…something. Sophie didn't move. Couldn't. Didn't want to.

Dana's fingertips were soft, gentle on Sophie's lips, stroking across them, feather-light, as if she was making sure they were there and not in her imagination, that she wasn't dreaming this whole thing.

No words.

They said nothing as Dana lowered her mouth to Sophie's. The kiss was slow, hesitant at first, and much as Sophie wanted to grab Dana's head with both hands and kiss the hell out of her, she also wanted to wait. To savor. To feel every single second of what was happening between them.

Dana tilted her head the other way and continued to kiss Sophie and gradually, oh so gradually, things deepened. Dana pressed into Sophie a bit more firmly. Lips parted slightly, then more. Tongues entered the action, tentatively at first, then more insistently. Sophie heard herself moan at the first touch of Dana's tongue to hers, and that seemed to spur Dana on, judging by the way she pushed her body into Sophie's, shifted herself so she was more on top and less off to the side of Sophie. Sophie helped by spreading her thighs and making room for Dana's hips to settle between them.

They kissed forever. Or so it felt to Sophie. She'd kissed other people. Men, mostly. A few recently. Only one other woman before, years ago, before she'd reached a level of fame where she had to be careful. But none of them had felt like this. And though kissing that woman had been infinitely more enjoyable than kissing any of the men…kissing her hadn't been this soft. Or this urgent. That was the perfect word. Kissing Dana had an urgency to it, an excitement, an anticipation that Sophie hadn't expected and wasn't quite sure what to do with, so she simply held on and kissed Dana back like there was no tomorrow.

Soon, lips, teeth, and tongues weren't enough and hands began to wander. Sophie didn't even realize she was sliding her hand up under the back of Dana's T-shirt until she felt the warm softness of her shoulder blade. Her other hand had somehow ended up under Dana's shorts, splayed over one cheek of her ass. Sophie dug her fingers in gently, pulled Dana into her, and the move forced a small sound from Dana that was throaty and sexy as hell.

Dana was not an innocent bystander in this scenario, and that was made clear to Sophie when she felt Dana's hand close over her breast through her tank top, knead gently. When her fingers zeroed in on Sophie's already hardened nipple and squeezed, Sophie gasped out a small cry, breaking the endless kiss.

They lay there, the two of them, chests heaving, and stared at each other. Sophie had never seen a more beautiful sight than that of Dana, staring down at her, all flushed cheeks and swollen lips.

"Maybe we should stop," Dana whispered, but it was more of a question than a suggestion, as if she wasn't sold on the idea.

"Maybe we should," Sophie said, and her inflection was the same.

Neither of them wanted to stop. That much was clear—to both of them, Sophie was sure. But they were in a house full of people, in Dana's childhood bed, and they hadn't talked about this even a little bit. Which was odd, right?

She was glad when Dana slid off her but didn't go far. In fact, she resumed her previous position and curled up into Sophie's side.

"Is this okay?" she asked quietly.

Sophie tightened an arm around Dana's shoulders, pulled her in closer. "It's perfect," she said, and had never meant anything more in her life. Her other hand, she dug into Dana's hair to cup the back of her head, hugged her again, and pressed a kiss to her forehead. A glance at the clock told her it was now 4:01 a.m. They could probably get a couple more hours of sleep before Thanksgiving officially began.

As if I'm gonna sleep now.

She managed to refrain from snorting at the thought, because the reality was, her body was on fire. Heated. Stoked. Ready. She wondered if Dana felt the same way. *We should talk about this.* More than once, she opened her mouth to say something, anything, but always closed it again, preferring the peace, the joy she felt from simply holding Dana's body against her own. Sophie felt her gradually drift off to sleep, her muscles relaxing, her body settling in closer, and again, her breathing evened out.

They wouldn't be talking about it tonight, apparently.

Sophie took in a deep, full breath and exhaled slowly. Then she did her best to relax, but part of her didn't want to sleep. She didn't want to miss a single moment of holding Dana.

She lay there, completely content, until the sky began to lighten.

❖

Dana loved to take long showers. The shower was her think tank. It was where she planned her day, came up with new ideas for clients, hashed out life issues. She could stand under the hot spray of water and let it pound on the back of her neck for what felt like hours. Thank goodness her father had long ago replaced the small water heater in the house or she'd be hearing it from her siblings about how she'd used up all the hot water because she stood there now, in the early light of the morning, and replayed the activities of a few hours ago.

Over and over and over.

My God, how had that happened? What was she thinking? What had gotten into her? And when could they do it again? Sophie was, hands down, the best kisser Dana had ever kissed…and she'd kissed her share of girls. Dana swallowed hard, turned in the shower, and let the water hit her square in the face.

She'd woken up still wrapped in Sophie's embrace, and the weirdest part about it was how *not* weird it felt. It felt right. Normal. Like Dana was exactly where she was supposed to be, tucked against her, leg thrown possessively over Sophie's.

And the way Sophie had looked at her in the dark, with such raw desire in her eyes? God…

Since when was Sophie into women? How did Dana not know that? How had Sophie never said anything, especially after the way Dana had poured out her heart about Laura? Was it new? No, it couldn't be new. Sophie was almost thirty. She had to have at least an inkling.

Dana turned the water off and grabbed a towel. Holding it over her face, she let out a muffled groan of frustration. Her brain was going to drive her crazy if she let it. And it was Thanksgiving. She needed to set her own crap aside and focus on helping her mother, enjoying time with her family.

Yeah. She could do that.

This stuff with Sophie would have to wait.

That line of thought lasted until Dana climbed the attic stairs back into her bedroom and saw Sophie. Sprawled on her stomach, arms up under the pillow, one bare leg completely exposed, tan shoulders begging for lips...

Jesus Christ, I'm in trouble.

She stood there with her pajamas held tightly to her chest. Frozen. Nervous. Ridiculously turned on.

Sophie moved then, stretched her arms out. Yawned. Opened those dark eyes that had been filled with so much last night. She blinked at Dana. Blinked again. Smiled.

"Good morning," she said, her voice throaty and deep.

"Hi," Dana said, forcing herself into some kind of movement. She crossed to the far side of the room, put her stuff down, and stood in front of the vanity her parents had gotten her for her fifteenth birthday. "The bathroom is free if you want to shower."

"Is that bacon I smell?" Sophie rolled over onto her back and sat up. The covers fell away from her tank top–clad torso and Dana pulled her gaze away.

"Yeah. My mom's probably been up since five."

With a determined nod, Sophie threw off the covers. "I'll take a quick shower so I can help with stuff."

Dana wanted to tell her to take her time. Not to worry. That there was plenty of time. But all the words died in her throat as she watched Sophie—in tank top and underwear—get out of bed and find her clothes. Dana was both grateful and disappointed when Sophie stepped into sweats and pulled on another shirt. At the door, she stopped, seemed to stare at her feet for a moment before turning to Dana.

"You okay?" she asked.

The soft quality of her voice sent a flutter through Dana's body and she nodded.

"Okay. See you in a bit." And she headed down the stairs.

Dana sat down at the vanity and plugged in the blow-dryer. Stared at her own reflection. Brought her fingers to her lips as she let herself remember again. Just for a minute. Then she let out a slow breath and clicked on the dryer.

❖

"Good morning, sweetheart."

"Hi, Mom." Dana kissed her mother on the cheek.

"You sleep okay? Did Sophie?" Connie flipped eggs over easy for her husband.

"We both did, yes." Dana had finished her hair and makeup and had escaped the attic before Sophie came up from the bathroom, all wet hair and clean-smelling, Dana was sure.

"I can't believe you're having breakfast, Dad." Bethany sat at the table with a cup of coffee in both hands and shook her head. "We are literally going to eat all day long."

"I have bacon and eggs every morning," he told her, the exact same sentence he'd said to her last year, when she'd made the same comment.

"This conversation has become a holiday tradition." Dana grabbed her own mug and filled it from the half-full pot of coffee as her father chuckled. She pulled out a chair and snagged a piece of bacon from her father's plate as she sat.

"Oh, crap." Dana looked up at the words from her mother. Connie was looking around the kitchen, opened the refrigerator. "Crap," she said again.

"What's the matter, Mom?"

"I thought I had more half-n-half." Connie spoke more to herself than to either of her daughters. "I was sure of it. I need it for the mashed potatoes."

Bethany picked up the now-empty half-n-half container on the dining room table and grimaced at Dana.

"Good morning." Sophie's voice came from behind Dana. It didn't startle her so much as settle over her like warm syrup, thick and sweet and comforting.

"Hi," Carter said with a friendly smile. "You sleep okay up there? Sean said you guys broke the cot."

Dana pretended not to see Bethany's eyebrows climb up into her hairline as Sophie answered, "Oh, yeah, I'm so sorry about that. Totally my fault."

"No worries. That thing was older than dirt. It was probably time to put it out of its misery."

Connie came in from the kitchen with a mug of coffee and handed it to Sophie. "Coffee, sweetie?"

"God, yes. Thank you." Sophie came around and into Dana's view to take a seat at the table. She was wearing dark jeans and a cozy-looking red sweater. Her hair was still damp, pulled back off her face, which boasted very little makeup.

"You warm enough up there?" Carter asked, then took a bite of toast. "Gets chilly."

"We had lots of blankets," Sophie said, then sipped her coffee.

Bethany's eyes went wide over the rim of her cup. Dana shot her a look.

Preventing Bethany from saying anything by laying a hand on her shoulder, Connie said, "Bethy, would you be a dear and run to Wegmans for me and get half-n-half? I know they're open until noon."

"Sure, Mom. Dana will come with me."

"I will?" Dana caught the look Bethany shot her way. "Yes. I will. Sure." With a turn to Sophie, she asked, "You'll be okay for a bit?"

Sophie's smile was beautiful, all straight white teeth and full lips. "Absolutely. I'll chat up your parents. Learn all your secrets."

How was it that those words simultaneously turned Dana on and sent her into a blind panic? How?

"Watch your driving," Carter said, as his daughters put on their coats. "It's starting to snow."

"We will." Bethany held the door open for Dana and just like that, they were outside in the brisk quiet of the morning.

Dana inhaled deeply, the upstate New York air so much different than that of the city. Fresher. Cleaner. Colder. She exhaled a visible cloud and pulled her coat tighter around her body as she strolled across the very light dusting of snow that must have just begun. Big, puffy flakes fell slowly and silently from the sky, and standing in that stillness, that calm atmosphere as it snowed had always been a favorite memory of Dana's childhood.

They were in the car and had driven for several minutes before Bethany finally spoke. "So, what's the deal with you and her?"

"Wow, that took you a long time. Was it killing you?"

Bethany had the good sense to chuckle. Her red hair was pulled back in a low ponytail today and her face was completely devoid of makeup, her visible freckles making her seem much younger than her fifty-four years. "It kinda was."

Dana's shoulders lifted as she inhaled. What was the deal with her and Sophie? "I honestly don't know, Bethy. I really don't." She could feel her sister's eyes on her.

"Wow." It was all Bethany said for a beat. "That's…wow."

Dana shot her a puzzled look. "What does that mean?"

"It means that my little sister always has her shit together. No matter what. She never doesn't know what's going on. Not ever. So…" She paused as she turned into the Wegmans parking lot, which wasn't full, but certainly wasn't as empty as it should be on a holiday morning.

She shifted the car into Park, removed the keys, and turned to Dana. "Do you want to talk about it?"

Dana dropped her head back against the seat and groaned. "Ugh. I don't know. I don't even know what to say, what I think. There's so much."

Bethany pulled the door handle and hauled herself out of the car. "Are you guys together?" she asked over the roof.

"What?" The question surprised Dana, for some reason. "No. Of course not."

Bethany squinted at her and Dana looked away as they walked into the store. "Then why are you acting so freaky?"

"I'm not," Dana snapped, then grimaced as she glanced at her sister. "Am I?"

"Little bit."

Nobody in Wegmans was walking slowly. Everybody apparently had someplace to be, and Dana would have taken a moment to be amused by that if her mind wasn't completely taken up by dark eyes. Soft lips. Silky skin...

"We made out in bed last night," she said, in a hissed whisper.

"Whoa." Bethany stopped in the middle of the produce section, her hand on Dana's arm. "How...what...who started that?"

Dana made an "oops" face as she admitted it had been her.

"Whoa," Bethany said again and resumed her trek toward the dairy.

"I know. I know."

At the coolers, Bethany opened a door, pulled out a half gallon of half-n-half. "She a good kisser?"

Dana felt her insides melt just a little as they headed for the registers. "God, yes," she said, before she could catch herself, be a little more diplomatic and a little less swoony.

"My little sister and Sophie James." Bethany paid for the cream and they left the store. "There's something I never thought I'd say. Wow."

Dana shook her head, suddenly panicked by the direction the conversation had gone. "No. No, no, no. That's not the case. We're not together."

"Do you want to be? 'Cause it sounds like it."

They got in the car and fastened their seat belts. "There are so many reasons why it's a bad idea," Dana said quietly.

Bethany scoffed as she shifted the car and turned them toward home. "Yeah, the heart doesn't usually give a shit about those things."

The heart?

Dana sat quietly, let Bethany's words sink in.

Were hearts involved now?

CHAPTER SIXTEEN

Sophie was kind of surprised to realize that she found the act of peeling and dicing potatoes relaxing. Calming. Mindless. She sat at the small table in the corner of the kitchen with a vegetable peeler, a knife, a huge pile of potatoes, a pot of water, and a cutting board.

"You okay over there?" Connie asked from the counter where she was literally stuffing a turkey, her hands deep inside.

"Totally. Thank you for letting me help." She liked Dana's parents. So much. They were kind and down-to-earth. They didn't treat her any differently than a normal houseguest, and Sophie loved that. Not that being treated like a celebrity was a bad thing; it rarely was. But sometimes, she wanted to just be…herself.

"You don't spend the holiday with your parents?" Connie asked.

"Not in a long time." Sophie dropped the chunks of potato in the enormous pot of water and moved on to the next one. "My dad's never really been in the picture."

"And your mother?"

"She's on a cruise." Connie didn't respond, but Sophie could feel her looking, sensed she had a comment. Sophie snagged her with a glance and smiled as warmly as she could. "It's okay. You can say it."

One corner of Connie's mouth turned down and she shook her head. "Not my place, sweetie."

"You're very kind." Sophie had the sudden strange desire to spill personal things to Dana's mother. She wasn't sure why. Something about the woman. She was warm and inviting, and Sophie hadn't felt so comfortable in someone else's house in…ever. "My mom is…she's interesting."

"How so?"

And the floodgates opened.

"Don't get me wrong. She's my mom and I love her. She worked hard when I was a kid." Sophie moved on to the next potato, having created a little routine for herself, and sliced into it.

"What does she do?" Connie continued to work on the turkey, her back to Sophie.

"She was a waitress. We didn't have a lot, but we managed."

"She's retired now?"

Sophie plopped the potatoes into the water. "She…kind of retired when I started making money."

Connie nodded, muttered a "Mm-hmm," but let Sophie continue.

"I can't really blame her." Sophie held a potato in one hand, the knife in the other as she looked off into the middle distance. "I mean, she never had money. Not as a kid. Not as an adult. She was always barely making ends meet. Then she had me, and kids take up so much; getting ahead must have seemed impossible. So, as soon as I could start buying her nice things, I did."

"Of course you did."

"I guess she kind of got used to that. Then there was a year I was touring and couldn't get home for Christmas. I was in the U.K. at the time and offered to fly her out so we could be together, but she didn't want to be in the cold. She said she'd been thinking of going somewhere warm…" Sophie swallowed hard and said the words she'd always thought but had never said out loud until that moment. "Which was her way of asking me to send her somewhere warm."

"Pay for it."

"Yeah." On to the next potato. "And it's been that way ever since. I started spending holidays with Ray instead. He was like a dad to me anyway."

"Ray is your old manager who passed away?"

"Right." Sophie cleared her throat in an attempt to alleviate the lump that had formed.

Connie turned to look at her then, and her loving eyes held Sophie's across the kitchen. "I'm so sorry about that, sweetie. This is your first holiday without him?"

Sophie could only nod, swallow. The next thing she knew, Connie was standing next to her, arms wrapped around her.

"I'm glad you're here with us, then."

There was no way Sophie could utter a word; she'd burst into sloppy sobs. But she did let herself sink into Connie's embrace, unable to remember the last time her mother had hugged her for any reason at all. Connie pressed a kiss to the top of Sophie's head and let her go. And just like that, she was back to working on the turkey.

The back door opened then, preventing any further discussion, as the brisk November air whooshed in along with Bethany and Dana and a bag that held a half gallon of half-n-half.

"We come bearing gifts," Bethany said, and handed over the bag with a flourish.

"Oh, thank you, honey." Connie took it from her. "Take off your shoes so you don't track snow through the house. Was it busy at the store?"

As Connie and Bethany discussed the trip, Sophie watched Dana. Her face was flushed, her cheeks a rosy pink and her eyes bright, and though Sophie still felt tears prickling her own eyes, she couldn't look away. Snowflakes melted into Dana's blond waves as she bent to untie her boots. When she looked up, an expression of concern crossed her face and her eyebrows met in a V above her nose. She mouthed, "You okay?"

Sophie smiled, tilted her head to one side, and nodded. The joy she felt at seeing Dana took her by surprise. The tingling in her legs, the warmth in her center. A different kind of lump appeared in her throat.

"I see you're on potato duty. Want some help?" Dana pulled out a chair and sat, and within a few seconds, Sophie felt Dana's feet on hers.

Sophie's grin appeared all on its own.

"Love some."

❖

Sophie couldn't remember the last time she'd been in a large group of people she didn't know very well and felt this at home. The Landons had made this a Thanksgiving she'd not soon forget.

Dinner was over. They'd all helped clean up the leftovers, load the dishwasher, and spread the desserts out on the table.

"Round Three," Sean had said, with a playful eye roll, when Sophie expressed her surprise at yet more food. "Breakfast. Then turkey. Now dessert."

"Three rounds." Sophie nodded. "Got it."

Coffee was brewed for those who weren't having wine or beer— or had had enough wine or beer. Bethany had brought an apple pie and a variety of cookies. Connie had made some sort of layered dessert incorporating chocolate pudding and graham crackers. Jeanine brought two pumpkin pies. On top of those things, a very large platter of fresh fruit sat in the middle of the table. Dana reached to pluck a grape from the pile and Sophie couldn't take her eyes off Dana's hand.

"I still cannot believe I'm having Thanksgiving dinner with Sophie James." It was the third time Bethany's daughter Lydia had uttered the same sentence.

"Oh, my God, Lid, give it a rest." Dana's tone was only half joking, and under the table, Sophie laid a hand on her thigh, gave it a squeeze to tell her it was fine.

"Well, I can't believe I'm having Thanksgiving dinner with *you*," Sophie said back to her, and Lydia blushed a pretty pink. "So there."

"And, Micah, for God's sake, stop staring at her like a creeper." Dana shot a look at her nephew, who immediately jerked his gaze away.

Chuckles went around the table.

Not only was Lydia a twenty-year-old college student, but she was majoring in music education and was a huge fan of Sophie's. The family had decided not to tell her ahead of time about Sophie's presence, in order to prevent her brain from completely overloading in anticipation. It had been the right call, Sophie decided, judging from the wide-eyed, speechless stare she'd gotten when she was first introduced to Lydia. That was followed a minute later by a squeal of the highest pitch Sophie had ever experienced. She'd fully expected to hear every dog in the neighborhood start barking. Since that introduction, Lydia had slowly begun to relax, but Sophie would catch her staring here and there. Finally, she'd ventured to ask Sophie a few professional questions about the art of singing, and those were fun.

Lydia's brother, Micah, was an eighteen-year-old boy, so staring at Sophie was about all he knew how to do.

Sophie was used to this kind of reaction, both the endless questions and the endless staring. Dana, apparently, was not, so Sophie spent much of dinner quietly reassuring her while also answering Lydia's questions and tossing winks or smiles at Micah just to let him know she saw him.

This is what it's like to have a family.

The thought had run through Sophie's mind more than once. Not really in sadness, but in wonder. She'd never really had anything like this. Even way back before she was working, there really hadn't been anybody else. Her grandparents died early on, and for most of Sophie's life, it was just her and her mother. This whole giant group of siblings and nieces and nephews was all new to Sophie. And she loved it. There was no doubt in her mind. She *loved* it. She'd taken a couple photos of the food—up close so you couldn't actually see where she was—and posted them on her Instagram account. She adored being surrounded by people who cared deeply for each other. She adored listening to their inside jokes and their affectionate teasing. She adored sitting next to Dana.

Yeah. That was a big one. She *adored* sitting next to Dana. Feeling the warmth of her thigh as it touched hers. The foot thing was still happening under the table, had been all day. The delicious smell of her perfume would make itself known every so often, tickle Sophie's nostrils in reminder.

Sophie was torn.

First of all, she'd never had such a warm and comfortable, fun time as she had with the Landons, and there was a part of her that never wanted it to end.

But second—and becoming much more prominent in her brain the more wine she drank—was the fact that eventually, she and Dana would head up to the attic. Together. Where they'd share a bed. The bed they'd made out in last night. That familiar tingling began in her legs again at the mere thought of it, at the mere recollection of Dana above her, of Dana's hips settled between Sophie's thighs, of Dana's warm body wrapped up against hers.

She grabbed her wine glass. Drained it. When she turned to Dana, she was looking at her, eyebrows raised, an amused expression on her face as if she knew exactly where Sophie's mind had taken her.

Exactly where.

Sophie felt her own face heat up, but the slight embarrassment was overshadowed by the knowledge that maybe—just maybe—Dana's mind went there, too.

"You girls leaving tomorrow?" Carter asked, pulling Sophie away from what would probably have been a very sexy daydream.

Dana nodded. "Our flight leaves late morning."

"You still doing your annual After Thanksgiving Cocktail Party, Dana?" Bethany scooped a forkful of pie into her mouth.

"Saturday afternoon, yes."

Sophie furrowed her brow. "What's this now?"

"Every Saturday after Thanksgiving, Dana has a cocktail party at her house." Jeanine explained the details. "Sean and I went one year when we visited New York. It's a cool gathering."

Dana, maybe at the sudden realization that Sophie knew nothing of her party, seemed to scramble. "It's just some folks I work with at Miracle, a few friends, that's all."

Sophie laid a reassuring hand on her forearm. "No worries. I'm not at all crushed that I wasn't invited."

Frazzled was a good way to describe Dana's demeanor as she obviously searched for words, and Sophie laughed, squeezed her arm tighter.

"Dana. Seriously. I'm teasing you."

Dana's relief was something Sophie actually felt, like it transferred through her skin into Sophie's hand. "Actually," Dana said, much more calmly, "I assumed you'd be in the studio, but I'd really like it if you came."

"I told the guys to take the weekend to be with their families and we'd get back to work on Monday." Sophie snagged a grape and popped it into her mouth. "And I'd love to come."

The answering smile Dana gave her was worth every second of life, right there.

Little by little, the evening died down, the conversation became a bit quieter, a little less exuberant. Carter and Sean fell asleep watching football in the living room. Eventually, Jeanine put Matthew to bed and didn't come back down. By midnight, the dining room and kitchen were clean and it was time for all to turn in. Good nights were exchanged, along with hugs. Lydia and Micah spread sleeping bags out on the living room floor. Everybody else headed upstairs.

In the attic, Sophie rested a hand over her stomach and said, "I'm so full."

"Oh, my God, me too." Dana smiled at her. "Go ahead and use the bathroom. I'll go after you."

Sophie was torn between performing the speediest nightly routine ever in the history of mankind and taking as much time as possible without pissing off everybody else waiting for the bathroom. On the one hand, she wanted to get back upstairs, into that bed, lights off, ready for Dana. On the other, she wanted to make sure she looked pretty, that she smelled good, and also look herself in the face in the mirror because oh, my God, what if she was the only one hoping the night would go…a certain way?

She never got this nervous before a show. What the hell was happening to her?

A gentle rap on the door startled her, and Dana's voice said softly through the wood, "Sophie? You okay?"

Sophie cleared her throat, gathered her things, and opened the door to that beautiful face, those soft blue eyes, and just like that, the nerves were gone. She smiled. "Yes. Sorry. Daydreaming. All yours."

They switched places. "See you in a bit." Dana shut the door.

Sophie headed for the attic door. At the bottom of the stairs, she looked up, blew out a slow, quiet breath, and put her foot on the first step.

Here we go.

CHAPTER SEVENTEEN

Dana Landon was not a stupid woman.

She knew exactly what was going to happen once she reached the top of the attic stairs she stood at the bottom of right now. Staring. Picturing. Worrying.

To be honest, the picturing was winning out over the worrying. By far, it was winning. So, that was good.

Suddenly, there was a warm hand on her shoulder in the darkness of the hallway, and Bethany whispered, "Stop thinking so hard and follow your heart for a change." Without waiting for a response, she kissed the top of Dana's head, crossed to the bathroom, and closed the door behind her.

Her sister's words in her head, Dana closed her eyes, pursed her lips, exhaled…and let her heart lead her right up the stairs.

Sophie's dark-eyed gaze met her from across the room and Dana shut the door with a quiet click. "Hi," she whispered.

"Hey." Sophie's smile was radiantly sexy, even though she wasn't doing anything any differently from usual.

Except lying in my bed.

Yeah. There was that. Dana dropped her clothes she'd changed out of onto a chair and, despite being clad in a pair of shorts and a T-shirt, she felt almost naked as Sophie watched her.

Never a woman to shy away from making the moves, Dana marveled at her own tension, at the unfamiliar anxiety running through her bloodstream like hot water. Sophie was beautiful, sitting up in the bed, clingy tank top and probably bikinis making up her pajamas. Like last night, her face was scrubbed and fresh-looking. She'd pulled her hair back and held a *People* magazine in her hands, which she indicated.

"Did you know the Jonas Brothers are the hottest new musical act around?" When Dana squinted at her, she glanced at the cover. "In June of 2008?"

Dana laughed. "Lydia must have left that up here."

Sophie closed it and set it aside, then Dana heard her take a deep breath, let it out very slowly, as if steadying herself. Dana watched as Sophie reached for the blankets on the other side of the bed and pulled them away, making room for her. "Come here."

Just like that, Dana's hesitation, her nerves, her worry all disappeared, and she crossed the floor in three steps, slid in under the covers, turned to Sophie, and kissed her.

And that was the end of the waiting.

Any indecision. Any misgivings. All the doubt. Everything was erased by the urgency Dana suddenly felt to be with Sophie. To touch her. To feel her. To hear her. To be a part of her. It was almost too much, and when she realized that she'd rolled completely over onto her, that Sophie was on her back beneath her, Dana's tongue deep in her mouth, she stopped. Pulled her head back an inch. Maybe half an inch. Smiled down at her, breathless.

"I'm sorry. I'm not usually this…fast." Her voice was a whisper. "Pushy?" She raised her eyebrows as Sophie's smile grew. "Bossy?"

"Oh, you *are* this bossy. Now shut up and kiss me." Sophie pulled Dana's head back down and they were kissing again. It occurred to Dana in the moment just how easy it would be to get lost in that kiss. Forever. To just stay there, kissing Sophie James until the end of time. Who needed food? Or water? Or even air? Yeah, she could definitely do this forever…

…or maybe it wouldn't be enough because Sophie's hand under her shirt only exacerbated the desire that had been building in her body since her first glimpse of Sophie still asleep in her bed that morning. It had been a slow burn all day, deep in her core, orange embers, glowing at first. Getting hotter. Every time she looked at Sophie—or Sophie looked at her—the heat would increase. They became flames the first time Sophie put a warm hand on her thigh under the dining room table, and those flames just grew every subsequent time they made eye contact. Every. Single. Time. It occurred to Dana right then that maybe Sophie had been doing that on purpose—the random touches and leg squeezes—but she didn't have time to think about it because before she knew it, Sophie had flipped them.

Dana blinked in surprise as she looked up at Sophie, at her beautiful face and those large, dark, expressive eyes.

"My turn," Sophie said, then brought her mouth down on Dana's in a soul-searing kiss that Dana was pretty sure melted her limbs.

Dana knew deep down that this was probably a bad idea. It was pretty much a no-brainer that you don't sleep with your clients. Also? She didn't care. This felt too good. It had felt too good all day long and she'd had to work too hard not to react.

She was ready to react now.

More than ready.

She wanted this. Badly.

Sophie sat up on her knees and pulled Dana to a sitting position where she lifted Dana's T-shirt over her head and tossed it to the floor. And then she just stared. Dana was sure she could feel Sophie's eyes as they skimmed over her skin, lingered on her breasts.

"You're so beautiful," Sophie whispered so softly Dana barely heard her. Reaching out her hand, she ran her fingertips across Dana's nipple and watched as it hardened. Then she did the same thing with the other, her expression almost reverent.

Dana's breath hitched, and she swallowed hard as she studied Sophie's face, her fascination with Dana's body. When she looked up, met Dana's gaze, her eyes were darker than Dana would've thought possible. They were heavy with arousal. With desire. Using both hands, she grasped Dana's face and crushed their mouths together in a heated kiss that was neither soft nor gentle. Dana's surprise was quickly eclipsed by her own rushing want. She found the hem of Sophie's tank top and yanked it over her head, baring her torso to Dana's feasting eyes.

Mouth still fused to Sophie's, Dana ran both hands up Sophie's ribs and cupped a breast in each one. When she rubbed thumbs over nipples, a guttural, sexy groan came from deep in Sophie's throat, so she did it again.

"Oh, my God," Sophie whispered. "Your hands...they feel so good..."

The surprise, the pure awe in Sophie's voice made Dana pause. A breast in each hand, she looked up at Sophie. "Have you done this before?" she asked, afraid of the answer, but not.

"Had sex? Of course I have."

Dana arched a brow at her. "You know what I mean."

Sophie cast her eyes down, seemed to study Dana's hands on her. "I do know what you mean." She closed a hand over each of Dana's, then looked her directly in the eye. "This is my first time with a woman, yes, and I am *so glad* it's you."

Dana had expected to panic. She'd expected all desire to fly out the window, chased by the spectre of pressure. But neither of those things happened. Instead, Sophie's words only lifted her, bolstered her, sent her arousal even higher—something she didn't think was possible, given how much she'd wanted her all day. But she did her best to rein it in, not wanting to scare Sophie.

Moving her hands again, running her thumbs over Sophie's nipples, she whispered, "We can stop any time, okay? If you need to, you tell me."

Sophie surprised Dana by taking her face in her hands. She tilted Dana's head up so their eyes met and then uttered the three sexiest sentences Dana had ever heard. "Shut up. Kiss me. Don't be gentle."

After that, details became a blur for Dana. Her brain checked out and her body took over. Instinct. *Very primal* instinct. She tried hard to focus and remember, to take inventory of every beautiful inch of Sophie's body, to memorize everywhere Sophie touched her and how and what it felt like, but it all melded together in one big canvas of sensation, and the next thing she knew, she was on her back, and Sophie was looking at her from between her spread thighs.

Their eye contact held, and Dana felt like she was tied to Sophie somehow. Like she couldn't look away, even if she'd wanted to. Which she didn't. Without breaking that eye contact, Sophie lowered her head slowly, touched her tongue lightly to Dana's center, and the blur of sensation was back.

Dana dropped her head back onto the pillow as Sophie increased the pressure, keeping a steady rhythm that Dana knew was going to send her over the edge in an alarmingly short amount of time because Jesus, Mary, and Joseph, Sophie knew exactly what to do. How was that even possible? Dana dug the fingers of one hand into Sophie's hair, not to direct her, but simply to hold on. With the other, she reached over her head and grasped the nearest pillow, pulled it over her face just in time to catch the sounds of the orgasm that ripped through her body like fire from a flame thrower. Her hips lifted off the bed with no direction from her, and she could feel Sophie's hands on them, holding tightly, trying to stay with her writhing body. Dana used both hands now to muffle the sounds Sophie was pulling from her, hoping to God one minute that nobody downstairs could hear her, and in the next minute, not caring at all if they did.

With no idea how much time had passed, Dana finally felt her body start to relax. Her hips settled back onto the bed, she removed the pillow so she could breathe, and her heart stopped feeling like it was going to pound right out of her chest.

"Oh, my God," she finally whispered, arms thrown over her eyes.

"That's good, right?" Sophie's voice was not only quiet but tinted with the smallest bit of uncertainty, and Dana moved her arms so she could look at her.

"Good?" she asked, eyes wide. "Good? Sweetie, that was well beyond good and closer to the realm of I might have blacked out for a minute. Are you *sure* you've never done that before?"

Sophie's expression then, even in the dark of the room, held so many things. Relief. Satisfaction. Pride. And still, like it had never left, huge amounts of desire. That was all Dana needed to see, and she sat up. Catching her breath was overrated.

"Come here, you," she ordered, as she pulled Sophie up to her and smoothly swapped their positions. "We are so very far from finished."

❖

It was the first time in her life Sophie had ever played the part of the big spoon, but she instantly loved it. Dana's warm, naked body was backed up against her front, and everything about that fact was amazing and wonderful. The skin of Dana's back against Sophie's breasts. Dana's shapely ass pressed into Sophie's stomach. Sophie's arm draped over Dana's middle, fingertips playing along the soft skin there. Sophie's nose buried in Dana's sweet-smelling hair.

I could lie like this forever.

Sophie grinned as the thought zipped through her head, and she pulled Dana in closer, even though that was probably impossible. Dana squeezed her forearm.

"Did I wake you up?" Sophie asked on a whisper. The bedside clock said it was 3:43.

"No. I've sort of been drifting in and out." Dana also spoke very quietly.

"Me, too. I think…" Sophie swallowed, pressed a kiss to Dana's head. "I think this has been so amazing that I don't want it to end. I figure if I stay awake, the night will take longer." She sounded silly; she knew that. But it was the truth.

Dana squeezed her again, pulled Sophie's hand to her lips and kissed it. "I know." A beat went by before Dana spoke again. "Can I ask you something?"

"Of course."

"You've really never been with a woman before?"

The tiny feeling of panic came out of nowhere and ran through Sophie's system like fire. She'd never really struggled with confidence, but this was different. This was Dana, and there was just something about her... Sophie cleared her throat. "Why? Was it not okay for you?" God, she sounded like a child. She squeezed her eyes shut. A petty child.

"Oh, my God." Dana turned in her arms. "No. Not at all. The opposite, in fact." She rested her hand on Sophie's cheek and her eye contact was intense, like she was trying to force reassurance into Sophie's brain. "I told you. You were *amazing*. I have never...I just... you were amazing, Sophie."

And just like that, Sophie felt relief. "Good." She kissed Dana softly.

"I was just curious, as I'd never seen anything or even heard an inkling about you maybe being gay. Or bi. And that's unusual. In my line of work, we're always privy to that stuff. It's common. I just wondered." Dana gave a half shrug.

"I didn't exactly have normal teen years." Sophie spoke quietly, but from the heart. She had the weirdest desire to be honest with Dana. Always. "I've had crushes. Lots of them. I just...I didn't know at the time what they were. I had no barometer, you know? I wasn't around kids my age, I was touring. So I didn't let myself give it too much attention. But it was there. And I wondered."

Dana turned in Sophie's arms, pushed herself up onto an elbow, and propped her head in her hand so she was gazing down at Sophie. She took a hunk of Sophie's hair and toyed with it, wrapping it around her finger, then unwrapping it, then repeating the move. "So, it's not new knowledge for you?"

"My attraction to women?" At Dana's nod, Sophie released an amused chuckle. "I'm twenty-nine, Dana, not fifteen. No, it's not new."

Dana didn't say anything, but her face was full of questions, like she was sifting through each one, deciding against it, and examining the next.

Sophie turned over onto her back and gazed up at the beamed ceiling. "I started on tour when I was sixteen." Her voice was low, quiet. She could feel Dana's eyes on her. "It wasn't really conducive for meeting anybody, let alone girls. I did meet one way back. In Las Vegas. She managed the venue where I was performing and was super nice. I think I was, maybe, nineteen? Twenty? We just had this sizzling connection and ended up making out in my dressing room before the show. But nothing beyond that." Sophie furrowed her brow. "I've never told anybody that."

"Never?" Dana seemed bewildered.

Sophie shook her head. "I tried to talk to Ray about it once. He kind of brushed me off and I figured he wasn't really listening. But almost immediately, he started suggesting guys I could date, that it would be good for publicity. So, I do wonder if he heard me and that was his way of telling me how he felt about it."

"I'm sorry, Sophie." Dana brushed Sophie's hair behind her ear. "That must've stung."

Sophie shrugged. "It did. Ray just wasn't terribly...open about that kind of thing. I think he would've come around eventually, though. He loved me like a daughter. He would have figured out how to accept it."

"There's been nobody since?"

Again, Sophie shook her head. "No. I got to a level of... recognizability where I really couldn't trust somebody not to go public about it, you know? The idea of the entire world knowing my business just..." She swallowed down the lump of fear and panic that the thought always jammed into her throat. "I can't even imagine. The whole drunken thing was bad enough, the way the press was all over that."

Dana nodded and lay down, and Sophie knew she got it. She had to, being in the business she was in. The press, the media, they were both a blessing and a curse. Often a necessary evil.

They lay quietly for a moment or two. Just as Sophie wondered if Dana was falling asleep, she propped herself back up and spoke. "So, I'm the only woman you've ever been with."

"Yes."

"The only woman you've ever brought to orgasm."

Sophie swallowed and felt a flutter low in her stomach. "Yes."

"And I'm the only woman who's ever brought you to orgasm."

The words were gone now, replaced with a level of arousal that astonished Sophie in its intensity. All she could do was nod.

"Then I guess I'd better become the only woman who's brought you to more than one in a night. Yeah?" Dana rolled closer, tossed her leg over Sophie's, and used it to pull Sophie's thighs apart. The kiss she gave her then was almost as sexy as the way she slid her fingers into the hot wet that was still clinging to Sophie's center.

Sophie let herself melt into the touch, dug her own fingers into Dana's hair, and pushed her tongue deeper into Dana's mouth.

Yeah, there wasn't going to be any sleeping tonight.

CHAPTER EIGHTEEN

By the time they flopped into their seats on the plane and got comfortable, Dana was already exhausted. For the first time in her life, she wished the impending flight was longer so she could get some sleep. A fifty-minute nap just wasn't going to cut it.

Next to her, Sophie looked just as tired as she felt. When those dark eyes met Dana's and Sophie smiled softly, Dana felt her insides go all gooey. And that scared her. She couldn't fall for this woman.

She could *not* fall for this woman.

Could she?

No. No, there were too many deterrents. She was Dana's client, first and foremost. It would not go over well with her bosses—though she was also pretty sure she wouldn't be the first manager to sleep with his or her client. The entertainment industry was all about sex. But still. It went against Dana's own code of ethics, and she was going to have to deal with that at some point. Also, Sophie was young. Yes, she was an adult. Of course she was. But there were a full ten years between the two of them. That was a lot, wasn't it?

Letting her head loll to the side, she studied Sophie, who was gazing out the window of the plane as they slowly began to move. Dana let her eyes roam over the shape of Sophie's face. The plane of her cheek. The straight slope of her nose. She followed Sophie's jawline from her chin to her ear and then down her neck and the flash she suddenly got of her own mouth on the skin there, how she'd used the flat of her tongue and licked from Sophie's throat up to her ear at 4:00 that morning, how Sophie had whimpered and dug her fingers into Dana's shoulder, sent a wet surge of arousal through her body and down.

She laid a warm hand on Sophie's thigh. Sophie turned to her and smiled.

"Can I get you ladies anything?" The flight attendant appeared as if out of thin air. Sophie immediately shifted her leg so Dana's hand fell away.

"I'm good," she said, smiling at the woman. Then she turned to Dana. "You?"

Dana shook her head. "I'm fine. Thank you."

The flight attendant moved on to the next passengers. Sophie went back to gazing out the window.

Dana gripped the armrests of her seat and faced forward for the rest of the flight.

Sophie stared at her closet, several different emotions coursing through her veins. This was the way she'd felt since she left Dana at the airport yesterday. Sophie had a car ready and waiting to drive them each home, but Dana insisted she was out of the way and would get her own ride, and there was something in her eyes that Sophie couldn't pinpoint, but it told her not to argue. So, she didn't.

Instead, she'd thanked Dana profusely for a wonderful Thanksgiving, hugged her tightly. Dana was initially a bit...stiff... but after a moment, she sank into Sophie's arms and hugged her back. They said nothing more, just went in separate directions, and Sophie hadn't heard from Dana again until later that night. A text inviting her to Dana's annual After Thanksgiving Cocktail Party.

Much wavering had happened since that text.

It was really sweet of her to invite me. I should go.

She specifically said it was for coworkers and colleagues, not clients. I shouldn't go.

I miss her. I want to see her. I should go.

She'll feel pressured to entertain me. I shouldn't go.

Back and forth since yesterday. Should go. Shouldn't go. Should. Shouldn't. She was currently on "should" as she stood and perused her clothing. It crossed her mind more than once to call Andrew and ask for his help, but if she did, she'd have to tell him where she was going and he'd ask questions, and she was a terrible liar when it came to him. He'd figure out what had happened and then he'd have *more* questions and Sophie just wasn't sure she was ready to answer. Any of them. She couldn't even answer her own. She tried. By writing.

A crowd at dinner
Can't wait
It's late
A double bed and her
Alone together
Top floor
Locked door
A double bed and her

They were good, the words. At least she thought they were. The song was really shaping up. Unfortunately, they didn't help her with her own issues. They only made them clearer to her.

Sophie groaned. Maybe she needed some guidance after all, so she swore a few times to get it out of her system, then picked up her phone and sent a text.

Less than forty-five minutes later, she heard Andrew's voice echoing through her living room, announcing his arrival.

"I'm in here." Sophie was lounging on the bed in her sweats, her closet still open, Gemma Day's catchy new song playing from the Bluetooth speaker on her dresser.

Andrew walked in, looking like he stepped out of a *GQ* magazine, all neatly tailored pants and a simple oxford. There wasn't a hair out of place as he waved a finger from the top of Sophie's head to her bare feet. "What's going on here?"

"How are you never wrinkled?" Sophie asked, sliding to the edge of the bed. "Do you just stand up all the time? Never sit?"

"I have special powers you will never understand." He went to her closet, a place he was way more familiar with than she was, and began sliding hangers. "So, you spent Thanksgiving with your hot manager and her family." It wasn't a question. More like he was stating the facts he already had, looking for confirmation.

"Yes."

"And you had a good time?" He kept his back to her, sifted through pants, tops, dresses.

"I had a great time."

"And you had sex with her." He never turned around.

She blinked, astonished. "How the hell did you know that?"

Andrew turned then, gave her a long put-upon look, like she exhausted his brain, then ticked off a finger for each point. "You posted food porn on Instagram, which you only do when you're really happy. You're not sure about going to this party. And your face is glowing." He pulled out a little black dress. "This."

Sophie blinked at him some more. Then she got off the bed and went to the full-length mirror where she checked her face. "I am *not* glowing."

"Oh, honey, you so are. Here. Put this on."

Sophie took the dress, squinted at the plunging V-neck. "This? Seriously?"

"Seriously. It's both sexy and sophisticated. You said industry folks are going to be there?" At Sophie's nod, he pointed at the dress. "You'll look classy for them and that neckline will get your girl's attention without a problem."

"But…" Sophie thought better of speaking at that moment, closed her mouth.

Andrew parked a hand on his hip and studied her. Which she hated because he saw right through her 99 percent of the time. It was his turn to go to the bed, and he took a seat on the edge. His voice was soft. "What's the matter, Soph?"

Much to her own horror, Sophie felt her eyes well up. "I don't know," she said with honesty.

He patted the bed next to him. "Come here and talk to me."

She sat, dress still in her hands, silent for a long beat. One of the things Andrew was best at was waiting her out, so he did that. Finally, Sophie swallowed down her tears and whispered, "I'm scared."

"Of?"

She shrugged.

"Her? Your feelings for her? Your sexuality? People finding out?"

Sophie's bitter chuckle held no humor. "Yes?"

"I see. A fear of multiple things."

How Andrew managed to say things like that without making her feel like an unreasonable idiot, she would never understand, but he did it. The tears were back.

"All normal. You get that, yes?" Andrew was not a physical guy, at least not with her, but he put his hand on her knee just then, squeezed. "I mean, I get that this is kind of new for you."

Sophie dropped her head back with a groan of frustration. "My God, I'm twenty-nine. You'd think I'd have gone through this crap by now."

"You didn't exactly have normal teenage years, you know."

A small snort escaped her lips, as she had said pretty much those exact words to Dana less than twenty-four hours ago. "True."

"Think about it as, I don't know. Getting a late start? Regardless of that, everything you're feeling is normal. Okay? Just breathe."

They sat together, two friends in companionable silence. Finally, Sophie stood up and peeled off her sweats to get dressed. Andrew stayed where he was, then came over and zipped up the back when she had the dress on.

"Have you guys talked at all about how you feel?" He stood behind her at the full-length mirror, watched her reflection. "Or was it just sex? Which is totally fine, you know. No judgment."

A mixture of feelings hit Sophie at the question. Wonder, relief, amusement, shame. "No. We haven't talked about it at all." She wanted to tell him about the plane flight home, how Dana had touched her and Sophie had subtly moved when the flight attendant could see. That a surge of panic had washed through her. How she was embarrassed and felt bad that she'd hurt Dana's feelings—because she had; she could tell—but that the panic and fear had overshadowed those things. How her fan base was having trouble with her dressing her age instead of like a middle-aged opera singer; how could she possibly expect them to handle the news that she was gay?

She didn't say any of those things to Andrew.

She didn't plan on saying them to anybody.

"Maybe you need to talk with her. I mean, she invited you to her party, right? You're obviously on her mind." Andrew cocked his head as he studied her in the mirror, and Sophie was sure he could see every thought she hadn't put a voice to. But he left it alone and shrugged. "Anyway. Just something to think about."

Sophie stepped into the heels Andrew had picked. Strappy and silver. Not too high, but fancy enough to warrant a second glance. He reached for her hair, pulled it up with one hand and tugged some curls free to dangle around her ears and the back of her neck.

"Like this," he said. She gave a nod and he dropped it back down. When she turned to face him, he said quietly, "Okay?" He wasn't talking about the outfit.

"Okay." Sophie stepped into his space and wrapped her arms around him, knowing he wasn't the hugging type, but hugging him anyway. "Thank you."

She couldn't stop her smile when she felt his arms around her as well. "You're welcome." Then he took a step back and held her at arm's length, stooped slightly to catch her eye. "You're going to be all right, Sophie. I promise."

The lump in her throat was suddenly back, but she swallowed it down. "Okay."

Andrew straightened, let his eyes wander over her, then waved a finger up and down in front of her. "Besides, that girl sees you? She won't remember what day it is."

Once he'd double-checked to see if she needed anything else and was gone, Sophie spent time in the bathroom doing her hair. She'd watched Michaela put her in enough updos that she had no problem creating something similar to what Andrew had suggested. She touched up her makeup, used a thin curling iron to curl the pieces of hair hanging down, put her phone, credit card, lip gloss, and keys into her silver clutch, and stared at her own reflection.

She looked good.

There was no denying that. She had a moment of "Am I overdressed?" but then wiped that away. She was a celebrity. Very famous. She should at least look like she made an effort. She hated seeing a well-known singer attending a gathering looking like a slob. In the park was fine. At the store was fine. Attending a party? Make an effort, dude. Some would argue with her, she was sure, but this was what she preferred. She wanted Dana to know that her invitation to the party meant something to her, was important.

What will Dana think?

She'd avoided that question for a good forty minutes, but now it cropped back up in her head. Because the truth was, she wanted the same reaction from Dana that Andrew had described, and she wasn't sure why it meant that much to her. Why she cared. She covered her face with her hands.

I have no idea what I'm going to do.

Then her eyes widened and she peeked over her hands at the mirror. From the nightstand, she grabbed a pen, jotted on the paper there, *What do I do? What do I say?* Good. Words were good.

Just as she was applying a coat of lip gloss, her buzzer rang. The doorman telling her the car had arrived. She pulled her long coat out of the coat closet and studied herself once more, this time in the full-length mirror on the closet door.

"You got this," she whispered to her reflection.

God, she hoped she was right.

CHAPTER NINETEEN

This was the best part of throwing a party to Dana: when she'd done everything she needed to do. When all she had to manage now was her own drink and mingling with her guests. She'd run her ass off all day, making calls, putting up decorations, arranging platters of food, setting up the bar area. There was a time a couple years ago when she'd made all the food herself. But the gathering got larger and she got busier with less free time, and she'd finally had to bite the bullet and hire a caterer and a bartender.

Soft music emanated from a speaker in the corner, light holiday jazz, something unobtrusive, and Dana stood near the bar, sipping a glass of champagne and taking in her own party.

It had started off as a dinner party the first year. Not a lot of folks at Miracle seemed to do things together, and Dana decided to see if she could fix that. So, she invited a handful of her closest colleagues and their spouses for dinner. They'd had a lot of fun. Good conversation. Dana had done the cooking. Lots of wine. But the next year, it had been harder to get people together, to find a date when everybody was available. Another year with a smaller dinner went by, but by the third year, she'd changed it to a cocktail party. She'd picked a start time in the late afternoon and told people to pop by any time they could, stay for a few minutes or all night. It had been a rousing success. Now, people started asking her in September if her cocktail party was still on.

The other benefit of people coming when they wanted and leaving when they needed to was that there was never a huge number of guests in her place at one time. Right now, three other managers from Miracle stood in the corner, drinks in hand, chatting about a client they'd all had. Two of the spouses had paired off and were talking about what Dana thought was knitting by the snippets she could make out. Maybe eight or ten people stood around the dining room table, eating the bacon-wrapped scallops and spanakopita and laughing.

"Another?" asked the bartender, an impossibly handsome young man—a server Dana figured was probably a struggling actor, like so many other servers in the city—when she set her empty flute down.

"Please." Dana turned to her right—the direction of the front door she kept open for the duration of the party—and she was pretty sure her heart stopped. Simply ceased to beat in her chest due to the sight before her.

Sophie stood in the doorway looking the tiniest bit uncertain. Her coat was draped over one arm and she wore a dress that was somehow the most stunning thing Dana had ever seen, despite the simplicity of it. Black. Snug. Cleavage. Those three words came to Dana one at a time. Nothing else. She couldn't manage anything else.

"Here you go."

Dana didn't even register the bartender's words for another moment. Finally, after exerting all the strength she had just to tear her eyes away, she muttered, "One more, please." When he handed her a second flute, she took them both and crossed the room to the door. "Sophie. You made it."

"I did." Sophie's smile was, like her demeanor, slightly uncertain. Dana wanted to reach out and smooth her thumb over that crease in her forehead, so it was a good thing her hands were full.

"I'm so glad. Here." Dana handed one glass to Sophie, then set her own on a nearby table, took Sophie's coat, and lowered her voice. "You look beautiful." She was rewarded by Sophie's cheeks tinting a soft pink.

"Thank you." She took a sip of her champagne while Dana hung up her coat. "Oh, this is good."

"I'm glad you like it." Dana picked up her own glass and tried to ignore the fluttering sensation low in her body. She cleared her throat. "Come on. I'll introduce you to some of my friends." It took every ounce of willpower she had not to touch Sophie's bare arm, let her hand slide down and entwine her fingers with Sophie's. But she forced herself to remember the plane flight, understand the situation, and clenched her fist instead.

The party was in full swing an hour later. People were coming and going steadily and the volume had increased a bit. Dana also remembered to invite her neighbors every year so they wouldn't be as bothered by any noise, and they all came, enjoyed mingling with people from the entertainment industry.

This year, Sophie was the big hit. Dana did her best to shield her. To make sure she didn't get cornered or her attention monopolized by two or three individuals. But she seemed to be holding her own. Dana exited the kitchen after consulting with the employees of the caterer, who stayed to make sure dishes were refilled and things stayed orderly, and she stood to watch Sophie chatting with the Hargraves, the elderly couple that lived above her. They were obviously enamored of Sophie, but, in watching to make sure Sophie wasn't trapped by them, Dana also realized that she'd gotten to know Sophie's face, her expressions, and the smile she sported now was genuine. When she glanced up and caught Dana's eye, and then her grin widened, Dana's heart melted in her chest. Just melted.

"Hey, sexy."

Dana jumped as the voice alarmingly near her ear scared the bejesus out of her. She turned to meet the green-eyed gaze of Laura.

"Hey," Dana said, slightly bewildered. "Hi." Before she could avoid it, Laura kissed her softly on the lips. Dana did her best not to snark at Laura's complete disregard of anything remotely resembling a boundary, but it wasn't easy. "What are you doing here?"

Laura cocked her head. "You mean because you forgot to invite me?" She tried to pull off "joking," but didn't quite get there. She was stung and Dana could tell.

"It's not that you weren't invited. It's a work thing." Not a complete lie. But she also purposely did not invite Laura.

"Good thing I remembered how much you enjoy throwing this party." Laura took off her coat without waiting for Dana, hung it up. Then she squeezed Dana's shoulder. "Don't mind me. I can find the bar." She winked and walked toward the young, struggling actor. Dana followed her retreat with her eyes and noticed that she wasn't the only one. Sophie was also watching her and the expression on her face was…

No.

Nope. Not going there.

Dana shook her head, refusing to entertain any of this right now. She was irritated enough that Laura had simply invited herself, thereby creating extra pressure Dana didn't need tonight. They were going to have a talk about boundaries. Laura wasn't taking any of her hints; it was probably time to be more direct. And in the meantime...

When she glanced back in Sophie's direction, her body had that same reaction. The one that was becoming regular. Standard when it came to direct eye contact with Sophie James, which was what she was getting right now. Her body reacted as if on cue. The heart skipping a beat. The flutter in the belly. The tingling in her lower body.

Let's not forget the lump in the throat.

She swallowed hard, took a large swig of her champagne, and swallowed again.

"I see Sophie James is here." Laura was back, right next to her. Again. Which made her tingle, but not in the good way Sophie did. In a weird, nerve-wracking way she didn't like.

"She is." Dana gave a nod, watching as one of her coworkers sidled up to her and introduced himself. Another followed suit.

"She certainly is charming." Laura's tone had changed. Her attitude. If Dana didn't know her well, she might not have noticed. But Laura seemed no longer entranced by Sophie's presence like she was at the studio. In fact, she seemed a bit...bothered.

Interesting.

"She *is* charming," Dana said. The desire to protect Sophie was strong, but she knew she needed to tread carefully. "And it's genuine. Most people are surprised."

"That she's not an obnoxious diva?"

"Exactly."

"Well. Jury's still out for me." When Dana turned to look at her, to watch her watch Sophie, Laura lifted one shoulder and downed the remainder of her bourbon and ginger. "What?"

Dana shook her head. "Nothing."

Laura put an arm around Dana then, squeezed the back of her neck and something about the timing, the purpose... Dana stepped to one side just enough for Laura's hand to fall away. She kept her voice low, but injected it with a firmness that surprised her. "Don't do that."

"Don't do what?"

"Get all territorial. You don't get to do that anymore."

Laura gave her a look of hurt confusion, but Dana was pretty sure it was fake. She dropped her hand to her side, and her expression was more irritated now than hurt. "I'm trying here, Dana. Give me a little credit."

I don't want you to try were the words Dana wanted to say. She managed to trap them in her head, felt her own upper lip curl slightly and she waited it out, forced herself to calm down. After counting to ten in her head, she turned to look at Laura and said, simply and calmly, "I am not doing this with you right now."

And she walked away, leaving her ex standing alone, blinking in shock. Dana had never done that before. Not with Laura. Dana considered herself a strong woman, assertive, a woman who took no shit. But not when it came to Laura. She'd always felt slightly trapped whenever they argued; like she couldn't leave. Like she had to stand there, because walking away would be rude. She wasn't sure what had changed, other than she'd had time after Laura left to get to know herself, to learn that she was worthy and not defined by her relationship. And goddamn, did it feel good. In that moment, she did exactly what she wanted to do. She felt a smile break out across her face as her confidence level soared.

She walked right into the circle surrounding Sophie and stood next to her, a hand on her back, as Mr. Hargrave was telling a story about New York City in the sixties.

Sophie leaned toward her. "Hi."

Dana looked up into those dark eyes. "Hey."

Their gazes held for a beat before Sophie whispered, "I need the restroom. Can you show me where it is?"

Dana never turned away. "I'll take you to the one in my room. More privacy."

"Perfect."

❖

Every ounce of concern or worry, every sliver of hesitation, each tiny drop of internal fear, all of it completely dissipated the second Sophie had seen Dana from the doorway of her apartment. Replacing them was stop-in-her-tracks, rip-her-clothes-off desire. Her body skipped right over the gently increasing arousal stage and flew instantly to full-blown I Want Her Right Now.

Dana was wearing a suit, but not her usual business attire type suit. No, this was made for an evening out. A party. The pants and blazer were black with faded white pinstripes. Under the blazer, she wore a white button-down shirt that was unbuttoned to just below that sweet spot between her breasts. Her blond hair was down, extra wavy around her face, and her heels were high and ridiculously sexy. She wore what Michaela would refer to as "evening makeup," and when Dana took a sip from the champagne flute in her hand, Sophie couldn't tear her eyes from the long expanse of throat that was exposed.

All those observations took place in about three-point-five seconds.

Sophie had managed to pull herself together, sip her drink, and mingle with Dana's guests, who turned out to be a nice mix of neighbors, friends, and colleagues.

One skill Sophie had perfected over the years of standing politely and listening to people blather on and on was a sort of multitasking. She could stand there, nod and smile, act just like she was enraptured by whoever was talking to her, and still be very aware of what was going on around her. Ray always marveled at how she always seemed to be engrossed in a conversation, but then she'd tell him later about the quiet argument going on across the room.

She put that skill to good use when Laura Clarkson had walked in, looking all smiley and comfortable and way too familiar with the guests, the apartment, Dana.

Dana wasn't happy about it. That much was clear when she'd shrugged off Laura's possessive arm-over-the-shoulder maneuver. Sophie almost snorted a laugh. And then Dana did something Sophie would never forget. Would never unsee. Would be burned into her memory forever.

Dana walked right toward her, stood next to her with a smile, and touched the small of her back.

I need to be alone with her. Five minutes. Three. Anything.

The thought shot through Sophie's head like rapid fire, until Mr. Hargrave's voice faded away. His mouth kept moving, but Sophie heard no sound, felt nothing but the gentle touch of Dana's hand, not at all possessive, but *there*. Solid. Steady.

The question about directions to the restroom came out of nowhere and Sophie specifically asked if Dana could *show* her rather than *tell* her where it was. Dana didn't miss a beat. She took Sophie's hand and led her away from the party, down a hall to the end where it seemed the rest of the world simply evaporated.

It occurred to Sophie, sort of tangentially, that she wanted to look at Dana's bedroom, take the time to study it, to see what kinds of colors she liked. Figure out her style of decorating. But she couldn't grab ahold of the thought because she had other things crowding it out of her mind. Mainly how badly she wanted to grab the lapels of Dana's blazer. Grab them. Pull her in. Hold her there. Keep her there.

She managed to wait until they'd crossed the bedroom and Dana had reached into the master bath and clicked on the light.

Then those lapels were hers.

Sophie grabbed the fabric, bunched it in each hand, and hauled Dana up against the wall by it. The surprise in those blue eyes morphed quickly into a darkened shade of desire and Sophie bent to capture Dana's mouth with hers.

Kissing Dana was everything Sophie remembered and more. Soft, hot, passionate, limb-melting, toe-curling. Dana wasted no time giving back as good as she got, and tongues came into play in a matter of moments. Suddenly, Dana flipped them so Sophie was the one against the wall. They kissed deeply. Thoroughly. Sophie became lost, with no idea where she was, who she was, what day it was. The only thing that existed was Dana. Dana's mouth on hers. Dana's tongue in her mouth. Dana's face in her hands. Dana's soft whimpers of pleasure.

After what might have been minutes or might have been years, Dana gently broke the kiss, moved across Sophie's jawline and down the side of her neck to that spot between Sophie's neck and shoulder. Sophie leaned her head against the wall, let out a small sound.

Dana looked up at her, smiling. "We should probably stop," she said on a whisper.

Sophie nodded. "You have guests."

"I do."

Another searing kiss.

Dana broke the kiss again. "Sophie." Still a whisper. "I really need to get back out there."

"I know." Sophie nodded, then rested her forehead against Dana's. "Okay."

Dana's focus dropped to Sophie's mouth, and she ran her fingertips across Sophie's bottom lip. She inhaled loudly, then blew it out through pursed lips, which made Sophie chuckle. One last peck and a stroke of Sophie's cheek and Dana left the room.

Sophie stepped into the bathroom, shut the door behind her, and fell back against it. Her lips burned with want. Her thong was damp with heat. Her entire body was on fire.

She moved to the sink and stared at her own reflection in the mirror. Her kiss-swollen lips. Her flushed cheeks. Her eyes that had gone even darker than usual.

Fingers to her lips, she smiled.

❖

"Jesus, Dana, don't you close the door to your bedroom when you have people over?" Laura's presence in the hallway startled Dana enough to force a small yelp of surprise from her. "Anybody could walk in."

She'd seen them. It was obvious by the inflection of her words as well as the flashing of her eyes. Laura had seen Dana and Sophie kissing. And before Dana could say anything, Laura confirmed her suspicions.

"Seriously? Sophie James?" Laura's voice was a harsh whisper. "What is she, twenty-one? What the hell are you thinking, fucking your own client? What happens if your bosses find out? I thought you were smarter than that."

Dana tilted her head and studied her ex-girlfriend. Laura wasn't even a tiny bit concerned about Dana's job. Dana knew her well enough to recognize that, to see through her overblown worries about Dana's bosses to the real truth. Which was that she was so jealous right then, she couldn't see straight.

"The least you could've done was reapply your lipstick."

Dana brought her hand to her lips before she could stop herself, then was annoyed by the accusation in Laura's words. "What are you doing back here, anyway?" Dana asked, purposely avoiding a response to anything Laura had pointed out.

Laura blinked once. Twice. Then got control over the surprise the question had caused and said quickly, "One of the girls from the kitchen was wandering back this way. I followed her to make sure she wasn't doing anything she shouldn't."

Dana made a show of standing on her toes and looking over Laura's shoulder to the hall behind her. "I don't see her."

"I sent her back to the kitchen."

"Well, thanks for that." Dana made a move to walk around Laura, who grabbed her arm.

"I'm worried, Dana. I just want to make sure you know what you're doing."

Dana poked the inside of her cheek with her tongue and gently removed her arm from Laura's grasp. "Honestly, Laura? What I'm doing is none of your business." She held her arm out toward the hallway, wanting to get her away from the bedroom as soon as she could. The last thing she needed was Sophie to walk out of the room and into the two of them. "After you."

Laura held her gaze for a moment, and Dana could see all the things she'd like to say zip across her face. To her credit, she stayed quiet and headed down the hall and back toward the party without further incident.

Dana swallowed down the irritation that had surfaced, straightened her jacket, remembered how Sophie had grabbed it and shoved her against the wall. She swallowed again, but this time, it had nothing to do with being irritated.

She cleared her throat, tipped her head from one side to the other like a boxer getting ready to fight, and headed back out toward her party. Only one thought was in her head.

How can I get Sophie to stay?

CHAPTER TWENTY

It was so lovely to meet you, Ms. James." Mr. Hargrave held Sophie's hand in both of his, his smile warm. Dana knew from experience that his grip was gentle and his skin was papery and soft. "I hope we see each other again."

"I hope so, too." Sophie smiled, genuinely, and took Mrs. Hargrave's hand as well. They were such nice people and Dana suspected that Sophie had honestly enjoyed talking with them.

Dana watched as they shuffled in her direction near the door and bid her a farewell, hugging her goodbye like she was their own daughter. They were the first neighbors she'd met when she moved in, and she was immensely fond of them both.

When they were in the hall and waiting for the elevator, Dana turned back to the living room where only a handful of guests remained. Wandering over to the bar to see how the bartender was faring in his cleanup duties, she surreptitiously watched the silent duel that played out before her. Laura was in one corner of the room, standing with two people from Dana's office. She wasn't talking; she didn't even seem to be listening. Instead, she was eyeing Sophie, who stood directly across the living room from her with one of the producers from Miracle and his wife. She moved away from champagne, and now, as Dana took a sip of her martini, Sophie raised her glass slightly in a silent salute to Laura...who glared.

Dana almost choked on her drink, both annoyed and amused. Annoyed because this was her party and her guests were expected to be adults. This little power play thing was not something she wanted to deal with. Also, Laura inviting herself to the party was still grating on Dana's nerves. It was very Laura, so she didn't know why she'd been surprised by her appearance. She was amused because Sophie...

Yeah. Sophie.

Unable to keep the grin off her face at the vision of Sophie cheering Laura from across the room, Dana simply shook her head and wondered how she got here.

She'd been surprised Sophie had come to the party. She'd been more surprised that she herself had even found the courage to invite her. She'd spent the hour-long plane flight trying not to dwell on the possibility that Sophie was ashamed to be seen with her. Like, *with* her. At the same time, she understood that Sophie was not an ordinary person. She was a celebrity, and the things she did and said got noticed. Affected her and her reputation, which, in turn, affected her livelihood. So Dana had done her best to shake it off, and later that evening while thinking about their goodbye hug, she'd impulsively sent a text with the reiterated invitation.

There were so many obstacles in the way of having a relationship with Sophie. Dana took another—very large—gulp of her drink because, God, was she actually thinking that far ahead? A relationship? She could hear her sister's voice in her head from the other day.

Stop thinking so hard and follow your heart for a change.

Before she had a chance to bask in those words, to take them in and let them warm her, Anya's voice echoed through her head.

All I'm asking is that you step carefully...there could easily be complications.

God, so many complications. What was Dana thinking?

A sense of melancholy settled over her instantly, and she felt it like a weight on her shoulders, pressing her down into the floor. She watched as Sophie and Laura subtly eyed each other from across the room as they also chatted with the few guests left, and she was suddenly so tired. Like, bone-weary. Like, I need to go to bed right this minute tired. Her energy was just gone.

In an attempt not to watch the two women—her ex who wanted another chance and her client she shouldn't be falling for but probably was, damn it—she went into the kitchen to see if the caterers needed any help cleaning up.

❖

Was it because she was famous? Sophie hated when she had to check herself. When she had to admit that she got special treatment—

or worse, was subconsciously annoyed when she didn't get special treatment—because of her career. Because she was a celebrity. That was one of the amusing, not to mention a bit unfair, things about being famous: She made a boatload of money but got a ton of stuff for free. Clothing, shoes, makeup. Fame got her all kinds of things.

Would it get her Dana?

An hour ago, she was pretty sure the answer was yes. Not so much would her fame get her Dana, but would she get Dana in general. Now, though? Now she was less sure. Something seemed to have shifted; she could see it on Dana's face. There was a...hesitation? An uncertainty? Whatever it was, it had parked itself in Dana's eyes and it worried Sophie in a way she couldn't explain. Was it because that fucking bitch Laura was here? Sending her daggers from across the room?

The couple she was talking to was very nice and Sophie did her best to focus on the restaurant they were talking about, but her brain was messing with her. Laura was probably really nice. *I mean, maybe.* But Sophie knew what Laura had done to Dana the first time around, so the fact that she was even standing in this room surprised Sophie. Dana was strong. She took no shit. So, why was Laura even here? Why was she even getting the time of day from Dana?

Sophie didn't understand it.

More than that, she didn't like it. She was feeling territorial and possessive, and those were very new feelings for her. She wasn't sure what to do with them.

"Well, we're gonna head home," the guy in front of her said.

"Date night is over," said his wife, a bit wistfully. "It was so nice to chat with you, Sophie. Wow. I still can't believe it." She shook Sophie's hand and then followed her husband to the coat closet. Dana came out of the kitchen and bade them farewell.

Across the room, the two people Laura had been talking to were also taking their leave. It took about five or ten minutes and then they were gone and it was Dana, Sophie, and Laura left. They stood in a triangle: Sophie in one corner, Laura across the room in another, and Dana at the door. Maybe it was just Sophie—and all the champagne she'd had—but it felt like they stood there for a long while, just looking from one to the other to the other.

Finally, Dana sighed, reached into the closet, and pulled out two coats. She held them up, her face shuttered a bit so Sophie couldn't quite tell what she was thinking. Doing her best to hide her surprise—

there was no way she wanted Laura to see that—she crossed the room and took her coat from Dana's hand. Laura followed suit. Dana didn't look at either of them for longer than a second or two.

"Thank you for coming," she said, and there was something in her voice…an edge? A hesitation? Or was it more like annoyance? Sophie couldn't put her finger on it, but she buttoned her coat as Dana buzzed the doorman to let him know to contact Sophie's driver and get a cab for Laura.

"Thank you for inviting me," Sophie said, and she meant it.

A look of mild surprise crossed Laura's face before she could catch it. Sophie wondered what that was about as Dana handed Laura her coat. It didn't occur to Sophie until they'd said goodbye to Dana and were in the hallway that she and Laura would ride the elevator down together.

Terrific. Sophie managed not to roll her eyes. Laura was a little less subtle. But Sophie was well practiced at being in the same space with people she couldn't stand. It was part of her job, really, so she called it up as the doors slid open and they stepped into the car.

"I see what you're doing," Laura said, her voice startlingly quiet.

"I'm sorry?" Sophie looked at her.

"You've hidden it well for years, but I see it."

Sophie squinted and a weirdly uncomfortable feeling started in the pit of her stomach. "I don't know what you're talking about."

Laura stared straight ahead. "What can you give her? Sure, you're rich and famous. But she's independent."

"I don't know—"

Laura cut her off. "Dana is her own person. Is she supposed to live in your shadow? In your closet? Because I can tell you right now, she's not going to do that."

Sophie swallowed, and her heart rate kicked up a notch. She scrambled for something to say, but words seemed to be playing hide-and-seek with her. And they were winning.

"She deserves better."

"And is that you?" Sophie blurted. "The person who left her for a job? Moved across the country without so much as a backward glance? Is *that* what she deserves?"

Laura's expression made it clear that she was surprised Sophie knew the details of their split, and Sophie silently gave herself a point.

Thankfully, the elevator doors slid open then and Laura stomped out ahead of her, her heels clicking loudly in the late night of the lobby.

The doorman smiled and tipped his hat. "Ms. Clarkson." She ignored him as he opened the door for her and she was out of the building by the time Sophie even made it to the front desk.

"Good evening, Ms. James," the doorman said.

"Hey, Jimmy."

His face lit up a little bit at her knowing his name, and he held the door for her. "Your car is ready."

"Thanks. Have a great night."

And then, she was safely ensconced in the back of the warm town car, part of her thinking it was a little bit obnoxious to travel this way, the other part feeling grateful that she could.

Watching the city go by as she gazed out the window, Sophie tried not to think. And failed miserably. She'd expected to stay the night. And after those few, very hot, minutes in Dana's bedroom, it had seemed like a sure thing. And while it was disappointing to be in a car on her way home, Sophie tried her best to shrug it off. Again, she failed miserably, mostly because Laura Clarkson's words came screaming back into her head.

I see what you're doing.

Was she doing something? Honestly? Was she?

More importantly, could she?

Sophie let her head rest against the window and sighed. God, she missed Ray. No, he hadn't been super open-minded about her sexuality, but it had been a while since the subject initially came up. She knew she could talk to him. He loved her. He'd listen.

If he were here.

Which he wasn't.

Sophie's eyes welled up, but she forced herself not to cry. It wouldn't do her any good.

No, she had to figure this out on her own.

The car glided to a stop in front of her building and her driver opened the door for her, held out a hand to help.

"Thank you, Ben."

"Have a good night, Ms. James."

In her penthouse, she walked through without turning on any lights—only then realizing she was slightly tipsy—and the lights of the city outside gave her more than enough to find her way to the bedroom, where she also left the light off. She stripped out of her clothes, leaving them in a pile on the floor that would give Andrew a mild stroke, and climbed into bed naked. Snuggling down under the comforter, she watched the city that she could see from her windows. It was something she'd done since she'd moved in: opened the blinds after she'd turned off the lights so she could watch the buildings in her view. She'd lie under the covers and make up stories about the various windows that were lit up at three in the morning.

Sophie was tired. Tipsy. Really should go to sleep. But her brain wouldn't stop, so she reached for the small notebook on the nightstand, grabbed her tiny book light, and sat up.

Might as well try to use up some of this excess energy.

It was going to be a long night.

CHAPTER TWENTY-ONE

"What the hell am I going to do with you?" Anya shook her head. Her tone held enough humor for Dana to not feel too stung by the words, but it was also clear that Anya wanted an answer.

"I don't know!" Dana dropped her head onto Anya's counter where she sat on a barstool and groaned. "I really needed you to be at my party last night."

"I know. I'm just so tired and I didn't want to be around all that alcohol and not be able to have any." Anya sounded sincerely sorry.

"I get it. But still, I can't believe you left me to fend for myself against these women."

"Yeah, it's hard to be you, two gorgeous women who want to be with you." Anya rolled her eyes and refilled Dana's water glass, added a fresh slice of lemon, then sat back down next to her. "Even though you know how I feel about Laura," she added.

Dana sat back up. "Anya. I'm so confused."

"All right. Lay it out for me."

Anya was good at this—logic and practicality—and it was a trait that Dana tapped into often for help with any number of life's problems.

"Wait." Anya held up a hand. "First, tell me one thing."

"Okay."

"How was the sex with the famous Sophie James? Was she passionate, like she is when she sings? Or is there not much beneath the shiny exterior?"

Dana gasped and playfully slapped at her friend. "That's so mean."

"It is. It's also an honest question I'd like the answer to."

Dana wet her lips, thought back to that night in her parents' house, in her old bed. "Sex with Sophie was…" She looked at Anya. "It was amazing. Truly, out-of-this-world amazing."

"Yeah?" Anya looked delighted by this fact.

"Yeah. Also…" Dana had intended to keep this tidbit to herself, but felt it was important in the grand scheme of things, and Anya was her best friend. "I'm the first woman she's ever slept with."

Anya's jaw literally dropped open. "You're shitting me."

"Nope."

"Well, fuck."

"Right? I've never been anybody's first before."

"No pressure."

Dana snorted. "*Tons* of pressure. But still. It was amazing." She felt the smile break across her face without her consent. Because it was true. Sex with Sophie had been wonderful.

"Is that the problem?" Anya asked, sipping her coffee. She reached for a cookie from the plate in front of them. "That you're the only one she's been with?"

Dana sighed. "I don't know. I mean, yeah. That would normally be kind of a big deal, but she's not exactly had a normal life. When would she have had a chance to explore her sexuality. What if she's not even gay?"

Anya furrowed her brow and tilted her head in obvious question.

"She could be bi. She could be experimenting." Dana shrugged. "I don't know."

"Did you ask her?"

"No."

"Mm-hmm."

Dana scrubbed her hands over her face. "And then there's Laura."

Anya chewed her cookie, studied Dana's face, stayed silent. Which made her thoughts pretty clear on that subject.

"I can admit that she seems different. At least a little. I know that sounds lame, but she does. She's making an effort."

"How so?" Anya propped her chin in her hand and at least looked like she was paying honest attention.

"Well." Dana took a sip of her water, wishing now that she'd taken Anya up on her offer of a mimosa after all. "She's suddenly way more attentive. Calls often. Checks in. She wants to do things, is always asking me to lunch or dinner. She pops in at my office, which she never used to do. I didn't say anything to her about the party, but she remembered and came anyway. Which really bothered me at first, but…" She poked at the lemon in her water with a finger. "No, there is no but. It bothered me. Still does. She's trying to worm her way back in."

"Don't let her."

"I know, but there were a lot of people there and I didn't want to make a scene. And then she and Sophie started with this weird silent battle like two frat brothers fighting over the same girl."

"Tough to be the one they're fighting over, huh?" Anya arched a brow and Dana knew she was half joking, half serious. She sipped her coffee again. "And what did you do with the two of them at the party?"

Dana groaned and dropped her head back down to the counter. "I threw them both out."

Anya snorted a laugh. "You what?"

"Well. I didn't throw them out. In fact, I was going to ask Sophie to stay. But then the two of them got into this silent glare battle across my living room and it was just ridiculous. They were acting like children, so I sent them both home. Which was dumb, but…they made me mad."

"It's interesting to me that you just sang the praises of all the things Laura is finally doing right, but you wanted *Sophie* to spend the night at your place."

"God, I know. I'm a mess. I should've just stood my ground and asked Laura to leave, but she caught me off guard."

"Were they surprised when you tossed them out?"

Dana let a small grin show. "Yeah, I think they were."

"Way to wield your power, my friend." Anya finished her coffee and pointed toward the table where Dana's purse, keys, and phone were. "While I love that you turn your phone to silent when you're with me, it's been lighting up like a Christmas tree. You'd better check it."

Startled, Dana slid off her stool to grab it. It was Sunday and she tried hard to make it a habit of not working much on the weekends; she mostly failed at that, but at least put in a smidgen of effort. She looked at her phone, then wished she hadn't. "Oh, my God," she said quietly, as she scrolled.

"What?" Anya returned to her seat and waited for Dana to fill her in.

"Oh, no. How the…oh, my God. Shit."

"Dana. What?" Anya was worried now. It was obvious in her voice, on her face. "Dana."

Dana covered her eyes with a hand and held the phone out for Anya to see.

"Oh, shit. Is that—?"

Dana nodded. "Sophie, yeah. And me."

"That's you? I mean, you can tell it's her, but nobody would know that was you. It's just your back and your head's down near—"

"I know, Anya," Dana snapped and snatched the phone back. Holding up a hand toward her friend, she apologized. "I'm sorry. I didn't mean to snark at you. I just…God, I have to call Sophie. She's got to be freaking out."

The photo was everywhere. Twitter. Instagram. Tumblr. Huffpost. Yahoo. The Hollywood Reporter. It was grainy and hard to see much detail other than Sophie's face. Which was tossed back in obvious pleasure, her eyes closed, her mouth slightly open. The only part of Dana visible was some of the back of her head as she kissed that spot where Sophie's neck and shoulder met. She remembered it well.

The headlines, speculations, comments…there were so many. So many. Some were brutal. Some were supportive. Some were confused. All of them were regarding Sophie's sexuality.

Dana held her breath as she dialed.

"Was it Laura?" Sophie answered in half a ring and didn't say hello.

"What?" Dana squinted. "Was what Laura?"

"The person who took the photo. And then leaked it. Was it Laura?"

Dana hadn't even gotten that far. She was still absorbing the photo itself. Next on her list of tasks would be how best to handle it. *Was* it Laura? "I have no idea," she said honestly.

"That bitch. I can't believe she'd do this." Sophie was obviously spiraling. Dana could picture her pacing, hands flailing animatedly.

"Just take a breath," Dana said, then knew immediately that had been the wrong thing to say.

"Take a breath? Take a fucking breath? Are you fucking kidding me, Dana? This is my life. My career. I haven't taken a breath since I saw the damn photo."

"Okay." Following her own advice, Dana took a breath instead, and put on her best calming voice, the one she reserved for her more difficult clients. "Listen. This isn't as horrific as you might think. It's 2019. People come out all the time. We just need to own it and spin it the way we want to."

"It should've been my choice, Dana. *My choice*." Sophie was near tears. Dana could hear it in her voice.

"I know." Dana started to walk around the round table in Anya's kitchen. She needed to move, to put one foot in front of the other. "But it's done, so we deal with it."

"Your ex is a piece of work. Who the fuck does she think she is?" The venom in Sophie's voice was a little bit shocking to Dana.

"We don't know it was her." Again, the words were out of Dana's mouth and she instantly wanted to snatch them out of the air and shove them back in.

"Are you defending her? Defending what she did? *It's nobody's goddamn business!*"

The line went dead.

Dana blew out a breath and set the phone down. Anya was looking at her, raised eyebrows, as she held her newly refilled mug in both hands.

"That sounded fun."

Dana sat back down on her barstool, elbows on the counter, chin in both hands. "Can I have that mimosa now? Easy on the OJ."

"Absolutely. I'll join you. But with just juice."

A couple of minutes later, they each had a flute. Dana took a very large gulp of her drink.

"She freaking?" Anya asked.

"Majorly."

"Can I ask a question?"

"Sure."

"Why? Why is she freaking? I mean, okay, so somebody outed her and that sucks. But…she's always been a class act. I would expect her to let this roll off. Or embrace it. Or something"—she shrugged—"classy. You know? Not this melting down that I could hear from over here."

Dana gave it some thought. Anya had a good point. "All I can think is that, because her formative years were spent in the spotlight, she's behind where any other person her age would be. She's doing things at twenty-nine that most of us did at seventeen and eighteen. You know?"

Anya nodded. "She's probably scared."

Scared. Dana hadn't thought of that. How? How had she not thought of that? Sophie had had sex with a woman for the very first time a mere three days ago. She was probably still absorbing that, and now, somebody had outed her to the entire world. No wonder she was losing her shit.

"What was the talk about Laura?" Anya's question pulled Dana back to the present.

"Sophie thinks Laura took the photo and leaked it."

"Did she?"

"I…" Dana hesitated. "No," she said, drawing the word out. "She wouldn't do that."

"No?"

Dana tilted her head to one side. "I don't think so. She's not like that."

"You haven't seen her in more than a year, Dana, and now she's back and wants to start up again with you. You don't think she'd do whatever she needed to?"

Dana hated that she wasn't sure. *Hated* it. She should call Laura and ask her, point-blank. Except she didn't want to because she was afraid of the answer. Dana downed the rest of her mimosa and set the empty flute down. "I have to go into the office. Do some damage control."

Anya nodded. She got it. She understood the job. "Okay."

"Thanks for…everything." Dana wrapped her friend in a hug, then headed down the hallway to where her coat was.

"Keep me posted." Anya opened the front door for her. "Call me if you need anything."

"I will."

Dana headed out into the brisk winter air, and it felt like her breath froze in her lungs. Normally, she'd take some time to admire the softly falling flakes of snow, but today, her mind was elsewhere.

There were so many questions.

There were so few answers.

She needed to find some.

"I'll kill her." Sophie paced from one end of her spacious living room to the other. The purple throw pillow in her hand was taking a beating, being twisted and crinkled, occasionally punched, and one time even screamed into, as she carried it with her around the apartment. "I will *fucking* kill her."

The TV was on, the entertainment channel making sure to keep

Sophie's ire up with its periodic mentions of how she was apparently a big ol' lesbian now.

"Do we know who the other woman in the photo is, Brandon?" the pretty blond TV show hostess asked the ridiculously handsome man next to her.

"We don't, Christie. Just speculation. All that's clear is that it's definitely Sophie James and she's definitely making out with a woman. Who knew?"

"Well, she's getting tons of support from LGBTQ groups around the country. I'm sure we'll hear more about this story in the coming days."

Her phone buzzed from the couch cushions where she'd thrown it. She really needed to turn her Google alerts off. The thing had been buzzing all morning long. There had also been unanswered calls from Andrew, Michaela, her agent, Brooks and Kettle (separately), and Dana.

Dana.

She didn't seem all that worried.

"Of course she didn't. She's out and you can't tell it's her in the photo anyway. What does she have to be worried about?"

What do you *have to be worried about?*

She heard the question in her head, in her own voice, which was weird. She flopped down on the couch, trying to simply breathe, when the phone rang. Again. It was Dana. Again.

"Hey."

"How're you doing?" Dana's voice was no different than it would've been on any other day. Friendly. Firm. Maybe a little less businesslike than normal, and for that, Sophie was grateful.

"Aside from having been outed to the entire free world? I'm fantastic."

"Let's talk options."

"You mean, I have some?"

"Of course you do. Why do you think you have me?" Dana was trying to make Sophie smile, and it worked. A little. Sophie heard a couple of keys being hit, then Dana went on. "Okay. One. You could deny it's you in the photo. That rarely goes well, but it could be done. Two. You can ignore it completely. News fades. New stories pop up every day. This will be old by the end of the week. The drawback to that is you have an appearance next week and they'll most likely ask. We could cancel that, but…"

"That would bring more attention."

"Exactly. Or there's number three."

"Which is?" Something in Dana's voice was interesting, and it made Sophie curious, made her sit up on the edge of her cushion.

"You embrace it. You own it."

Oddly, that hadn't occurred to Sophie at all.

And she wasn't sure how to feel about it.

"Like, come out for real?"

"Exactly."

"But it isn't anybody's business," she said vehemently.

"I know." Dana's voice stayed calm. "I know it isn't. But you're in the public eye. You're a celebrity, and, unfortunately, normal rules don't always apply to you. So, we have to do what we can. But it's totally up to you how we handle it."

"Can I sit with it for a bit? I mean, this is all kind of…fresh for me still. You know?" She wanted to say so much right then. So many things to Dana. About their night together on Thanksgiving. About that kiss the night before.

"I do know." Dana's voice went very soft, and this time, she wasn't talking to a client. She was talking to somebody she cared about. Sophie could feel it. "Just don't take too long, all right?"

"All right."

"Good."

"Was it Laura?" Sophie couldn't seem to let go of that, and she hated how angry her voice sounded.

"Does it matter?" Was that Dana's way of saying yes? The soft tone was gone. Back to business. "It's done."

Sophie ground her teeth but said nothing. Dana was right.

"Look. Take some time. Think about it. This doesn't have to be awful, Sophie. It can actually be something we can use to our advantage. But it's going to depend on how you want to handle it. It's your life."

"Damn right it is." The words were muttered, but Sophie felt them from the top of her head right down to the tips of her toes.

"You're in the studio tomorrow?" Dana asked, redirecting the conversation.

"Yeah."

"Can you swing by my office at some point after? We can talk, then I can put some things in motion and we'll take the control back."

"Okay."

"And, Sophie? Try to stay off your phone. No Instagram. No Twitter. Watch Netflix or something."

Sophie could hear the smile in Dana's voice, and it made her feel the tiniest bit better. "Yeah, okay."

"Call me if you need me and I'll see you tomorrow. It'll be better then."

They hung up and Sophie tossed her phone down next to her, flopped back against the couch. It immediately buzzed another alert. With a sigh, she picked it back up and turned off all of her notifications. Maybe Dana was right.

Maybe everything would be better tomorrow.

CHAPTER TWENTY-TWO

Davis Silverstein rarely made personal appearances. He liked to greet the heavy hitters when they visited the Manhattan headquarters, show his face, throw his weight around. Once in a while, he'd make an appearance to do superficial damage control, again, just to show his face and be intimidating. Other than that, he rarely left his office unless it was to go to the golf course or walk a red carpet. He hardly ever even showed up to meet new clients unless he had inside information that they'd be huge. No. For the most part, he stayed behind the scenes, made occasional blustering phone calls to remind everybody he was the boss, and that was it. And Dana was fine with that.

So, when he showed up in the door of her office, nobody was more surprised than Dana. But one of the things she'd learned to do over the years of working in this business was to master her poker face. She remained calm, acted like Davis stopping in unannounced was an everyday occurrence, even though her thoughts were racing and she was already thinking up some damage control.

"Davis. Hi. What a nice surprise. What brings you to this floor?" She stuck out her hand and put on her best mask of innocence; she knew exactly what brought him to this floor.

He closed his meaty hand over hers and held tight. "Tell me you have this Sophie James thing under control, Dana." His voice was low, his eye contact alarmingly direct.

"I do." Dana nodded. "I promise."

"It's bad enough she's started dressing like a stripper and singing club music. This isn't going to sit well with her demographic."

Dana could have argued with him. She could have debated with him about how wrong he was about the older generation and how open-minded a large percentage of Americans were these days—despite the situation in Washington, DC—about how he should have a little more faith in Sophie and her talent. But she didn't even attempt it. "I know," she said instead.

"I looked at that photo very carefully," he said. This time his voice dropped even lower and he squeezed her hand. "Any idea who the other woman is?"

Dana was saved from responding by a knock on her door. It opened and Laura stood there, a cup of coffee in each hand and an uncertain smile on her face.

"Hi?" she said, looking from one to the other.

Thank God. She'd never been so happy to see Laura in her life.

Davis let go of her hand but narrowed his eyes at her knowingly. "Handle it," he said as he pointed at her, then left her office, nodding to Laura as he passed. "Ms. Clarkson. Good to see you again."

"Likewise." Laura watched him go, then crossed the office and handed Dana one of the cups. Her voice low, she asked, "What was that about? Are you okay? You're all pale."

Dana blew out a breath and went around her desk to her chair. Fell back into it with a groan.

"Let me guess." Laura sat down without being asked. "Was that about the Sophie James photo?"

Dana nodded, hand over her eyes, took a moment. Then she moved her hand and looked directly at Laura. "Please tell me it wasn't you."

Laura's mouth fell open, and her expression of shock seemed genuine to Dana, who liked to think she knew her, even after more than a year apart. "Of course it wasn't me. I can't believe you think I'd stoop that low. Jesus, Dana. I'd like another chance with you, but I'd like to earn it on my own, not because I sabotaged the competition." She shook her head, clearly disgusted.

"I'm sorry. I didn't think it was you, but I had to ask."

"I bet the famous Ms. James thinks it was me."

Dana grimaced.

"I figured. I'm telling you, it was that sneaky little caterer girl. I told you I followed her down your hallway."

That memory suddenly made itself known to Dana. "Oh, right. You did." With a sigh, Dana picked up a pen and jotted herself a note to call that caterer and let them know what had happened, because Laura was probably right. It wasn't uncommon in this industry. The caterer had probably gotten a nice chunk of change for selling that shot and having it go viral.

"Social media." Laura scoffed. "It's unpredictable, but really, it's totally predictable."

Dana chuckled. "Right? So totally predictable."

They sat quietly for a moment.

"Hey, Dana? I'm really sorry about Saturday night. I acted like a child."

The apology was unexpected, and Dana held Laura's gaze for a moment. "You both did."

"I'm not going to pretend that seeing that photo didn't feel like a punch to the gut. It's obvious, at least to me, who she's kissing."

Dana felt a flash of anger zip through her at the audacity of Laura thinking it was any of her business who Dana kissed, but she clenched her jaw and did her best to keep the words in.

Thankfully, Laura redeemed herself. "Not that I have any right to be upset. I know that."

"Good," Dana said, and felt the anger recede just a touch.

"Listen," Laura said. "I know you're busy and this isn't the time or place, but...I'd like to talk. I mean, really talk. Can we do dinner again maybe?"

So much was in Dana's head in that moment. She was confused. She was angry. She was frustrated. And because of those emotions, she missed a lot that Laura represented. Familiarity. Somebody who knew her. Those were the big two, especially the familiarity. Familiarity was comfortable and safe and warm. She missed feeling that way, really needed to right then, and that was the only reason she agreed. "Yeah, okay. Tomorrow night?"

Laura's face lit up so fast, it was almost comical. "Yes! Tomorrow would be great. I'll pick you up—"

She was stopped by Dana's upheld hand. "I'll meet you."

They made plans, set the time and place. Laura stood up, grabbed her coat, and walked around the desk to wrap her arms around Dana's shoulders. She squeezed hard, held on for a long moment. Dana let her, even hugged her back just a bit. But she admitted to a small sense of relief when Laura finally let go and stood up straight. The smile on her face was beaming, and Dana couldn't remember the last time she'd ever seen her ex that happy.

"I'll see you tomorrow," Laura said, as she bent forward. She placed a kiss on the top of Dana's head and then left the office.

There was so much work to do. Calls to make. Emails to return. But instead, Dana sat at her desk and stared into space as her thoughts swirled and mixed in her head. Thoughts of Laura and that warm comfort that came with having spent many years together. But also the memories of how badly things had gone, how much pain there'd been when it had ended. Closure would be a good thing. And while she was sure Laura would disagree, it was something Dana now knew she desperately needed so she could move forward. As if on cue, her thoughts shifted, became thoughts of Sophie and the newness, the passion, the trepidation of being with her. Also, the excitement, the promise, the possibility.

So much.

❖

Recording was going all right. Surprisingly, as Sophie had expected her worries and concerns to get in the way of her focus. But she was in the middle of recording one of the new songs she'd helped write. It had a beat, a little zing that Tim had given it by adding a guitar riff that carried through the entire song.

Slashing her hand across her throat in the universal sign for stop, Sophie spoke into the mic as she looked at the guys through the window. "I'm really liking this." The guys both nodded and Damon shot her a thumbs-up. "What do you think if we…" Her voice trailed off as she watched Tim turn to his right, see something out of Sophie's line of vision, and completely lose his smile.

The door to the recording booth opened and Davis Silverstein himself walked in, shut it behind him as if he thought that would give them privacy despite the fact that there were microphones everywhere.

"Sophie," he said, his voice laced with equal parts friendliness and condescension.

"Davis. What a nice surprise." Sophie was surprised. Surprised that she felt utterly calm, completely in control, rather than nervous and jerky like she expected to. "What brings you by the studio?"

Davis's bushy gray eyebrows furrowed until they looked like a furry caterpillar crawling across his forehead. "We at Miracle are a little concerned, Sophie." The tone of his voice changed to Boss Mode, complete with extra condescension. Sophie tried hard not to stiffen but knew she failed. "The public drunkenness, the questionable clothing, that photo." He waved a hand toward the window to the sound room. "Now this shift in your music." He made a face of distaste. "I've said it before, but you're apparently not hearing me. Maybe you don't understand that you have a demographic and they expect certain things from you. Your *record company* expects certain things from you." As if to punctuate, he looked at her expectantly.

Sophie wasn't sure which words did it exactly, but she thought it might have been all of the *expectation*. Whatever it was, something inside her snapped. Not violently, so maybe snapped was too strong a word. Faded into nonexistence? Went dark? Stopped caring? All she knew was that she'd had enough. She straightened her stance so she stood her full height, making her about half an inch taller than Silverstein.

"Let me tell you what I do understand, Davis. I *understand* that I've been recording music for Miracle for ten years now. I also *understand* that I have made Miracle a veritable shitload of money. I am happy to continue to do that, but I also have a need to change and grow creatively. I *understand* how the market works, that not everything sells well, and I plan to pay careful attention to that. I don't plan on continuing something that makes no money because while I *understand* that you think I'm a helpless female who needs direction from big strong men like you, I also *understand* this business. Which means I *understand* that there are any number of other—some bigger—record companies who would happily take the money I'd make them and put me on their label. So, if you'd rather I take my music elsewhere, just say the word. No hard feelings."

The silence in the booth right then was deafening. Davis and Sophie stood, face-to-face, a standoff of sorts. She never broke eye contact, just blinked calmly as she watched her words penetrate his rich, white, chauvinistic being. His surprise at her gumption was written all over his face in wide eyes, raised brow, flushed cheeks.

"Well," he said, and cleared his throat as he pointed a sausagelike finger at her. "Just know that we'll be keeping a close eye on things with you."

"I would expect nothing less."

With that, he turned quickly and left the booth. The sound room, too, judging from the way Tim and Damon followed his retreat with their eyes. Sophie knew he was completely gone when the guys turned and high-fived each other.

"Prick," Sophie muttered as the door to the booth flew open, Damon breezed in and wrapped her in a bear hug before she even knew what was happening.

Tim followed and Sophie watched him over Damon's shoulder as he said, "Oh, my God, that was *amazing*! The mic was on, so we heard everything." He grimaced. "I mean, we probably should've turned it off…"

Sophie laughed and waved him off. "No worries."

Damon finally let go but held her by her upper arms as he looked her in the eye and spoke with so much sincerity, Sophie could actually feel it. "Thank you, Sophie. Thank you. Davis Silverstein is such a blustering bag of wind who treats people like they're beneath him, and seeing him put in his place"—Damon shook his head—"it was a beautiful sight. You made my year."

"I have to admit, it felt pretty damn good." Not just to see the look on Davis's face when somebody had the audacity to stand up to him, but *that*: She'd stood up to him. She'd stood up for herself and her music, and she was hugely proud of herself right then. "All right." She clapped her hands once. "Let's make sure this is the terrific album I know it's going to be and show Silverstein so in the only language he understands: money."

Both sporting wide smiles, the guys headed back to their seats behind the sound board while Sophie donned her headphones. She had the strangest sensation that she'd grown up a little bit in the past twenty minutes.

Her only regret was that Dana hadn't been there to see it.

❖

"I'm sorry," Sophie said with a sigh. She waved a hand and shook her head. "Can I take a quick break and then try again?"

"Absolutely. Take all the time you need." Damon's salt-and-pepper hair hung in a ponytail again today, and he regarded Sophie through the window to the booth with gentle eyes. His voice softened in her headphones. "You're doing great, Soph. Don't worry so much." She heard his kindness, his support, and was more grateful than she could put into words.

Sophie pulled off the headphones and moved toward the chair in the corner of the booth, exhaling a long, slow breath as she went. Mug of tea with honey in hand, she sank into the seat, balanced her head in her hand, and tried not to think about anything but the music.

Which was impossible. Because of course it was.

She couldn't remember a time in her life when her head had been this full. And she'd led a pretty busy life. Still, all the new music and the pressure to sell well and the appearances and the awards shows where she met idols of her own and the new cities she traveled to... none of that stuff had made her feel so incredibly...she searched for the right word. *Heavy*. That was it. She felt heavy.

Completely aware of the issues weighing her down—confrontation with Davis aside—she'd spent the past two days trying to decide if it was better to analyze them—ad nauseam, as that was the only way she knew how to analyze—or do her best to let them go—ridiculous, because she'd never been able to let anything go).

Ray was on her mind. For some reason, she felt his absence more acutely today than she had in a while, again probably because of the words she'd had with Davis. She wondered if he'd have been horrified by her behavior or proud of it. Probably a little of both. But if she dwelled on Ray too long, she'd crumple into a ball of sobs—something she'd already done twice that morning. Maybe it was because of the photo, the outing. She knew he'd have opinions, could almost hear his voice in her head. *What is the matter with you, Sophia? Why would you do this? What were you thinking? Do you know how much damage this could do to your reputation? I told you, this is not you.*

"But it is me," she said softly, into the empty room. "It is me."

And she realized, right then, that it was the first time in her entire life she'd fully accepted her own sexuality. The tears came instantly.

Thank God she was in the corner and couldn't be fully seen. The guys were doing their own thing anyway—they'd been very respectful of her when she needed time and they did their best not to sit at the sound board staring through the window at her until she was ready.

The tears flowed. Sophie knew better than to try and stop them when she felt like this. It was better to ride it out. They'd stop eventually. Unfortunately, they'd mess with her voice a bit, so it would take her longer than usual to get back into singing shape.

She took a sip of her tea and let her head drop to the back of the chair as Dana's words came back to her.

You embrace it. You own it.

She made it sound so simple. Like, "Hello, world! I'm gay, FYI. Just wanted you to know."

God, Ray was probably spinning in his grave right now.

Why was she so scared? That was the big question. It was 2019. While not necessarily accepted by everybody, homosexuality had become fairly common. It wasn't the shock it used to be when somebody came out publicly. Sophie knew this. She'd seen enough singers and actors come out during her career. And no, announcing her sexual orientation to the world was not something she was hugely comfortable with, but why did it terrify her so much? She'd had a couple of awkward public moments in her life—the recent drunken escapades came screaming into mind—and she'd survived them, as had her career.

So why was this so paralyzing?

As if the Universe was talking to her, the answer to her question walked right into view in the window.

Dana leaned a bit, off to the side so she could see Sophie, and then gave her a wave and that smile.

Sophie sent a halfhearted wave back, and Dana made some gestures that amounted to "can I come in there?" Sophie nodded.

"Hey," Dana said, closing the door behind her. "I thought I'd swing by here instead of you having to make another trip to my office. The guys said you've had quite a day. You okay?"

Sophie shrugged and wondered how it suddenly felt like all the air in the room had been taken. She'd always been so easy with Dana. So effortless. Why was it hard to breathe now?

Dana found a stool and dragged it over to the chair. Her phone started to slip from the back pocket of her pants, so she set it on the floor, then sat. Her knees touched Sophie's and Sophie both loved and hated that. "Talk to me."

"About what?" Sophie asked, then realized immediately how childish she sounded. She sat forward and patted Dana's knee, tried not to rub it, to circle her thumb on it like she really wanted to. "I'm sorry. I don't mean to be snarky. I'm just…" She blew out a breath and sat back. "Like you said. It's been a day." She relayed the conversation with Davis Silverstein and was kind of thrilled when Dana let out a full-on laugh.

"Oh, wow, I wish I'd seen that. If anybody needs to be knocked down a peg or twelve, it's him. Good for you." Dana took a minute, seemed to bask in the story of her boss being cut down to size, before she got serious again. "Unfortunately, we need a decision on how you want to handle the photo." One side of her mouth tugged down in a half grimace.

"Yeah." Sophie gazed off into the distance, letting the word hang there in the air between them. Finally, she returned her gaze to Dana's and tried not to get lost in the blue of her eyes as she asked, her voice barely above a whisper, "What would you do?"

Sophie couldn't be sure, but it almost seemed as if Dana had been ready for this question, had an answer all planned. "Like I said yesterday, I'd embrace it. If you own it, you have the control."

Sophie listened, nodding slowly.

"Nobody has any power over you that way. You can be all, 'yeah, so?' Which usually shuts them up."

"Usually?" Sophie arched a brow.

Dana shot her a half grin. "Not all of my publicist methods are foolproof, but I do okay."

And just like that, Sophie felt relief. "How do you do that?" she asked, bewildered.

What the hell was wrong with her? It was like being on a roller coaster. A very unpleasant roller coaster. Up, down, way up, way down. She felt a little bit like she was going crazy.

"Do what?" Dana raised her brows in question.

"Make me feel better so easily."

"It's my job." Dana shrugged, but the way her eyes darted away from Sophie's told her there was much more she wanted to say.

Sophie nodded.

"Listen." Dana put her hand on Sophie's knee, then as if thinking better of it, removed it. "Let me go hit the ladies' room. You take another few moments to chill, drink your tea, and when I come back, we'll talk about a plan. Yes?"

"Sure." Sophie braced her elbows on her knees as she watched Dana go. The door clicked shut behind her just as the phone Dana had left on the floor buzzed. Sophie looked down in time to see the notification of a text from Laura.

Can't wait for tomorrow night.

That simple line was followed by about seventeen red heart emojis. Sophie felt ill. She sat back in her chair, picked up her mug of tea, then set it back down again, certain even one sip might send her heaving up her lunch.

A few minutes later, Dana was back, that smile on her face. "The guys said you're okay on time, so let's talk about how you want to deal with this." She reclaimed the stool, took a seat.

Sophie just looked at her for what felt like an hour. Just looked at her.

Dana tilted her head. "What's wrong?"

"You're seeing Laura?"

Dana's eyes widened in surprise, and Sophie glanced down at the phone.

"You got a text. I saw the notification."

"We're having dinner tomorrow night. Yes."

"Why?" Sophie knew she didn't really have a right to ask. Did she?

Dana shifted on the stool and seemed uncomfortable with the question. She inhaled slowly, let it out. After so much time passed that Sophie thought she just wasn't going to answer at all, she said quietly, "Because I feel like she and I have unfinished business. I feel like I need to hash it out."

Sophie felt her own eyes go very wide. "Hash it out? She left you, Dana. Without so much as a backward glance, from what you told me."

"I don't know how else to explain it, Sophie." There was a flash of chagrin in Dana's blue eyes now. "We have a history."

"*We* have a history," Sophie snapped, gesturing between the two of them.

"I know. I know. We do. We definitely do and I..." She seemed to want to say more, but caught herself and just exhaled instead. A beat went by before she whispered, "It's all so fast." She immediately looked surprised that she'd said the words out loud.

Okay. Sophie took that as she stared at the floor. Swallowed hard. Gave herself a moment to breathe. "I know." When she looked back up at Dana, who was still pacing, she was mortified to feel her eyes well up. "Did it mean anything to you?" she asked, her voice barely a whisper. "Our night together? The kiss in your bedroom?"

Dana stopped pacing, and her entire being softened. Everything seemed to relax. Her shoulders. Her face. Her eyes. "Of course it did," she whispered back.

Sophie held her gaze and the entire room felt electrified, like there was a sizzle in the air. "Then give us a chance."

"Sophie..."

Sophie stood up, paced the floor.

Dana cocked her head. "Can you just trust me?"

Giving herself no time to think, to second-guess, to panic over the fact that Dana was going to have dinner with her ex, Sophie crossed the room, took Dana's face in her hands, and kissed her with every fiber of her being. She poured everything into that kiss: her heart, her soul, her very essence. And Dana felt it. She must have, because she kissed her back. Hard and with more intensity than Sophie had ever felt. She moved her hands, slid them farther into Dana's thick hair, pulled her even closer as they kissed.

And kissed.

And kissed.

They finally eased apart and Sophie had no idea how long the kiss had lasted. When her vision cleared and she could see more than Dana's beauty, she noticed Damon and Tim. Both stood in the window of the booth, both were staring, both had mouths hanging open.

"Yeah," Dana said quietly as she saw them, too. "Making out with me in front of people? Probably not the best way to deny your gayness."

Sophie grinned and turned back to Dana. "I'm not denying it."

Dana's brows went up. "No?"

"No. I'm taking my manager's advice. I'm owning it."

Dana's expression held a lot right then. Surprise. Satisfaction. Maybe a little bit of pride. "Okay then. I'll get on it."

"Good." Sophie clasped her hands together to prevent them from shaking and giving away the nervousness that suddenly washed over her like an ocean wave. She was doing this.

Holy fucking shit, she was doing this.

Dana picked up her phone, pocketed it, and strode to the door. When she turned back to look at her—those darkened eyes, the kiss-swollen lips—Sophie's entire body felt like it melted into a pool of uselessness on the floor. "No worries," Dana said. "You got this." She pulled the door open.

"Dana?"

"Hmm?" Dana stopped in the doorway and turned her head back.

"She's not good enough for you."

Dana blinked at her.

"Come back to me, okay?" Sophie grimaced at her own words, didn't like feeling that vulnerable, but she couldn't seem to help it.

The smile Dana offered was so much more than enough. Then she glanced quickly down at her feet for a beat before walking through the door and pulling it closed behind her. Sophie inhaled a big breath and let it out slowly.

Her tea was cold now, but she took a sip anyway. Then she found the headphones and put them back on. Tim and Damon were in their seats at the board, both looking at her with knowing smiles. She could hear them in her headphones.

"That was the best break I've had in a long time," Damon said, then turned to his producing partner. "What about you, Tim?"

Tim shrugged. "I mean, two hot girls making out? Can't really go wrong with that."

"Right?" Damon agreed, with a vigorous nod.

Sophie tried to mask her grin, sifted through the music in front of her, but failed as a small chuckle escaped. "I hate you both right now."

"Yeah, but we like you," Tim said. He paused and Sophie could feel eyes on her. She glanced up and the two men were studying her.

"You okay, kiddo?" Damon asked softly, and the tenderness in his voice brought tears to Sophie's eyes.

"I will be."

"All right then. You ready?"

"Let's do this," Sophie said, and music filled her ears, a familiar tune she'd been singing to for most of the day. She let herself hear it. Feel it. Absorb it.

For the rest of the day, the remainder of the session, Sophie sang for the one person who mattered most.

CHAPTER TWENTY-THREE

"I have ten minutes before my next client. Fill me in quick." Bethany always spoke more quickly when she was at work than at home, something that always amused Dana. The funny part of their relationship was that it rarely occurred to them—either of them—not to spill every last crumb of the truth. Anya was her best friend, and Bethany was her true north.

"Brace yourself." Dana clicked through the day's schedule on her computer screen as she spoke. "Sophie wants to come out officially. I'm having dinner with Laura tonight. She wants to talk again about restarting our relationship—no thanks. I told Sophie that Laura and I have unfinished business, which is true. Sophie proceeded to tell me Laura isn't good enough for me. Also, she kissed my face off in the middle of the recording studio."

Silence on the other end of the phone.

"Bethy?" Dana waited a beat. Then, "You there?"

"I'm here," Bethany finally said. "I'm just trying to absorb all of what the hell you just said."

"Take your time. It's a lot, I know."

"You're going out to dinner with Laura. Tonight."

"Yes." Dana called up the notes she'd taken for the phone calls she needed to make that morning.

"Why?"

Dana remembered Sophie asking her the same question. But Dana was more honest with Bethany than she'd been with Sophie. "I don't know." She sighed. "Unfinished business?"

"So you said. Seems like a catchphrase more than the real deal."

Dana sighed. "No, you're right. I guess...I guess it just felt weird to say no." That was the truth.

Bethany snorted. "She give you the lit-up face and excited puppy dog eyes?"

"She did." It made Dana laugh to be reminded how well her sister knew Laura. But she sobered quickly. "And then, there's this whole thing with Sophie, which scares me. It makes dinner with Laura seem... less scary. I don't know what I'm saying."

"The devil you know?"

"Something like that. Ugh. Do you think I'm weak?"

Another snort. "You're not weak if you're fighting off a woman like Sophie James. I am a hot-blooded, heterosexual woman and a *very* big fan of the penis, as you know, but I have to tell you, *I'd* jump in the sack with her if the opportunity presented itself. That girl is *hot*."

On any other day, that would have made Dana burst into laughter. But not today. Today, some of those old insecurities she'd had early on in adulthood came screaming to the forefront. It was kind of crazy how you could think you'd buried them for good and then somebody comes along and it's like they took a shovel and dug them right back up. Suddenly, there were reasons that maybe being with Sophie was a bad idea. Logically, Dana knew she was being silly. But emotionally? "She's ten years younger than me, Bethany. Ten years. An *entire decade*."

"Your point? Sweetie, that only makes *you* look good."

"She's famous."

"So? You deal with famous people every day like it's your job. Cuz it is."

Dana groaned in frustration. "She's not even out yet."

"But she will be. You said so yourself. Besides, you've already been with her. Remind me again: How awful was the sex?"

Instead of a groan, Dana let go of a whimper. She was fully aware that her sister had put on her therapist's hat and was shrinking her. She also knew it was something she probably needed.

"Yeah, that's what I thought." Bethany's low chuckle rumbled over the phone. She waited a beat, then went on. "So, what's dinner going to be like?"

Dana blew out a breath, her only answer.

"She's going to turn on the charm—you know she can—and she's going to have a list, a grand plan that details how it'll all be perfect. That's how she operates. She's going to overwhelm you with all the good information so that you forget the bad shit. Mainly, that she's selfish and will always put herself first." Bethany's voice softened. "You know this."

Dana opened her mouth to comment, to reassure her sister that she would not be bulldozed by Laura, not this time, but she heard voices other than Bethany's on the line before she could say anything.

"Damn, Dana, I have to go. Just…think about what I said. Get some closure and get the hell out of there. I'll text you later." And she was gone.

Dana set the handset back in its cradle, then turned to gaze out the window. A light snow was falling, fluffy flakes drifting past her office on their way down to the New York City streets. Holiday decorations were in full swing and twinkling lights were visible even in the daytime. Dana loved Christmas in New York. It was her absolute favorite time of year. But lately, she had trouble grabbing onto that festive feeling she'd usually held solidly by now.

Everything felt fleeting.

It was such a strange feeling. Dana was an in-control person. She was diligent and organized and had become more so after Laura had left. That whole situation had made her feel so untethered, so at the mercy of others, that she locked everything down and took control of each aspect of her life. She didn't need a therapist to tell her that. She was a smart woman. She'd figured out all on her own that one moment in time can completely alter your personality.

It didn't necessarily mean she enjoyed being a control freak. Sure, it was nice to know where everything was and how everything was going to play out, but it was also hard to be the person that nobody could ever surprise because she knew everything ahead of time.

Sophie had surprised her.

Actually, maybe that wasn't quite true. Maybe it was that *she* had surprised *herself* with Sophie. Because, job aside, she had been anything but in control when it came to her.

And then, just like that, her mind took her back upstate. Back to her parents' house. Back up to the attic, to the bed, to Sophie's naked body under hers. *Women think about sex an average of eighteen times a day.* She'd read that somewhere and thought it was a little high, but since Thanksgiving, she'd thought about sex with Sophie about a hundred times a day. Maybe more.

She scares me.

The thought seemed to come out of nowhere as Dana continued to watch the snow, and she furrowed her brow as it registered. She blinked rapidly several times, then turned back to face her desk, palms down on the surface.

"She scares me."

Saying it aloud seemed to help a bit, grounded her. Dana could work with facts. She was good with facts. Studying her hands, she asked herself, *Why? What am I afraid of?*

Good question.

Her phone rang then, and instead of being annoyed by it, she was relieved. She needed a path away from this train of thought before it derailed and drove her mad. There was a lot of work to be done, comments and responses for Sophie, appearances and interviews to set up. She could focus on that for now so she didn't have to focus on the other thing.

What was she afraid of?

❖

Sophie stood behind Damon and Tim where they sat at the sound board. They made adjustments, slid levers, turned knobs, punched keys, and Sophie's voice came out of the speakers mounted in the ceiling.

She brought her cup of tea to her lips as she listened carefully. "Right there," she said suddenly, and Damon stopped the recording. "You hear it?"

Damon went back, played the snippet again, heard the small click. "Yeah, what is that?"

Sophie sighed. "No idea, but let's do it again."

"From the top?"

"From the top."

"Okay." Tim rolled his chair down the board and hit a few buttons.

"Hey, Sophie?" Damon said as Sophie reached for the door to go back into the booth. When she met his eyes, he smiled warmly. "It's a great song. And at the risk of sounding too…fatherly…I think you're crazy brave with the pronouns."

"I'll take fatherly right now." She smiled at him. "I'm good with fatherly."

Inside the booth, she set down her tea and slipped the headphones on. She did a couple of quick vocal warm-up exercises, then nodded to the guys.

They'd done a beautiful job putting music to her lyrics. Yes, it was a ballad, but it was modern and sensual and even kind of hip. She waited for her cue, then began to sing.

I don't recognize myself when I'm with her
But I like this version of me
How do I hold on to her?
Can I hold on to her?
Can I hold on?

As she had every time she sang it, the words filled her, warmed her, took over. She closed her eyes and let herself get lost in the melody. She didn't have to look at the words in front of her; she knew them by heart, could sing them in her sleep.

I want to scream, just give us a chance
But the fear steals my words, so we do this dance

Her mind filled with Dana's face as the notes glided up from her throat and emanated from her mouth. Dana's blue eyes that went all dark and sexy when she was turned on. Dana's hair, soft and wavy and so many shades of gold. Dana's body—God, Dana's body. Warm and soft and curved in all the right places, the way it moved under Sophie's hands, her mouth, the sounds she was able to pull from her, this stoic, in-control woman who opened herself just for one night to Sophie. Let her see inside…

Sophie stuttered to a stop. She'd lost her place.

She looked up at the guys in the window and could feel the heat in her face as she grimaced an apology.

Tim smiled and Sophie squinted at him because that smile was *knowing.*

God, was she that obvious?

Her shoulders moved as she chuckled. Yeah, she probably was.

"Okay. One more time," she said into her mic, and the music started up again.

❖

Miracle Records had several recording studios they used, both in New York and in LA. A variety of artists recorded music, comedy, even audiobooks in all of them, often simultaneously.

Sophie's studio was in a larger building that housed several others, so Dana checked herself in at the front desk, then went wandering. One of the most amazing things about a giant recording studio was all the different music you could hear while walking to your destination inside. She passed a studio where a rap group was recording. Each studio had a speaker mounted in the entry room, which was the room *before* the sound room, which was the room *before* the recording booth. And if the main door to the entry room was open, you could hear what was being recorded as you walked by—the other rooms were soundproofed. The rappers went along amazingly fast for about ten seconds before somebody tripped over a word and hoots of laughter came from the entry room. Dana smiled as she walked by, passed several more studios. Some were quiet, some full, some contained folks she knew and she waved at them in greeting.

Sophie was recording in Studio 119 today, and Dana opened the door quietly when she saw the red *Recording* light on, not wanting to disturb anyone. She stepped into the room but stayed to the side, out of view of Brooks and Kettle as well as Sophie. Leaning against the wall, she folded her arms and listened as Sophie's smooth-as-silk voice filled the air.

A crowd at dinner
Can't wait
Gets late
A double bed and her.

Dana's eyes went wide.

Alone together
Top floor
Locked door
A double bed and her.

Dana's heart rate picked up speed and goose bumps broke out across her arms as the chorus kicked in, background vocals adding to the depth of the song.

What do I do?
What can I say?
All I want is for you to stay.

A hard swallow couldn't ease the lump in Dana's throat as Sophie kept singing.

The fear is real
I don't know what to do
The fear of falling, falling for you.

Dana clamped a hand over her mouth and stood there, riveted to the floor, knees shaking, thoughts a jumble...but not. Not a jumble at all. In fact, in that very moment, life seemed clearer than it had ever been before. Unsure what to do with that, she listened a bit longer until Sophie cut the music and chatted with Brooks and Kettle about some pop in the air that Dana hadn't noticed at all. A smile broke out across her face as she realized how much she liked Sophie's voice, even when she was only talking.

Dana inhaled deeply, slowly exhaled. She heard Bethany's voice in her head yet again.

Stop thinking so hard and follow your heart for a change.

Everything was clear. Just like that. Her path was laid out before her, as bright and obvious as the Yellow Brick Road.

All she had to do was follow it.

CHAPTER TWENTY-FOUR

Dianetti's smelled like simmering tomatoes, oregano, and parmesan cheese, and Dana's mouth watered the second she'd stepped through the door. The restaurant was packed, as any well-known Italian restaurant in New York City usually was. Dana remembered when she'd first moved to the city, remembered her first week at Miracle. She'd worked well into the night and was starving by the time she left the nearly deserted office. On the way out, she'd asked the security guard if he could recommend someplace to get dinner. He gave her directions to Dianetti's, which was literally around the corner from her office. She'd walked in at almost ten p.m. and stood there in shock at the fact that there was barely an empty table. She'd ended up eating the best lasagna of her life while sitting at the bar and watching the waitstaff run around like squirrels getting ready for winter.

It was her first real taste of how the city really didn't sleep.

Laura was waving at her from a table in the back corner and Dana carefully maneuvered her way back there, zigging and zagging like she was in a game of *Frogger*, the frog trying to cross the busy highway without being run over.

It didn't escape Dana's attention that Dianetti's was also the location of her very first date with Laura. She was sure that was the reason Laura had suggested it—which was slightly surprising, given that Laura didn't really have a sentimental bone in her body. And also not surprising, given Laura's skill at manipulation.

Dana reached the table and slid her coat off as Laura stood up and kissed her on the cheek.

"Hi, sweetie," Laura said.

She looked gorgeous—she rarely didn't look gorgeous—in a black dress with a low-cut V-neck. Her hair was pulled back and clipped at the nape of her neck, leaving her sharp cheekbones and stunning green eyes as the focus. "Hi." Dana took a seat and picked up a menu as Laura filled her glass from the already-opened bottle of Merlot on the table—also the same wine they'd had on their first date. Apparently, Laura was pulling out all the stops.

Glass held up, Laura offered a toast. "To possibilities."

Dana narrowed her eyes slightly but decided touching her glass to Laura's couldn't hurt anything. They sipped.

"You look beautiful," Laura said, propping her chin in her hand.

"Thanks." Dana had purposely come right from work, purposely didn't fuss over how she looked.

The waiter stopped at their table to see if they were ready to order.

"Yes," Laura said, smiling widely at him. "I'll have the pasta primavera and my gorgeous date will have the eggplant parmesan."

The waiter gave a nod, but Dana caught his attention.

"Actually, I'd like the lasagna, please."

He nodded again, took the menus, and was gone.

"You always get the eggplant," Laura said, her face a combination of confusion and irritation.

"No, you always order me the eggplant."

"Oh."

How that was news to Laura, Dana wasn't sure, but she didn't push. "I had the lasagna the very first time I came here, so I feel like having it again."

Laura nodded, forced a smile—something Dana recognized as one of her coping skills when she was embarrassed. Normally, this would be the place where Dana felt that old familiar guilt and went out of her way to make Laura feel better. It was a feeling she'd had around Laura a lot when they'd been together, because she never seemed to do anything right. Laura was always correcting her, making decisions for her, answering for her. And Dana had allowed it. That was one of the things she'd realized—after months of therapy—once Laura had left: that Dana, an intelligent, independent woman, had let Laura take over her life. Any time she'd made even the feeblest of protests, Laura would make her feel guilty and ungrateful. Which she also learned from her therapist were emotions that nobody else could *make* her feel; she was responsible for them. In that moment, she made the conscious effort to *not* feel guilty.

"So? How was your day?" Laura's attempt at righting the ship.

"It was good. Busy. You know."

"I see Sophie James is stepping out into the big lesbian spotlight, huh?"

Dana could tell Laura worked hard to keep the sarcasm out of her voice, but she failed. *Top floor, locked door, a double bed and her.* Sophie's voice suddenly rang through her head. Dana did her best to shake it away. "She is. Decided to be open about the photo rather than denying it or ignoring it."

"Will she be open about who else is in the photo?" No attempts to hide the sarcasm this time.

Dana shrugged, took a sip of wine. *Can I hold on to her? How can I hold on to her?* "No idea. I mean, it's not that hard to find out. I'm kind of surprised it hasn't been announced yet."

"Me, too. Did you contact the caterer?"

"I did. They had already fired the girl, said they'd had similar complaints about her."

"Ah."

They sat quietly for long moments, sipping their wine, watching the other patrons. Their food arrived, putting a temporary stop to the awkward, as they doctored their dishes, added salt, let the waiter grate fresh cheese. Then they each took bites, made the appropriate noises, ate from each other's plates like old times.

"This is nice," Laura said, and this time, her smile was its normal, genuine self.

Dana nodded because it was. It was nice. This was the kind of thing she missed after Laura had left. That familiarity of sharing your dinner with someone. That level of comfort that came with knowing somebody well enough to let them eat off your fork. But that's all it was: a nice memory.

Laura took an audibly deep breath as she stared at her plate. When she looked up at Dana, her eyes shimmered and her smile was there, but uncertain. She was nervous. Dana knew her well enough to see that.

"I want us to try again." Laura's voice was quiet. Tender. Filled with hope.

Dana's stomach churned unpleasantly. "Laura…"

Laura held up a hand. "Wait. I know we already touched on it a few weeks ago, but…just let me say this. Okay?"

Against her better judgment, Dana nodded once and stayed quiet.

"Do me a favor. Just think about how great we were." Laura cocked her head almost comically and added, "I mean, before I lost my mind."

Dana kept her expression carefully neutral.

Apparently seeing her attempt at humor fall flat, Laura went on. "I'm back now. And I'm not that same stupid person. I like to think I've grown up a bit. And I missed you." Her voice dropped. "I missed you so much." She reached across the table, picked up Dana's hand in both of hers, turned it, ran a fingertip in circles on Dana's palm. "We can be the way we were again. I know it."

Dana looked at their hands because it was easier than looking at Laura's face. There was too much hope there. It was too open. Too expectant. Too sure of the answer. "I've changed, too," she said, her voice gravelly.

"I know," Laura said, enthusiasm lacing her tone. "I've seen it. You're amazing."

"Thank you." Dana used her free hand to finish her wine. Laura reached for the bottle to pour more, but Dana stopped her.

"We can start slow. Date. You can set the pace."

Dana took a deep breath, eased her hand free of Laura's. "This all sounds great on paper, but…"

The light in Laura's eyes dimmed just a touch. "You're over me."

That surprised Dana. "What?"

"You're over me." Laura sat back in her chair. "I'm not over you, but you're done with me."

Dana felt a tiny bubble of anger start to simmer in her gut. "Laura." She waited until her ex made eye contact, and she kept her voice low, aware of how close other tables were. "You left me without so much as a 'take care of yourself.' More than a year ago. What did you think was going to happen?"

"I guess I thought…" Laura let her voice drop off, and her expression looked like she'd eaten something sour. She pulled her napkin from her lap and tossed it onto the table. "I don't know what I thought. I guess I just hoped."

Dana hated seeing the sadness, the dejection on her face, but she knew it was better this way. Yes, it might be easier to allow that slow pace, to allow a date here and there, but what would be the point? So many thoughts shot through her head then, different words to utter. Some would be angry—no less than Laura deserved. Some were apologetic, because she knew this night wasn't going to go the way Laura had hoped. So many words to choose from, but instead…

Instead, she remembered Sophie singing. Not just singing, though. Singing a heartfelt, emotional song that she'd written. For Dana. So obviously for Dana. And not only did it express the fear Sophie felt about them, it also echoed Dana's…something she was only realizing in that very moment, sitting across from her ex who wanted her back. *I want to scream just give us a chance, but the fear steals my words, so we do this dance…*

"I waited too long, didn't I?" Laura's voice broke into Dana's thoughts and hauled her back to the table.

"I don't know that there was a time limit," Dana said honestly. "But you broke me. You did. If you'd come back sooner…I don't know." Dana shrugged. "Maybe we could have tried again. Maybe not."

Laura's green eyes filled. Her throat moved as she swallowed. "I guess we'll never know, huh?" They sat quietly for a beat. "I'm so sorry, Dana."

Dana looked at her, knew it was the truth. "I know." She reached across and took Laura's hand again. "I forgive you."

Rather than uncomfortable and awkward, the remainder of their dinner was actually nice. Familiar. Laura pulled herself together—she always could make a whiplash-inducingly fast recovery—and it felt to Dana as though they suddenly went from being exes to being old friends, a wonderful shift as far as she was concerned. They ordered a piece of chocolate raspberry cheesecake to share, had coffee, and talked about both old times and new ones.

Dana was surprised by how okay she felt.

Outside the restaurant, Laura hailed a cab, held the door open for Dana. "Share?"

"Actually…" Dana began, suddenly clearer than she'd ever been on what she needed to do next. Laura gave her a knowing grin.

"Going the other way?"

Dana nodded and felt her cheeks heat up even in the cold of the December night.

Laura waved her into the cab. "Take this one. I'll grab another."

Before she even realized what she was doing, Dana wrapped her arms around Laura and hugged her tight. She felt Laura's arms around her body, felt the squeeze from a person she'd once loved more than anything and now still loved, but on a completely different level. It was weird and wonderful at the same time.

She slid into the back seat and Laura leaned in. "I hope you find what you're looking for." With a nod, she slammed the door.

❖

It had been about an hour since Sophie turned her Google alerts back on and her phone hadn't stopped buzzing since. There was such a mix of reactions that she couldn't decide if all the buzzing was a good thing or a bad thing. All she knew was it was a thing and she was obsessed.

The wine probably wasn't a great idea. Not because she'd had too much, but because she should be drinking something a bit gentler on her throat, as she had to record some more tomorrow. But scrolling and surfing and reading had made her nervous, and she needed something to steady herself. And if she was going to be honest with herself, she also knew that the knowledge of Dana having dinner with her ex that night was slowly eating her alive from the inside out.

She slugged some more wine.

Sophie paced her living room, strolling from one side to the other, wine in one hand, phone in the other. The Instagram photo of her and Dana making out had been shared over 200,000 times, and while she tried hard not to read all the comments, she got sucked in sometimes. She could hear Michaela's voice in her head telling her, "Never read the comments! That's where all the world's trash lives." They were a mixed bag, the comments, ranging from disgust to support to disturbingly inappropriate remarks. Websites for all the variety shows had posts about her. Dana said she'd been contacted in the past week by GLAAD and the HRC, both asking if Sophie would be interested in talking to them. Dana had already lined up four appearances for her: one late night show, one morning show, one news show, and one radio show.

Yep, Sophie was coming out.

Not subtly. Not quietly. No, her career didn't really allow for that. No, she was kicking the closet door right down. It was going to be big and loud. Hell, it already was.

The buzzing of her intercom surprised her, and she checked the time on her phone. It was after ten.

"Yes?" she said into the speaker.

"I'm sorry to bother you, Ms. James," the doorman said. "You have a Ms. Landon here to see you?"

Dana. Dana was here. At ten o'clock on the night she'd had dinner with her ex. What did that mean? Something bad? Something good? God, did she have Laura with her? So many thoughts zipped through her head, took her focus long enough for the doorman to poke at her.

"Ms. James?"

"Yes. I'm here. Sorry. Send her up."

She ran to her bedroom and checked herself in the mirror, and something kind of surprising occurred to her. She was wearing worn yoga pants and a sweatshirt that was so old the cuffs on the sleeves were frayed and there was a hole in the collar that got bigger every time she washed the thing. Her hair was in a messy bun on top of her head and she'd taken her makeup off when she'd gotten home. This was her. This was Sophie James, at home just being herself, and she felt zero need to change that. For any other visitor, she'd be speeding around her room like a crazy person, trying to make herself look like people thought she was supposed to: glammed up, all flawless makeup and perfect hair and envy-inducing fashion sense. For the first time, she really understood that with Dana? She could be herself, because she always had been with her.

Her doorbell rang and she took a deep breath, held it in, then let it out slowly before heading for the door.

Dana was alone. And she looked amazing.

Jesus Christ. What else is new?

"Hey," Dana said, and there was something…different in her demeanor. Something slightly…Sophie didn't want to say "off" because the shift wasn't a bad thing. It was somehow softer. Gentler. Tender.

"Hi," Sophie said, shaking herself back to the here and now. "Come in." She stepped aside, let Dana enter. Dana slipped her coat off and Sophie took it, hung it up. She looked down at herself, then up at Dana's skirt, blazer, and heels, her perfect makeup and hair like spun gold. "I, um, was just having a little wine—okay, maybe a little more than a little—while I paced my apartment looking at my phone while wearing the rattiest clothes I own." She shrugged. "You caught me at my best."

Dana's smile was radiant and lit up her whole face. "I think you look super cute."

"Seriously?"

"Seriously. I love your hair up like that." Without waiting for an invitation, Dana crossed to the kitchen and helped herself to the open wine bottle, pouring herself a generous glass. "I read somewhere that, like, seventy-five percent of women change out of their work clothes and into sweats the second they get home."

"Well, I guess that makes me feel better." *Yeah, not really.*

Dana held the bottle up with raised eyebrows.

"Why the hell not?" Sophie said with another shrug. So much shrugging happening right now.

Dana brought the bottle into the living room, topped off Sophie's glass, then set it on the coffee table and dropped herself back onto the couch. She blew out a breath and took a sip.

Sophie watched all of this with interest, wondering if Dana was happy, sad, relieved, frustrated, all of the above, none of the above... She sat down next to her—leaving a respectable distance between them—and sipped her wine.

"Been looking at your phone, huh?" Dana asked.

"Yeah." Sophie hung her head in defeat, and as if paying attention to the conversation, her phone buzzed another alert.

"Turn that off." Dana's voice held some humor, though, and not a shred of assertiveness.

Sophie obeyed and felt instant relief. She flopped back against the couch, lifted her legs to set them on the coffee table, crossed them at the ankle.

"How are you feeling about it all?"

Well. That was the million-dollar question, wasn't it? Sophie turned her head against the back of the couch so she faced Dana, who was looking at her with those blue eyes like there was nobody else in the world. Sophie felt a flutter in her stomach. And lower. "I honestly don't know," she said finally, and they were the truest words to come out of her mouth in what felt like a very long time.

Dana nodded slowly. "That makes sense." She sipped her wine as she gazed forward into the living room, and it occurred to Sophie how funny they must look, the two of them, slumped down on the couch, feet up on the coffee table, like two annoyed teenage girls who were just totally done with life today. "I've been keeping track of posts and headlines and such. I feel like it's leaning more toward the positive than the negative. Don't you?"

"Hard to say."

"Well, sure, the negative stuff is…louder somehow, huh?"

Sophie widened her eyes. "Sure feels that way."

"You see the support, though, right?" Dana turned to look at her and Sophie swore she could *feel* it. Feel Dana's eyes roam over her. Like fingertips. Like lips. "I don't know how you feel about being a spokesperson or a gay icon of sorts, but you totally could be. You just have to say the word."

Sophie blinked and tried to let that idea sink in.

Sophie James had had some degree of fame since she was sixteen years old. It had only gotten bigger as time went on, and it had certainly taken some getting used to. She'd traveled to more countries than she could count, done thousands of interviews, signed tens of thousands of autographs, had been recognized in public on a regular basis, and there were times when it could feel...heavy. But none of that—not one iota of it—felt like a *tiny fraction* of the weight of being some kind of a figurehead for being gay.

"It's a lot, I know," Dana said, interrupting Sophie's panic. "I'm just saying, it's a possibility. Something to think about."

Sophie nodded. "Okay." Because thinking about it was all she could do right now.

They sat in silence for what felt like a long while. And it wasn't uncomfortable at all. Well. With the exception of the elephant in the room. Sophie stared at it, its enormous girth, its gray skin and soft, surprisingly understanding eyes, before finally deciding she'd had enough.

"How was your dinner?" she asked, not really wanting the answer, but knowing it had been driving her crazy all evening.

"I stopped by the studio today," Dana said at the same exact time.

"You did?" Sophie furrowed her brow. "I didn't see you."

"I didn't come all the way in." Dana glanced down at her wine, over toward the window seat, at the ceiling. Anywhere but at Sophie's face. "I just listened."

"You did?" Sophie said again. She was confused. It was fine that Dana stopped by, that she listened. None of that was unusual. But she hadn't made her presence known, and that was unusual. "Why didn't you say hi?"

Dana's throat moved as she swallowed. She sat forward and reached for the wine bottle so she could refill her glass. She poured the remainder into Sophie's, set the empty bottle down, then sat back. She didn't utter a word the whole time.

"Dana? Are you okay?" Sophie hated to see her this...what was she? Torn? Frightened? Uncertain?

"It was the song."

Again, Sophie didn't follow. "What song?"

Dana turned to her then and the blue of her eyes was so deep, so complex as she spoke, that Sophie's heart squeezed in her chest a bit. "'Fear of Falling.' You were singing 'Fear of Falling' and I..." She let her voice trail off, looked away, took a sip of her wine.

"Ooohhhh..." Sophie understood then. She'd kept the lyrics a secret for a reason and this was it. Right up until that morning, she wasn't 100 percent sure she was even going to record it. It was so personal. So telling. But it was in her heart, just like Dana was. It was in her *soul*. Just like Dana. She'd had no choice. Even if things never went any further, she felt like she *needed* to get it out. The silence stretched on, and she finally ventured to ask, very quietly, "Are you upset with me?"

When Dana met her gaze, that depth and complexity still sat deep in her eyes. Her expression softened, from the lines on her forehead that relaxed to the corners of her mouth that turned up just a touch. She reached a hand toward Sophie, wrapped a finger around a hunk of hair that had escaped from Sophie's messy bun, played with it, tugged gently. "No."

"Okay. Good. That's good." How was it possible that Dana's one finger playing with a little bitty fraction of all of Sophie's hair could have such an effect on her? Because that fluttering in her stomach kicked up and her heart rate increased, and she suddenly couldn't swallow enough.

"I thought it was beautiful. I'd like to hear the whole thing."

"It's kind of simple, as far as the words go, but it's mine. I wrote it." Sophie lifted one shoulder and Dana switched from playing with her hair to running her fingertip around Sophie's ear. "But the guys came up with some great music."

"I thought about it all day."

"Even through dinner with your ex?" Sophie didn't mean it to sound snarky, and it didn't, but it wasn't super kind either.

"Even through dinner with my ex," was Dana's response, and it surprised Sophie. In a big way.

"Really?"

Dana nodded slowly, her cheeks now lightly pink. From the wine? Or something else? Her eyes were still magnetic. "Yeah. I couldn't get it out of my head."

Sophie wasn't sure if she should feel bad about that or giddy, so she said nothing.

"Is it true?" Dana asked.

Sophie smiled. "'A crowd at dinner, can't wait, gets late, a double bed and her'? Yeah, you were there, remember?"

"I do." Dana sat up then, set her wine glass down, and turned so she was facing Sophie, one leg bent and up on the couch. She grabbed a throw pillow, began picking at some nonexistent something. "I mean, the fear part. Is that true?"

Now they were getting into the nitty-gritty. The down-and-dirty. The real stuff. Sophie could play this off. She could be dismissive. She could make a joke of it, wave it away. It would be easy.

Or she could be honest.

That wouldn't be quite as easy.

But right then, sitting next to the most beautiful woman she'd ever seen, the woman who made her feel wanted and sexy and important and loved—the woman who made her *feel*—she knew she had to lay all her cards on the table. She studied the wine glass in her hand, noted the deep purple of the liquid, the delicacy of the crystal, and then took a breath.

"Yes." It came out not much louder than a whisper, and Sophie cleared her throat, tried again. "Yes, it's true. The fear part." Forcing herself to look at Dana, she met those eyes with her own and said, very softly, "You terrify me."

Sophie watched as a line of emotions chugged across Dana's face like train cars. Surprise, sadness, understanding, relief, delight, confusion. They were all there, taking their turns moving through her, stopping to look through her eyes and out at Sophie before moving on to allow the next feeling. Sophie was shocked by how clear it all was. All the feels. Dana had them.

"Well," Dana said finally. She turned back to her previous position, feet up on the coffee table. "Right back atcha."

They sat there on the couch, both slouched, both with their heads against the back and turned to face each other. Their eye contact held. Sophie had never felt so content, so completely, inarguably comfortable looking directly into the eyes of another person as she did in that moment.

"What are you afraid of with me?" she asked Dana.

Dana let out a light scoff. "What am I *not* afraid of with you?" When Sophie didn't say anything, she turned her gaze to the ceiling and ticked things off on her fingers. "Let's see. I'm afraid of being your first girlfriend. Hell, your first relationship as far as I can tell. I'm afraid you're too young for me. Or I'm too old for you, I'm not sure which. I'm afraid of your fame. I'm afraid for my job. I'm afraid this has all happened way too fast." She stopped suddenly, and Sophie watched her swallow. Dana's voice got very soft as she turned to Sophie and added, "I'm afraid of how I feel about you."

Sophie took in a slow breath, let it out. "Wow. That's a lot of fears."

Dana's smile was small. "Yeah." They sat quietly again before Dana spoke again. "What about you? What are you afraid of?"

With a shrug, Sophie said simply, "I'm afraid of not being with you."

Dana blinked at her, stayed quiet, blinked some more. Finally, she asked, "That's it?"

Sophie pursed her lips and nodded. "That's it."

"Huh."

"I'm really a very simple girl, Dana." Sophie gave her a half smile.

With a chuckle that sounded laced with something like sarcasm, but gentler, Dana said, "Oh, you are far from simple, sweetheart. Far from simple."

"You give me too much credit. And you never told me how dinner went." Part of Sophie didn't want to know, but a bigger part knew she needed to. "She wants you back, doesn't she?"

"She does." Dana stared straight ahead and gave one slow nod.

"And are you going back?" Sophie felt her entire body brace. Her muscles tightened. Her heart slowed. Her right hand balled into a fist and she tucked it next to her thigh so Dana wouldn't see. Her fingers curled around the stem of her wine glass so tightly, part of her expected it might snap.

Dana rolled her head so she was looking at Sophie again. And those eyes. Those damn gorgeous blue eyes of hers held...too much. Sophie looked away as Dana spoke. "Do you think I'd be here right now if I was?"

Sophie swallowed down the lump of hope that had instantly formed in her throat. She wet her suddenly dry lips. "Maybe? Maybe you came here to let me down easy?"

"No."

Sophie swallowed. Again. God, what was wrong with her throat? "No?"

"No."

Barely, barely a whisper now, Sophie asked, "Then why?"

Dana tucked some hair behind her ear and breathed in deeply. "I wanted to ask about the song, to know if that's how you really felt."

"Okay."

Dana's hand was warm as she took Sophie's wine glass and set it on the table. Then she took Sophie's hand in her own, pulled it into her lap. She held it in one hand and stroked a fingertip from the other along the inside of Sophie's wrist. Traced the outline of the tattoo, followed each ray of sunlight.

Sophie's heart began to pound. "If I'd said no? It's just a song?"

Dana pushed the sleeve of Sophie's sweatshirt up past her elbow, then ran her finger along the inside of Sophie's forearm. "I would've talked to you a bit about your upcoming appearances and then I'd have gone home."

"You would have pretended you came on business." The simple contact of her hand cradled in Dana's and that one fingertip was doing all kinds of erotic things to Sophie's body in the moment. She tried to focus.

"Exactly."

"At ten o'clock at night."

Dana gave a half shrug. "The entertainment industry keeps crazy hours."

"I see." The fluttering in Sophie's stomach had gone from butterfly light to Canada goose insistent, and her thighs clenched without her even thinking about it. "And what was your plan if I'd said yes, the lyrics were absolutely the truth of how I feel about you?"

Dana switched then from a fingertip to her palm, running it down Sophie's arm to her hand, entwining their fingers—which fit perfectly together, Sophie noticed, her olive skin against the creaminess of Dana's, yin and yang. Dana brought their linked hand to her lips, kissed Sophie's knuckles. She held Sophie's hand against her lips for a sweet and tender moment before saying, without looking at Sophie, "Then I was going to spend the night here."

"Oh, *really*?" Sophie let the fun come through in her tone, the teasing, because in all honesty, she was practically giddy at Dana's words. "A little presumptuous, wouldn't you say?"

Dana turned and met her gaze, and Sophie was surprised to see a sheer tint of uncertainty there. "Was it?"

Sophie freed her hand and used both of hers to grab the lapels of Dana's blazer. "God, no." She tugged Dana toward her until their mouths met in a searing kiss that left both of them breathless. Tugging some more, she finally made her point, and Dana got the idea. She tossed her leg over Sophie's, straddling her lap, which caused her skirt to ride up and expose her smooth thighs. Which Sophie instantly took advantage of, running her hands up and down them as Dana brought her mouth down onto Sophie's once more.

This is it. This is everything.

The thought ran through Sophie's mind, loudly, as Dana pressed into her. As Sophie pushed Dana's blazer off and threw it to the other end of the couch. As Dana pulled the elastic band out of Sophie's hair so it came tumbling down around her shoulders.

They stopped then, stopped for a moment and just looked at each other. Just stared. Just felt. Sophie moved her hand and pressed it flat against Dana's chest, where her heart was. Dana stacked her own hand over it and they sat, stared, as something tangible floated between them, between their chests, their hearts. Sophie felt her eyes well up, and she tried her best to swallow down the lump in her throat, but she couldn't. It stayed firmly there, as if ordering Sophie to say the words in her head, as if that was the only way to clear her throat completely.

This is everything.

Dana brushed the hair off Sophie's forehead, tucked it behind her ear, never stopped gazing into her eyes. Her smile was soft. Warm. Tender. In that moment, Sophie had never felt so loved.

She knew it. She knew it was time, and just like that, all the worry, the nerves, the trepidation were gone. She felt solid. Sure.

She felt home.

"I love you, Dana," she whispered, and then watched as this time, Dana's eyes filled. "I love you so much."

A tear spilled over, ran down Dana's cheek, and Sophie caught it with her thumb. "I love you, too," Dana said, and a gentle sob pushed its way up softly from her chest. "More than you know."

Sophie looked up at her, at this woman in her lap, at this beautiful soul, this tenderhearted person she'd only known for a short time. But in that instant, in that one moment in time, she knew. She felt it just as sure as she felt the couch under her body or Dana's silky skin beneath her fingers. She just knew.

This is everything.

Epilogue

Four months later...

The green room for *The Almost Wee Hours* felt nearly deserted. Normally, there were a good dozen people in there milling around while the show was on the air, but tonight, there were only Dana, Andrew, Michaela, and one other person, and enough food to keep them all comfortably full for a good two weeks.

The wall-mounted monitor allowed them to watch as Jeff Cruze talked with Sophie about her self-discovery, her coming out, and last but not least, her new album. The audience had gone nuts when Sophie walked onto the stage, waving and...blushing? Dana had squinted at the screen to make sure. Yup, Sophie James, internationally renowned singer-and-now-songwriter, famous for the past fifteen years, was blushing on national television.

It was actually super cute.

Which was not the description she'd used when she'd entered the dressing room earlier and had seen Sophie all ready for the show. Andrew had outdone himself. Sophie wore what was sort of a pantsuit. Black. Slacks that couldn't have fit better and a matching jacket buttoned low. She wore nothing underneath that jacket—which had caused Dana to do a double take when she first saw it—and Andrew had chosen a complicated silver necklace that hung perfectly in that large expanse of bare, olive-colored skin that Dana had been seized with an almost irresistible urge to lick. Sky-high heels, her hair down and wavy, and Michaela's makeup magic had finished off the look, and when Sophie had turned to face her, Dana had been speechless. Literally speechless. Had no words. Just stood there. Gawking like a teenage boy.

"I'm gonna go out on a limb and guess that you like this outfit," Sophie had said with a little grin.

Dana had simply nodded. Still no words.

Sophie had waved her finger up and down in front of Dana. "This is good, this reaction. I'll take this reaction any day of the week." Then she walked up to her and kissed her sweetly on the mouth.

"Hey," Michaela had complained. "Lipstick."

Sophie had given Dana a sexy little grin, then turned to her makeup artist. "Sorry."

Michaela shook her head and touched up Sophie's lips, ensuring they were red and glossy.

"Wish me luck," Sophie had said when the production assistant came to get her.

"You don't need it," Dana assured her, finally finding some words. "But break a leg."

And now Sophie was sitting in the guest's chair as Jeff Cruze sat behind his big, square desk.

"So," Jeff said to her now as Dana watched the monitor. "You're really embracing the new you."

Sophie smiled. "It's not really a 'new me,'" she said, making air quotes with her fingers. "It's just the genuine me. If that makes sense."

"It does." Jeff turned to the large screen mounted behind them and a colorful photo of Sophie surrounded by a gaggle of teenagers appeared. "You've been doing a lot of work since you've come out. Fill me in here."

"These are kids at the LGBTQ community center in the East Village. I spent some time there a couple weeks ago, just talking to them, hearing their stories." Sophie shifted her gaze from Jeff to the audience. "I know we're in 2019 and things are significantly better than they were twenty, even ten years ago. But we still have a long way to go, and the best way to start helping that journey along is to listen." She gestured back to the photo. "These kids had so much to say. They just need to feel like they're being heard and they're being supported. If you can volunteer somewhere, even for just an hour a week, please do that. It means so much to them."

The audience erupted into applause and cheers, and there was that blush again. Dana would never get tired of seeing it. The pinkened cheeks, the eyes cast downward. It really was so sweet that Sophie was suddenly embarrassed by her popularity.

Jeff shifted gears. "So, let's settle this once and for all." He waved his hand and the photo of the kids changed to the photo of Sophie and Dana kissing. "The photo that started the storm," he said to the hoots and catcalls of the audience. "Who is that...standing very much in your personal space?"

Sophie's blush deepened, but she wasn't surprised. Jeff had cleared this all with her ahead of time. *Perks of being longtime friends with the host*, Dana thought.

"That's my girlfriend. Dana."

This time, among the cheering of the audience, there were some boos and a few groans.

"And millions of lesbians around the world just burst into tears," Jeff said to laughter and more applause. "So, this Dana...she was your manager, yes?"

"Still is," Sophie said, and Dana could see her relax into the conversation. Her heart warmed, as she'd been worried Sophie might balk at such direct talk. Instead, she seemed to settle more comfortably into her chair and crossed her legs. She didn't get into the details of how she'd had to put her foot down with Miracle, how they'd been less than enthusiastic about her writing her own stuff, how her best sales in years had shut them right up. And she didn't get into the fact that yes, Dana was still her manager, but that she'd left Miracle and was now working at Starshine for Anya. She stuck to the lighter stuff, the stuff she knew the audience was much more interested in.

"She hot?" Jeff asked, in typical guy fashion.

Sophie played along, which didn't surprise Dana at all. "You have no idea, Jeff."

"Well, at least now I know why you refused to go out with me all those years ago." Jeff pretended to shuffle papers on his desk.

"Okay. We'll go with that."

The audience cracked up.

"I was going to go through the whole, 'how did you win her over' thing, but...you used the oldest trick in the book: You wrote her a love song."

"I did."

"Pretty ballsy move." Jeff's tone said he was impressed.

"Hey, it worked, didn't it? I got the girl." Sophie's grin was wide and sent the audience into crazed cheers.

"Would you sing it for us?"

"I'd love to."

Sophie stood and crossed the stage to the mic stand that was waiting for her as Jeff announced, "Ladies and gentlemen, Sophie James."

The lights dimmed, the spotlight shown on Sophie, the music started up, and she began to sing "Fear of Falling."

Dana didn't think she'd ever get tired of hearing that voice. It was like velvet. Melted chocolate. Warm silk. Any other smooth thing you could think of, Sophie's voice was smoother. Richer. Had more depth.

"Goddamn," Andrew said quietly.

Michaela nodded her agreement. "She never doesn't blow me away. On a bad day, she sounds better than anybody I've ever heard."

"Right?" Andrew's eyes were glued to the monitor. "And she looks fucking amazing."

Both Michaela and Dana laughed softly; it was true. The lighting made Sophie's outfit seem iridescent, glimmering gently like stars in the night sky. Her makeup was perfect as she closed her eyes and held a long note with what seemed like minimal effort.

Dana was entranced and wondered if she'd ever not be. They were still so new. Only a few months in. But to her, this was it. She knew it in her bones. And at night, under the covers, wrapped up in each other, she looked deep into Sophie's eyes and knew she felt it, too.

This was everything.

On the monitor, the music swelled and Sophie raised her arms up as she sang the big finish. The audience exploded.

Jeff shouted over the cheers, "My friend Sophie James, everybody. Her new album, *Fear of Falling*, is available now. We'll be right back."

The show cut to commercial and Dana moved out of the green room into the hallway where she could see the path Sophie would take from the wings. Her appearance was finished tonight and she was free to go. Dana waited and a minute later, Sophie turned the corner and came into view.

Andrew and Michaela clapped as she approached and she tossed a grateful smile their way, but she only had eyes for Dana and Dana knew it. Could see it on her face, the love, the trust, the commitment. She walked straight toward Dana and right into her arms, a quiet sigh of relief leaving her body under Dana's hands.

"You were amazing," Dana whispered against her throat, then looked up, craning her own neck and laughing. "God, these heels make you so freaking tall."

Sophie instantly stepped out of them, bringing her down to a still-taller-than-Dana but much more palatable height. "Better?"

"Much." Dana kissed her. Softly. Lovingly.

"Ugh. Get a room," Andrew said, but his disgust was feigned and Dana knew he was teasing. His eyes were filled with happiness for his friend. Anybody could see that.

As she and Sophie headed to the dressing room so Sophie could change, Dana said, "You know, it'd be a shame to waste that outfit. Dinner out? Show it off?"

Sophie pulled her through the dressing room door, then closed it by backing Dana up against it. She kissed the side of Dana's neck, causing goose bumps to break out along her skin and a gentle throbbing to make itself known between her legs. "I have a better idea." Sophie kissed up to Dana's ear and whispered, "How about we go to my place, have dinner in and you can *take* it off?"

"That is a *much* better idea," Dana agreed, and let herself get lost in the feel of Sophie's mouth on her for a moment before forcing herself to focus. "Okay." She was breathless. "Okay. Get your things together. I'll go get us a car."

Sophie nodded and turned away to gather her belongings.

"Hey, Sophia?" Dana called softly, her hand on the doorknob. When Sophie turned those dark eyes on her, she said simply, "I love you."

The smile that broke out across Sophie's beautiful face was worth everything Dana could ever give and she felt tears well up in her eyes as Sophie responded. "I love you back."

Yes. This was everything.

About the Author

Georgia Beers is the award-winning author of more than twenty lesbian romances. She resides in upstate New York where she was born and raised. When not writing, she enjoys way too much TV, not nearly enough wine, spin class at the gym, and walks with her dog. She is currently hard at work on her next book. You can visit her and find out more at www.georgiabeers.com.

Books Available From Bold Strokes Books

Daughter of No One by Sam Ledel. When their worlds are threatened, a princess and a village outcast must overcome their differences and embrace a budding attraction if they want to survive. (978-1-63555-427-4)

Fear of Falling by Georgia Beers. Singer Sophie James is ready to shake up her career, but her new manager, the gorgeous Dana Landon, has other ideas. (978-1-63555-443-4)

Playing with Fire by Lesley Davis. When Takira Lathan and Dante Groves meet at Takira's restaurant, love may find its way onto the menu. (978-1-63555-433-5)

Practice Makes Perfect by Carsen Taite. Meet law school friends Campbell, Abby, and Grace, law partners at Austin's premier boutique legal firm for young, hip entrepreneurs. Legal Affairs: one law firm, three best friends, three chances to fall in love. (978-1-63555-357-4)

The Last Seduction by Ronica Black. When you allow true love to elude you once and you desperately regret it, are you brave enough to grab it when it comes around again? (978-1-63555-211-9)

Wavering Convictions by Erin Dutton. After a traumatic event, Maggie has vowed to regain her strength and independence. So how can Ally be both the woman who makes her feel safe and a constant reminder of the person who took her security away? (978-1-63555-403-8)

A Bird of Sorrow by Shea Godfrey. As Darrius and her lover, Princess Jessa, gather their strength for the coming war, a mysterious spell will reveal the truth of an ancient love. (978-1-63555-009-2)

All the Worlds Between Us by Morgan Lee Miller. High school senior Quinn Hughes discovers that a broken friendship is actually a door propped open for an unexpected romance. (978-1-63555-457-1)

Falling by Kris Bryant. Falling in love isn't part of the plan, but will Shaylie Beck put her heart first and stick around, or tell the damaging truth? (978-1-63555-373-4)

An Intimate Deception by CJ Birch. Flynn County Sheriff Elle Ashley has spent her adult life atoning for her wild youth, but when she finds her ex, Jessie, murdered two weeks before the small town's biggest social event, she comes face-to-face with her past and all her well-kept secrets. (978-1-63555-417-5)

Cash and the Sorority Girl by Ashley Bartlett. Cash Braddock doesn't want to deal with morality, drugs, or people. Unfortunately, she's going to have to. (978-1-63555-310-9)

Secrets in a Small Town by Nicole Stiling. Deputy Chief Mackenzie Blake has one mission: find the person harassing Savannah Castillo and her daughter before they cause real harm. (978-1-63555-436-6)

Stormy Seas by Ali Vali. The high-octane follow-up to the best-selling action-romance *Blue Skies*. (978-1-63555-299-7)

The Road to Madison by Elle Spencer. Can two women who fell in love as girls overcome the hurt caused by the father who tore them apart? (978-1-63555-421-2)

Dangerous Curves by Larkin Rose. When love waits at the finish line, dangerous curves are a risk worth taking. (978-1-63555-353-6)

Love to the Rescue by Radclyffe. Can two people who share a past really be strangers? (978-1-62639-973-0)

Love's Portrait by Anna Larner. When museum curator Molly Goode and benefactor Georgina Wright uncover a portrait's secret, public and private truths are exposed, and their deepening love hangs in the balance. (978-1-63555-057-3)

Model Behavior by MJ Williamz. Can one woman's instability shatter a new couple's dreams of happiness? (978-1-63555-379-6)

Pretending in Paradise by M. Ullrich. When travelwisdom.com assigns PR specialist Caroline Beckett and travel blogger Emma Morgan to cover a hot new couples retreat, they're forced to fake a relationship to secure a reservation. (978-1-63555-399-4)

Recipe for Love by Aurora Rey. Hannah Little doesn't have much use for fancy chefs or fancy restaurants, but when New York City chef Drew Davis comes to town, their attraction just might be a recipe for love. (978-1-63555-367-3)

The House by Eden Darry. After a vicious assault, Sadie, Fin, and their family retreat to a house they think is the perfect place to start over, until they realize not all is as it seems. (978-1-63555-395-6)

Uninvited by Jane C. Esther. When Aerin McLeary's body becomes host for an alien intent on invading Earth, she must work with researcher Olivia Ando to uncover the truth and save humankind. (978-1-63555-282-9)

Comrade Cowgirl by Yolanda Wallace. When cattle rancher Laramie Bowman accepts a lucrative job offer far from home, will her heart end up getting lost in translation? (978-1-63555-375-8)

Double Vision by Ellie Hart. When her cell phone rings, Giselle Cutler answers it—and finds herself speaking to a dead woman. (978-1-63555-385-7)

Inheritors of Chaos by Barbara Ann Wright. As factions splinter and reunite, will anyone survive the final showdown between gods and mortals on an alien world? (978-1-63555-294-2)

Spinning Tales by Brey Willows. When the fairy tale begins to unravel and villains are on the loose, will Maggie and Kody be able to spin a new tale? (978-1-63555-314-7)

Love on Lavender Lane by Karis Walsh. Accompanied by the buzz of honeybees and the scent of lavender, Paige and Kassidy must find a way to compromise on their approach to business if they want to save Lavender Lane Farm—and find a way to make room for love along the way. (978-1-63555-286-7)

The Do-Over by Georgia Beers. Bella Hunt has made a good life for herself and put the past behind her. But when the bane of her high school existence shows up for Bella's class on conflict resolution, the last thing they expect is to fall in love. (978-1-63555-393-2)